Final Target

Iris Johansen

RANDOM HOUSE
LARGE  PRINT

Library of Congress Cataloging-In-Publication Data
Johansen, Iris.
Final target / Iris Johansen.
p.   cm.
ISBN 0-375-43114-4 (lg. print)
1. Children of presidents—Fiction. 2. Victims of
terrorism—Fiction. 3. Psychic trauma—Fiction.
4. Virginia—Fiction. 5. Sisters—Fiction. 6. Revenge—
Fiction. 7. Large type books. I. Title.

PS3560.O275 F56 2001b
813'.54—dc21
2001018577

1 3 5 7 9 10 8 6 4 2

FIRST LARGE PRINT EDITION

This Large Print edition published in
accord with the standards of the N.A.V.H.

*To Linda Howard, Catherine Coulter, Kay Hooper,
and Fayrene Preston. Fantastic writers and the very
best friends. Thanks for all the wonderful years, guys.*

Final Target

Prologue

Wind Dancer.
Get to the Wind Dancer.
Blood was everywhere.
He was coming toward her.
Cassie screamed and ran from the bedroom.
"Come back here!" The man in the ski mask leapt after her.

Her white nightgown flying, she ran down the hall and the stairs, her breath catching as sobs choked her. She had to get to the Wind Dancer. She would be safe if she could just get to it.

"Stop that kid, dammit." The man was now leaning over the banister. The man who had shot Pauley in her bedroom after Pauley had thrown himself in front of her. He was yelling at the three masked men in the hall below. More blood. More bodies lying on the floor . . .

She stopped in terror a few steps from the bottom. Daddy . . .

But Mama and Daddy weren't here. They were in Paris. She was alone in the house with Jeanne, her nurse, and the Secret Service men. Where was Jeanne?

"Come, little one." There she was, standing in the doorway to the study. The Wind Dancer was in the study too. She would be safe if she could get to it.

Jeanne smiled. "Come, Cassie."

Couldn't she see that those three men were between her and the study? But maybe she could get past them. The study was to the left of the staircase. She jumped over the banister and landed running.

"Clever girl." Jeanne whisked her into the study and locked the door.

Cassie threw herself into Jeanne's arms. "He shot Pauley. I woke up and he was standing by the bed and . . . Pauley was bleeding. . . ."

Jeanne patted her back. "I know, Cassie. It must have been terrible for you. But you're with me now."

Cassie's arms tightened around her in panic. "They're in the hall. They'll break down the door. They'll shoot us."

"They won't shoot us. Don't I always protect you?" She gently pushed her away. She nodded at the Wind Dancer on the pedestal in the corner. "Now go and see your friend while I think of something to do."

"I'm scared, Jeanne. They'll break down the door and—"

"Stop crying." She turned away. "Trust me, Cassie."

She couldn't stop crying. She did trust Jeanne, but they would come in. Nothing could stop them.

The Wind Dancer.

She ran across the room and looked up at the statue. They needed magic and everyone said the statue had magic. Cassie knew it did. She always felt it whenever she was near the Wind Dancer. Even though this wasn't the real statue, Daddy had said the hologram was like it in every way. So surely it had enough magic to save them.

"Help us," she whispered. "Please. They're going to hurt us."

The Pegasus stared at her with brilliant emerald eyes that seemed to know everything. It would be all right. The warmth that always comforted her when she was with the statue was gradually banishing the chill. She had Jeanne and the Wind Dancer. Nothing could hurt her. They would be safe now that—

A knock at the door.

She whirled to face it. Jeanne was walking toward the door, she realized in horror.

"No."

"Hush."

She ran across the room. "No, Jeanne. He's going to—"

Jeanne pushed her aside and opened the door.

It *was* him, the man in the mask. "I told you—"

"It's about time," Jeanne said. "Where the hell have you been, Edward?"

"Finishing up. This place was teeming with Secret Service. I knew you had her secure, so I took care of business." He walked into the study. "The helicopter is coming. I'm ready for the kid now."

"Then take her. Get it over with." Jeanne crossed her arms over her chest. "This night has left a nasty taste in my mouth."

"Because you're such a delicate soul. But not too delicate to take the money and run." He looked at Cassie. "Come on, Cassie. We have places to go and people to see."

"Jeanne?" She backed away from him. "Jeanne, help me. . . ."

"Go with him. He won't hurt you as long as you mind him like a good girl." Her voice was hard, not like Jeanne's at all.

This man had shot Pauley and left him lying on the rug of her bedroom with the blood pouring out of his chest. How could Jeanne say he wouldn't hurt her? How could she tell her to go with him? Why was she looking at Cassie that way? "Daddy," she whimpered. "Daddy."

The man's green eyes gleamed through the slits in the ski mask as he came toward her. "Daddy's not here. No one's here to take care of you, so don't cause me any trouble."

She kept on backing away. "Jeanne?"

"Stop it," Jeanne said harshly. "I can't help you. I don't want to help you. Go with him."

Cassie felt the cold marble of the Wind Dancer pedestal touch her back, and she suddenly felt a surge of hope. "No, I won't go. You can't make me go. He won't let you."

"He?"

"She's nuts about that crummy statue," Jeanne said. "She thinks the damn thing can do anything."

"Crummy?" He stared at the hologram. "That's almost sacrilege, Jeanne. It's magnificent. Have you no appreciation?"

"I appreciate the money the thing could bring us."

"But it's not real and Cassie is very real. Go get her."

"Get her yourself."

"If you want to be on that helicopter, you'll earn your passage."

"I've already earned it. You'd never have been able to do this if I hadn't given you the setup and opened—" She met his gaze. "Oh, very well." She strode across the room. "Come along, Cassie. You can't fight us. You'll only be hurt if you do."

Take me away, Cassie prayed. *Take me away. Take me away.*

Jeanne put a hand on her shoulder.

Take me away.

"You don't want him to shoot you like he did Pauley? He'll do it. You have to mind him or—"

"She doesn't seem to believe you," the man said softly. "I think she needs another example."

"What do you—"

Jeanne's head exploded.

Cassie screamed as brain matter splattered her chest. She crouched on the floor, her gaze on Jeanne's ruined face.

Take me away.

"Stop screaming."

Take me away.

"Stand up." He reached down and jerked her to her feet. "You shouldn't mind my getting rid of her. She insulted your friend the Wind Dancer, and she was a Judas. Once a Judas, always a Judas. Do you know what a Judas is, little girl?"

Take me away. Take me away. Take me away.

It was happening. He was fading, as if he were at the end of a long tunnel.

"But I won't do that to you if you don't cause me problems. Just do what I tell you and it will— What the shit!"

Gunshots.

He let go of her and ran out into the hall.

She sank back down on the floor next to Jeanne. Blood. Death. Judas. She wasn't afraid any longer. She was going away. She was the one in the tunnel now and the darkness didn't frighten her. As long as she stayed in the tunnel, nothing could touch her and she'd be safe. With every moment she was moving deeper into that darkness.

"Cassie?"

A man was kneeling before her. No mask. Dark eyes like her daddy. "I'm Michael Travis. The bad people have gone away. You're safe now. I'm going to touch you and check to make sure you're not hurt. Is that okay?"

She didn't answer. She didn't have to be afraid any longer. He'd made the monsters go away. Soon he would go away too, but it didn't matter what happened outside the tunnel.

She felt his hands on her arms and legs and then they were gone.

"Come on, baby." His lips tightened as he glanced at Jeanne. "Let's get you out of here. I'll take you into the kitchen and we'll get you cleaned up while we wait for your mom and dad." He picked her up and moved toward the door. "I know it's hard to believe, but everything's going to be okay."

It wasn't hard to believe. Not now. In the tunnel, everything was shadow and she wasn't afraid of shadows. As they reached the doorway, she looked over Michael's shoulder at the Wind Dancer. Emerald eyes stared at her across the room. Strange. They looked fierce and cruel like the picture of the dragon in the book Daddy had given her. But her Wind Dancer was never cruel.

And nothing else was cruel anymore either. Not here. Not now.

But just to be sure, she went even deeper into the tunnel.

1

May
Cambridge, Massachusetts

"I'm sorry to have to throw this at you during finals, Melissa." Karen Novak's voice was hesitant. "If there was any other way . . ."

"You want me to move out." It was no surprise. Melissa had known the decision was coming.

"Just until you have this problem under control. We've scouted out an efficiency for you about a block from here. You can move in right away."

Melissa turned to her other roommate. "Wendy?"

Wendy Sendle nodded miserably. "We think you'd be better off in an apartment by yourself."

"And you certainly would be better off without me." She held up a hand as Wendy opened her mouth to protest and said gently, "It's okay. I understand. I'm not blaming you. I'll pack up and be out by tonight."

"You don't have to be in a hurry. Tomorrow would be—" Wendy broke off as Karen gave her a pointed glance. "We'll be glad to help you pack."

Melissa had known they wouldn't want to risk another night with her. "Thank you." She tried to smile. "Now, stop looking so guilty. We've been friends for years. This isn't going to change anything."

"I hope not," Karen said. "You know we love you. We took it as long as we could, Melissa."

"I know. You've been very tolerant." She should have moved out weeks ago, but she'd felt safe here. "I'll just go into the bathroom and pack my toiletries."

"Melissa, have you ever thought of going back to Juniper?" Wendy moistened her lips. "Maybe your sister can help you."

"I'll think about it. Right now Jessica's pretty busy with a new job."

"You're very close. If she knew, I think she'd put her project on hold."

"It's hard to put off. Don't worry, I'll be fine." She closed the bathroom door behind her and leaned against it, her heart pounding. Calm down. So she'd be alone tonight. Maybe it wouldn't happen. Maybe it would go away.

But it hadn't gone away in the last few weeks. It had started hazy and far away, barely discernible in the swirling darkness. But lately it kept coming closer. She knew she'd be able to see it clearly soon.

Oh, God, don't let her see it.

Juniper, Virginia

"Cassie's had another nightmare," Teresa Delgado said as she stood in the doorway of Jessica's bedroom. "A bad one."

"They're all bad." Jessica Riley rubbed her eyes before she sat up and reached for her robe. "You didn't leave her alone?"

"There are other people around here who know their jobs besides you. Rachel's with her." She made a face. "But Cassie might as well be alone. She's curled up in a ball with her face to the wall. I tried to comfort her, but, as usual, Cassie's acting as if she can't hear me. As deaf as a fence post."

"She's not deaf." Jessica passed her and started down the hall. "She's aware of everything around her. She's just rejecting it all. The only time she's vulnerable and lets anything in is when she's sleeping."

"Then maybe you should treat her when she's sleeping. Try hypnotism or something," Teresa said. "You're sure not doing very well when she's awake."

"Give me a break. I've had her for only a month. We're just beginning to know each other," Jessica said. But Teresa was right, there had been no obvious progress. The child had been caught in a prison of silence since the incident at Vasaro eight months before. Surely there should have been some breakthrough by now, she thought, then tried to dismiss her doubts. She was just tired. Jesus, a child lost in a catatonic state for eight months was nothing compared to other children she'd treated. But acceptance was difficult when her patient was a seven-year-old child who should be running and playing and living life to the fullest. "And it's better if she makes the first steps back herself. I don't want to force her."

"You're the doctor," Teresa said. "But if a lowly nurse can offer some advice, I'd—"

"Lowly?" Jessica smiled. "Where did that come from? You've been telling me what I should do since my first year of residency."

"You needed it. I'd been around for over

thirty years by then and I had to set you straight. You were one of those hotshot doctors who never knew when to stop. You still don't. You could let us deal with the kid for one night and get eight hours' sleep."

"She's got to know I'm here for her." She shrugged. "And I wouldn't have been able to sleep much longer anyway. Her father's coming to see her. He said he'd be here by three A.M."

Teresa gave a low whistle. "The great man is paying us a visit?"

"No, Cassie's father is coming to see his daughter." Many people considered Jonathan Andreas one of the most popular presidents the United States had ever had, but Jessica didn't think of him in those terms. From the first time she had met him a month ago, she saw him only as a father who was terribly worried about his child. "And you should know that. You've seen him with her. He's just a man with a giant problem."

"So you put your life on hold and let him use your family home for a treatment center for his daughter. The damn place is an armed camp. You can't even take a walk without being shadowed by some Secret Service man."

"It was my idea. The President wanted her hidden from the media, and this place has a certain amount of privacy and is easy to secure. Cassie has to be protected. Look what happened at Vasaro."

"What if the same thing happens here?"

"It won't. The President assured me that the security is infallible."

"And you trust him?"

"Sure." Andreas inspired trust. "And besides, he loves his daughter. He's racked by guilt over Vasaro. He'd never risk another tragedy."

"You're very generous. I've noticed he's been pretty cool to you."

"That's okay. I've an idea he's sick and tired of dealing with psychiatrists. Besides, a family usually feels some resentment when they have to turn over their child to a stranger. We'll work it out." She nodded at Larry Fike, the Secret Service agent stationed outside Cassie's door. "Hi, Larry. Did they tell you the President is paying us a visit?"

He nodded. "Poor guy, not a good night."

"No." Though there were few good nights for Cassie Andreas. "But he has to come when he can get away without suspicion. We don't want reporters descending on us."

"Yep, then we'd all be having nightmares." He opened the door for her. "The little girl was screaming pretty badly. If it hadn't happened before, I'd have burst in there with gun drawn. I'll give you notice when the President reaches the gates."

"Thanks, Larry."

"Do you need me?" Teresa asked.

She shook her head. "Go make some coffee for the President. He may need it." She nodded to the nurse sitting in the easy chair. "Thank you, Rachel. Anything I should know?"

"What you see is what you get." The young woman rose to her feet. "She hasn't moved a hair since Teresa left the room." She smiled at Cassie. "See you later, baby."

Jessica sat down and leaned back in the chair. She didn't speak for a moment, letting Cassie become accustomed to her presence. The child's color was good, but her face was pinched. Making sure she ate enough was already difficult; if she deteriorated even more, she would have to be fed intravenously. What a sad contrast this Cassie was to the pictures Jessica had seen of her before Vasaro. She'd been the darling of the White House with her long, shiny brown hair and luminous smile. Full of vitality and mischief. America's poster child . . .

When are you going to learn? she told herself. Don't get all choked up. Her esteemed colleagues never passed up a chance to tell her that a doctor's emotion never healed a patient.

Screw them. If you didn't let it blind and hogtie you, love could do a hell of a lot.

"Pretty scary dream? Would you like to tell me about it?"

No answer. She hadn't expected one, but she always gave Cassie the opportunity. Someday a miracle could happen and Cassie might be tempted to come out of the darkness and answer one of her questions. "Was it about Vasaro?"

No answer.

It was probably about Vasaro. Terror, death, and betrayal were the stuff of nightmares. But what element was the primary catalyst that had driven her away? The nurse she had loved and trusted and who had been prepared to hand her over to killers? The murder of the Secret Service guard and the nurse? It could be a combination of causes. "Your daddy is coming to visit you soon. Would you like me to brush your hair?"

No answer.

"It doesn't matter. You look very pretty anyway. If you don't mind, I'll sit here until your daddy comes and we'll talk a little." She smiled. "Well, I'll talk. You seem to have given it up for a while. That's okay. You'll catch up when you decide to come back. My sister, Mellie, is a real chatterbox these days, and she was as closed as a clam for six years. I hope you won't see fit to stay away that long. Mellie's much happier now." Were Cassie's locked muscles relaxing a little? "This is Mellie's room you're in right now. She loves yellow and I had to talk her out of lemon and ease her into wheat-colored wallpaper. The brighter the better for Mellie. But it's a cheerful room, isn't it?"

No answer, but Jessica hoped that wherever she was, Cassie was listening. "Mellie's at Harvard now, studying to be a doctor like me. I miss her very much." She paused. "Like your mom and dad miss you. Mellie calls me every week and we talk and that helps. I bet your daddy would really like you to talk to him tonight."

No answer.

"But he'll love to be with you whether you talk to him or not. He loves you. Do you re-member how he used to play with you? Yes, I know you do. You remember everything, the bad and the good. And the bad doesn't hurt you where you are, does it? But it does hurt you when you go to sleep. If you'd come back to us, the dreams will stop, Cassie. It will take a little time, but they'll go away."

She could sense that Cassie was beginning to tense again.

"No one's going to make you come back until you want to do it. Someday you'll be ready and I'll be here to help you." She added softly, "I know the way, Cassie. Mellie and I traveled the same road. I wonder where you are. When

Mellie came back, she said it was like being in a deep, dark forest with a canopy of trees over-head. But some other children who have gone away say they went to a nice cozy cave. Is that where you are?"

No response.

"Oh, well, you'll tell me when you come back. I'm a little tired, do you mind if I just rest a little until your daddy gets here?" Dear God, she was weary of questions. *Answer me just once, sweetheart.* She closed her eyes. "If you want to sleep, go ahead. I'm here. I'll wake you if the bad dreams come."

Paris

Gleaming emerald eyes, teeth bared to tear into him!

Edward bolted upright in bed, his heart pounding. He was drenched with sweat.

Only a dream.

How ridiculous to become so upset that he was actually dreaming about the statue. It had to be the humiliation he had experienced at Vasaro.

Not his fault. The plan had been perfect. If it hadn't been for Michael Travis, he would have had the child. How had the son of a bitch known about the raid? There had to have been a leak. He would find it and then he would find Michael Travis and blow the bastard's brains out.

Wide awake now, he decided to go to the room. Just the thought of it was bringing him peace.

He got up and made his way downstairs. The intricately carved door gleamed richly in the soft light. And once inside the room he would be able to relegate the small failure at Vasaro to the back of his mind, where it belonged. There was no question that he would persevere and get what he wanted soon.

Including the death of Michael Travis.

Georgetown

"Where the hell is Michael Travis?" Andreas demanded when Ben Danley got into the limousine. "It's been eight months. How long does it take the CIA to find one man?"

"We're close." Danley sank down in the seat across from Andreas. "We've trailed him to Amsterdam. You don't understand, Mr. President. He's been mixing with the criminal underground since he was born. His father was a thief and a smuggler and he was brought up all over Europe and Asia. He has contacts that—"

"So you've told me." And Andreas didn't want to hear it again. He wanted Travis and no excuses.

"I'm only trying to explain that he moves in circles that leave few tracks. We expect to locate him within two days." He paused. "You haven't told us what to do when we do find him, sir."

Andreas turned to look at him.

"Do you wish him to have . . . an accident, Mr. President?"

Andreas smiled sardonically. "Why, Danley, you know the CIA no longer does sanctions. You've cleaned up your image."

"I didn't say we'd do it," Danley said. "I merely asked if that was your wish."

"Very cagey."

"It's a natural question. If Travis is the man behind Vasaro, I can see why—"

"Travis wasn't behind it. I don't want him hurt," Andreas interrupted. "And you don't know jack about what happened at Vasaro."

"Your pardon, sir, but naturally Keller at the Secret Service shared his files with us since the attempt on your life was made outside the U.S."

"It wasn't Travis."

"Then why have we spent eight months searching for him?"

"Because I told you to." He looked out the window at the darkness. "And I wanted you to have a damn good reason to find him. What did Keller tell you?"

"That there was an attempt on your life and the nurse and six men had been killed and three wounded. Fortunately, you and the First Lady had gone to Paris."

"Fortunately?" His tone was biting. "Do you realize that my daughter hasn't spoken a word since that night? And that my wife was on the verge of a nervous breakdown after six months of trying to cope with a child who looked at her as if she were a stranger?"

"I'm sorry. A slip of the tongue. I only meant—"

"I know what you meant." Andreas closed his eyes. "I shouldn't have jumped on you. I've been under a hell of a strain lately."

"But I understood Cassie was doing much better and would be coming home soon."

"That's the statement to the press to keep the reporters from searching for her. She's the same as she was when we brought her home from Vasaro. We've tried four different psychiatrists, and they've done zilch."

"Perhaps a little more time and—"

"I want her well now." His eyes opened. "And I want to keep her safe. Find Travis."

"Keller and his men will keep her safe. They know their ass is on the line."

"They didn't keep her safe at Vasaro. If Travis hadn't shown up, she'd be dead or held hostage."

"What?"

"Travis and his team came in minutes after Vasaro had been taken. They killed three of the attackers, one got away. Travis called me in Paris and told me what had happened."

"He saved your daughter?"

Andreas nodded. "And stayed with her until we got there. He had a helicopter waiting and slipped away in the confusion after we arrived."

Danley gave a low whistle. "Which left Keller with a copious amount of egg on his face."

"He couldn't clap him in custody. Travis was the hero of the hour . . . we thought."

"Have you considered the possibility the rescue was a setup?"

"No, one of the wounded Secret Service men verified that Travis wasn't one of the attackers and did save Cassie."

"But you're not searching for him to give him a medal."

"I asked how he knew about the attempt and

he said he dealt in information, among other commodities."

"That's true. He's bartered several bits of information to us over the years. But if he wanted to interfere, why didn't he just call the Secret Service and warn them?"

"That was my question. He said he'd found out too late and the attack was already in progress."

"Fishy."

"He'd just saved my child. It wasn't the moment to give him the third degree. We thought we had plenty of time. And we knew right away that something wasn't right with Cassie. She was our first priority. She still is." His lips tightened. "Travis told me I might not have been the target. They might have wanted Cassie."

"What?"

"What better way to bend a father's will than to threaten his child?"

"Did he name names?"

"If he had, don't you think I'd have given them to you? He said he didn't know. He knew only that there was going to be an attack on Vasaro."

"Did you think he was lying?"

"How do I know? But if he's so good at gathering information, then he can damn well find out who was behind the attack. You don't seem to be doing the job."

"The three dead men had terrorist affiliations."

"But also were known to work for hire. You haven't come up with any solid leads."

"We're working on it."

"Then work harder. And bring me Travis." He spoke to the driver. "Pull over, George." After the limousine glided to a stop, he leaned over and opened the door. "I'll have George place a call and have you picked up. I want to hear something positive from you within twenty-four hours."

Danley got out of the car. "I'll do my best, Mr. President."

"Do better than that." He slammed the door and leaned back on the seat. God, he hoped he'd lit a fire under Danley. There was something seriously wrong when it took all this time to track down just one man.

"Juniper, Mr. President?" George asked.

"Yes." Take him to the serene beauty of that old house in the country and let him sit beside Cassie, who existed in a world he could never enter. Cassie, who seemed to be fading away more and more with every passing day.

He blinked rapidly as he felt tears burn his eyes. Jessica Riley had said that Cassie was not any worse, but God knows how she could tell.

Maybe she could though. Maybe dealing with children like Cassie had given her a sixth sense about them. It was his wife, Chelsea, who had urged him to try Jessica Riley. She'd read a book Jessica had written about her work with her younger sister, Melissa, who had been in a state similar to Cassie's for over six years. Melissa was now attending Harvard, apparently completely cured. He'd checked Jessica out and found that she had excellent qualifications, but her treatments were sometimes unorthodox and controversial.

Well, maybe they needed unorthodox. He had no faith in any psychiatrist, but he'd do anything if it meant getting Cassie back.

And keeping her safe.

And to keep her safe he needed information, the information Michael Travis might be able to give him.

Where the devil was Travis?

2

Amsterdam

Was he being followed?

Travis's heart jumped as he saw the shadowy figure in the darkness behind him.

He cut down Kerkstraat to Leidestraat, went through an alley, and then ran two blocks north. His breath was labored as he ducked into an alcove and waited.

No one.

He moved quickly down the street. Ten minutes later he was climbing the steps to his flat. He checked the door for booby traps, then flung it open.

Darkness.

He always left the lights on. He whirled and tore down the stairs.

"Is that any way to treat an old friend?" Sean

Galen was leaning over the banister. "You'd think you didn't want to see me."

"You turned the lights off, damn you." Travis started back up.

"I was resting my eyes. I've had a long day." He grinned. "Besides, I wanted to see how sharp you were. You're a little on edge."

"A little." He followed Galen into the flat and closed the door. "What are you doing in Amsterdam? I thought you were going back to California."

"I was about to take off from Paris when I happened on a bit of information. Since you've been on the fly and incommunicado since Vasaro, it took almost a week to locate you." His smile faded. "You have blood on your temple."

"Do I?" He went into the bathroom and washed his face. "Just a scrape."

"Maybe made by a bullet whistling a little too close?"

He didn't answer as he dabbed at his face with the towel. "How did you find me?"

"Don't worry, no one else knows about this place here . . . yet. I wouldn't have been able to trace you if not for your old friend Van Beck. My God, what have you gotten yourself into, Michael?"

"Something immensely profitable, but it takes careful handling."

"I hear both the Russians and South Africans are after you."

"True. But there's always a chance they'll trip over each other trying to get to me."

"I wouldn't count on it. You take too many risks."

"The pot calling the kettle black. Is that what you came to tell me?"

"I came to tell you the CIA has traced you to Amsterdam."

Travis stiffened. "Oh, have they?"

"I told you to leave the kid and get out of Vasaro before Andreas got there."

"That wasn't an option."

"Any more than it was an option not to go to Vasaro."

"You never know when you need a favor from the President."

"Bull. You knew it would be trouble."

"You came along."

"I owed you. I still owe you. You had the good taste to save my neck that time in Rome and I value my life highly. But I didn't hobnob with Andreas. We were lucky to get you out. The place was crawling with Secret Service and French police, and none of them were pleased that they'd screwed up on the job."

"But you did get me out."

"And then you ran straight to Moscow and into the lion's mouth."

Travis smiled. "But he has such bright, sparkling teeth."

"I think you have a death wish."

"No, I have a life wish, the life I want, exactly the way I want it." He added, "It's going to be a beautiful bonanza, Galen. I wouldn't mind sharing it with you."

Galen raised his brows. "And what do I have to do?"

"Nothing that you haven't already done. Van Beck is taking care of the negotiations. I'd just like you along on the gravy train. You've always been a good friend to me."

"Damn straight I have." He shook his head. "I don't want to profit from just sitting on my ass, and I don't get a thrill out of walking tightropes anymore."

"Neither do I."

"The hell you don't. You don't know any other life."

"I intend to learn."

Galen shrugged. "Then get out of Amsterdam."

"My thought exactly."

"Do you need any help? I could make arrangements."

It might not be a bad idea. Besides his main occupation of troubleshooting, no one was better than Galen at slipping in and out of difficult situations. Travis thought for a moment, then shook his head. "No."

"Suit yourself. Anything else?"

"Yes. Who's heading the CIA team?"

"Big stuff. Ben Danley."

"What do you know about him?"

"Not much. Why?"

"Just looking for a way out."

"Try the nearest airport." Galen's gaze narrowed. "I can see the wheels turning. What are you up to?"

"Do me a favor. Send the CIA here."

"What?"

"Make sure the CIA finds out where I am. I don't have much time. I want them bursting in here within the next few hours."

"What are you up to?"

"I was wondering how I could get out of Amsterdam. Isn't it lucky Andreas wants me in Washington?"

"Or he may want you dead."

Travis shook his head. "I don't think so. I would have heard if there was a sanction. Give me two hours to make some preparations and check out a few things and then send them to pick me up."

"I can't talk you out of it?"

"It's the best way."

"Whatever." Galen turned but stopped at the door. "How *did* you find out about that attack on Vasaro?"

"I have my sources."

"Damn good ones. I didn't hear a murmur about it."

"You think I knew about it because I was part of the plot?"

"It occurred to me."

"A very logical supposition to a man of your cynical nature. But then why should I go to the trouble of a double cross?"

"How do I know? I've never met anyone capable of more convoluted machinations." He waited. "You're not going to tell me."

"I don't usually use kids in my plans."

"But you're not saying you didn't this time." He opened the door. "It was a pretty foul game at Vasaro. I wouldn't like to think you'd drawn me into something that dirty. Tell me who your source was."

"You know me. We've been friends for seven years. If that's not good enough, you'll have to think what you like."

Galen swore softly. "Damn you. Give me *something.*"

"I don't make excuses or explanations. You take me as I am or not at all."

"I'm supposed to trust you blindly?"

Travis didn't answer.

Galen sighed. "You're a tough friend to have, Michael. I don't think you were in on the setup at Vasaro, but the CIA may have a different view. I hope you know what you're doing."

He hoped he did too, Travis thought as the door closed behind Galen. The situation here was very dicey, and he didn't know how long he could stay on the run. He needed a safe haven while he negotiated a way to stay alive and get out with all the marbles in the game.

And keep the marbles from falling into the hands of the CIA. He'd have to do some fast talking and even faster manipulating to place himself in a position to bargain with Andreas.

So what was new? It was what he'd been doing all his life. Deception, manipulation, sleight of hand, and balancing on the tightrope Galen said he wanted nothing to do with any longer. He wasn't sure he wanted it either. God, he was tired.

Snap out of it. The adrenaline would come back in a rush when the CIA came through that door. Think of the challenge. It wasn't every day a man got to match wits with the leader of the free world.

★   ★   ★

Juniper

The nurse who opened the door was middle-aged, her red hair peppered with gray. "Dr. Riley is with your daughter, Mr. President. I'm afraid she's having a bad night."

"How bad?"

"Just a nightmare."

He knew about the nightmares and the almost catatonic withdrawal that followed. "I'll go to her right away, Teresa. Will you have some coffee made for my driver and the Secret Service men in the other car?"

"It's already made. Shall I bring some up to you?"

"Thank you." He was climbing the oak steps to the second floor. The house breathed of ages past and the same genteel warmth his own house in Charleston possessed. If Cassie came back, this place might remind her of all the weekends she had spent there.

If? She would come back. He couldn't tolerate anything else.

He threw open the door to Cassie's room without knocking. "How is she?"

Jessica Riley looked up. "She's fine. She had a bad time, but it's over now and she's resting. Isn't that right, Cassie?"

He strode over to the bed. "God, she looks—"

"She's resting," Jessica interrupted, standing up. "And I think we'll leave her to rest while we get a cup of coffee." She turned to the little girl. "We'll be right back, Cassie."

"I don't want to—"

"We're going to get a cup of coffee." Jessica's voice was steely with determination. "Now."

He met her gaze, then turned on his heel and followed her from the room. "Well?"

"I've gone over this before. She's not deaf and she's not in a coma, so you will not act as if she is."

"She lies there like a dead person. She won't speak or respond and you say she's—"

"If you accept her the way she is, it will only encourage her. I won't let you make my job harder by—"

"Won't let me? Who the hell do you think you are?"

"Your daughter's doctor. Who the hell do you think you are?" She paused and then her lips curved in a faint smile. "The President of the United States?"

His anger suddenly left him. "So I'm told, but evidently that doesn't impress you."

"It impresses me. You've been a good president. But that doesn't mean you know more than I do about your daughter's condition. If you want me to treat her, I have to be the boss."

He stared thoughtfully at her. She was quite small and her short, curly blond hair and luminous complexion made her look much younger than her thirty-two years. But there was intelligence in those brown eyes and an incisive boldness in her manner that definitely was not childlike. "I'm not accustomed to taking a backseat, Dr. Riley."

She smiled, the aggressiveness gone. "I know. It's very difficult for you. But you've got to accept it."

"How do I know you're right? How do you know you're right?"

"I don't. We can study, guess, and second-guess, but the mind is still a mystery to us. But I've been through this many times before and I have a better chance than you of hitting on the answer."

"You think she's fully aware?"

She nodded. "More than aware. I've found in cases like this the senses become terribly acute. It's as if rejecting the outside world and turning inward releases some power that's usually inhibited."

"The other doctors never mentioned anything like that."

"I can only tell you what I've experienced."

"With your sister?"

"With Mellie and others." She rubbed her temple. "You knew I was a bit of a maverick when you hired me. I can only do my best based on what I've learned. If that's not good enough, then fire me. But don't try to take control. Conflict might send Cassie deeper and further away from us."

He didn't speak for a moment, then said gruffly, "I . . . didn't mean to go against your instructions in there. You have no idea how different she is now. I've never known a stronger child than my Cassie. She's the last kid anyone would pick to go under like this. There was nothing fragile about her. She was always such a fighter. When I saw her all curled up like a— I felt so damn angry that I—"

"I know." She added deliberately, "And you don't really trust me."

"I don't trust anyone when it comes to Cassie. I'm her father and I should be the one to help her, not some—"

"Shrink?" She nodded. "I agree. But sometimes it doesn't work like that. Sometimes they totally reject familiarity. So the shrink has to take over. Now, are we going to work together, or do you want to find someone else?"

"It sounds more like you're opting for sole guardianship."

"No. Just don't put barriers in my way."

"And do as you say."

"Right."

He thought about it. "Okay. We'll see how you do as commander in chief."

"And if I don't measure up, you'll fire me in a heartbeat?"

"Exactly. Now, if there's nothing else, I'll go sit with my daughter."

"There's something else. I need more information."

"What kind?"

"About Vasaro."

"We've told you what happened."

"Before the attack, did your daughter like Vasaro?"

"She loved it. Who wouldn't? Vasaro grows flowers for the perfume trade, and what kid doesn't like farm life? Acres of lavender and lilies and far away from the strictures of D.C."

"She'd spent time there before?"

Andreas nodded. "Often. Caitlin Vasaro is her godmother and they're very close. She lets Cassie work in the fields and pick the flowers for the perfume." His lips tightened. "It's damnable Cassie will never be able to go back now."

"Why?"

"If you could have seen her that night, you'd know why. She was covered with blood and gore. The trauma made her what she is now. If we get her back—*when* we get her back—there's no way I'd ever let her go to Vasaro again."

"I see."

His gaze narrowed on her face. "Why did you want to know about the place?"

"As you said, that night made her what she is, and it happened at Vasaro. I need to know everything I can about both. You were there because you were lending the statue to Caitlin Vasaro to publicize her new perfume?"

"I was actually lending the Wind Dancer to the Museum d'Andreas for a few months. That's why my wife and I were in Paris that night. We thought the publicity surrounding the loan would remind everyone of Caitlin's first perfume, which she named after the Wind Dancer."

"The Wind Dancer wasn't at Vasaro?"

"No, it had been couriered to the museum." He made a face. "Cassie was so disappointed, we had to set up the hologram Caitlin bought years ago. It's truly remarkable and it satisfied Cassie. Why are you so curious about the statue?"

"I went through the family album you sent me and pulled a few pictures to test Cassie's reactions. I think she had a response to the photo of her with the Wind Dancer in the library at your house in Charleston."

He stiffened. "What kind of response? What did she do?"

"Nothing physical. Nothing I can put my finger on."

His eagerness vanished. "Then how do you know she had any response?"

"It's just . . . a feeling."

"You think she was afraid?"

"I'm not sure. Was she afraid of the statue?"

"Not before that night. The Wind Dancer has belonged to my family since the thirteenth century. She grew up with the statue and was never happier than when she was allowed to play in the same room with it."

"It must have seemed magical to her. A golden Pegasus is the stuff a child's dreams are made of. Just the image of a horse flying through the clouds . . ."

"She used to make up stories about it."

"What kind of stories?"

"Oh, adventures. Her own fairy tales about flying away with the Pegasus and rescuing princes from dragons and such."

"She must have a wonderful imagination."

"Marvelous. She was very bright."

"She *is* very bright."

"Of course, that's what I meant." He opened the door. "I'll try anything you want me to until

I decide it's not working. How do you want me to treat her?"

"Talk to her. Ask her questions. Show her you love her."

"You said that she rejects familiarity."

"It never hurts anyone to know that love is waiting. But don't show her you're upset when she doesn't respond. It will only cause her to draw away."

"That's a big order."

"You're a big man." She paused. "I'll bring you a cup of coffee. How long can you stay?"

"Two hours." He sat down in the chair by Cassie's bed and felt his heart twist as he looked at her. Come back to me, sweetheart. "I have to be back at the White House by seven." He took Cassie's hand and his voice lowered. "But that's long enough to tell you all about what's happening, Cassie. I miss you. Your sister, Marisa, called from Santiago and told me to remind you that you'd promised to go down and help her train the new baby dolphin. She can't wait to show you what they're doing now. Your mama sends her love. You know she'd be here if the doctor hadn't ordered her to stay in bed. Do you remember that you're going to have a new little brother next month? He's proving a little rambunctious and the doctor doesn't want him coming into the world too soon. He's a strong little guy and wants to establish his place in the family. He reminds me of you and the way—" He had to stop a moment to even his voice. "Your mama says she really needs you. She wants to talk to you about names for your brother. So you just think about it and maybe you'll have a suggestion when you come back. We had some acrobats from the Cirque du Soleil two nights ago. Remember when we took you to see . . ."

Jessica felt her throat tighten as she stood watching Andreas from the doorway. Dear heaven, how he loved his child!

She had made progress with him tonight, but she knew he had a long way to go before he would trust her entirely. Who could blame him? She would feel the same if Cassie were her own daughter. But, in a way, Cassie was her child. They were all her children until they came back and she had to give them up. They heard her voice, and if she was lucky, there came a time when she could coax them back.

But sometimes persuasion didn't work. Sometimes it was necessary to insert a different element to help the process along. It was a hurdle she didn't want to face when she'd barely managed to earn a tentative trust from Andreas.

She could imagine the explosion if she told him she might have to take Cassie back to Vasaro.

"We've got him, sir," Danley said. "We found him in a flat on the Amstel River."

"You didn't hurt him?"

"You gave us our orders. He was actually pretty tame. He didn't give us any trouble."

Tame wasn't the word he'd use for the man he'd met at Vasaro, Andreas thought. Michael Travis had been quiet and respectful but also exuded wariness. Andreas had gathered the impression Travis was a force to be reckoned with. "How unusual."

"He knew he was outnumbered. You want me to take him to Langley?"

"No, the Justice Department. I don't want anyone to know anything about him. I'll use the tunnel from the White House at midnight tomorrow. Have him there."

"Yes, Mr. President." A pause. "He asked us to give you a message. He said if you want his cooperation, he expects cooperation in return."

"What kind of cooperation?"

"He wants you to send *Air Force One* for him," Danley said. "The son of a bitch doesn't seem to realize he's the one behind the eight ball."

Air Force One. Why would Travis want that concession? Arrogance? To establish a position of strength? He'd judged the man to be too smart to let conceit or arrogance guide his actions, and his message gave promise he wasn't averse to working with him. Let him have his little power play. It might make him feel more secure. "Where is the plane?"

"D.C. and ready to go."

"Then tell the pilot to pick up Travis and bring him here."

"It's not necessary, sir. With all due respect, you shouldn't give in to that bastard."

" 'That bastard' saved my daughter's life. We're not sure he had any other involvement. Send the plane."

3

Paris

"You haven't found him yet?" Edward Deschamps asked. "It's been almost eight months. What kind of fool are you, Provlif?"

Provlif's hand tightened on the receiver. He wished it were Deschamps's throat. Patience. The money had been good so far, and no one knew better than he did how deadly Deschamps could be if crossed. "I have a strong lead. He has a connection in Amsterdam. A Jan Van Beck."

"Why didn't you say so?"

"You wanted concrete information. I had to dig very deep to find Jan Van Beck. They used to be partners, but Travis has been on his own for years."

"And what have you found out about Cassie Andreas?"

Silence.

"Nothing?"

"Naturally, we've been concentrating on Travis."

"Dammit, I told you, I need to know where she is."

"You can't be thinking of a second attempt on her? It would be crazy."

"That's none of your concern, Provlif. Your job is to find her."

"It's not as if she's an ordinary kid. The President put a security blanket around everything connected with her. We finally managed to trace her to a clinic in Connecticut, but the President took her from there over a month ago. We're still trying to find out who's treating her now and where she—"

"Where she was a month ago is no help to me. I need to know where she is now."

"I have three men working on it."

"Then hire more."

"I'll need additional cash." He had to walk very carefully, Provlif thought. Deschamps was one of the most coldly brilliant men he'd ever met, but that didn't mean he was always in control. He'd seen him explode on more than one occasion. And the word was out that since he'd become obsessed with finding Travis, Deschamps had become even more volatile.

"You'll get your money," Deschamps said softly.

"I'm leaving at once for Amsterdam."

"No. Get on a plane to Washington and find Cassie Andreas. I'll go to Amsterdam myself and follow up on Jan Van Beck."

"But he may be difficult to—"

"Provlif, you may remember that when I first started in the business, I became very well known for finding people."

Oh, yes, Provlif remembered. Finding them and then ridding the world of them. "I meant no disrespect, Edward."

"Then get on a plane and find that kid."

Lousy son of a bitch.

Deschamps hung up and strode toward the closet. He tossed a suitcase on the bed and began throwing clothes into it.

Prick. The nerve of Provlif to bother him about money. Did he have so little vision?

In spite of Provlif's doubts, the plan was sound and it would still work. But he had to have Cassie Andreas. She was paramount in the scheme of things.

Just as Jan Van Beck was the key to finding Michael Travis.

He slammed the suitcase shut and fastened it. In an hour he'd be on a flight to Amsterdam.

No, wait. First he would go to the room.

Then he would be ready for Amsterdam.

"I want to come home to see you," Melissa said as soon as Jessica picked up the phone the next afternoon. "Is that okay?"

"I thought you were studying for finals."

"I can study at home."

"You always told me that you studied better at your apartment. By the way, how are your roommates?"

"Fine. I decided I wanted a little more privacy, so I moved into an efficiency."

"But I thought you loved living with Wendy and Karen."

"I did. I still see them every day. I guess I'm going through growing pains." She paused. "I want to come home."

"Something's wrong."

"Just because I want to see you? You're my sister, for God's sake. I do like to see that baby face of yours every now and then."

"What's wrong?"

"Can I come or not?"

"I've told you what's going on here. If you

come, you won't be able to do anything but study. And I've given Cassie your room."

"That's okay. I'll take the blue room even though it's a disgustingly boring color. Maybe in my spare time I'll paint it orange."

"Don't you dare."

"Just kidding."

"When will you be here?"

"I can't get away before the weekend. That's four days—enough time to get me security clearance with those Secret Service men all over the place." She paused. "They're still there, aren't they?"

Jessica stiffened. "Of course they are."

"That's good."

"You won't think so when they start following you all around the grounds."

"I can live with it. See you Saturday morning."

"Mellie."

"I've got to go now."

"What is it?"

"I just miss you."

Jessica moistened her lips. "Is it the dreams?"

"I'll see you Saturday." She hung up.

Jessica slowly put down the receiver. It was probably okay. Mellie was completely cured now. There was no danger of her falling back.

So stop panicking. Besides, if something was wrong, she could handle it.

Unless it was the dreams.

How the hell would she handle the dreams?

Justice Department

Michael Travis was sitting on the leather couch reading when Andreas walked into the office. "These law books are very dry fare," Travis said. "It's no wonder most lawyers leave something to be desired. Their minds must have atrophied in school."

Andreas crossed to the desk and sat down in the executive chair. "Have a good flight, Travis?"

"Excellent. Thank you." He smiled. "Better than the Concorde. How much did it cost the taxpayers?"

"Not a dime. I made sure the expenses came out of my pocket."

"Very ethical. But only what I'd expect from you. You're one of those rare, old-fashioned phenomena, a man of honor. But you really could have charged it to the government. Your life is valuable not only to yourself and your family, it's essential to the smooth running of the country."

"I'm fully aware of that. But I didn't have to send *Air Force One* for you. I could have had Danley bring you by regular means."

"But you didn't want to piss me off even though the demand was unreasonable. You didn't want to start negotiations on the wrong foot."

"Negotiations?" Andreas shook his head. "I don't have to negotiate with you. I can have you charged with accessory to assassinating the President and stick you in prison."

"But you won't do it. As I said, you're an honorable man. You wouldn't punish the man who saved your daughter."

"I would if I thought there was a chance you might be a threat to her in the future. How did you know about the attack?"

"I told you, I have sources."

"Who are they?"

"And have Danley and his men descend on them like a swarm of locusts? Sources have to be protected. It's the way I make my living."

"Among other rather nefarious enterprises, I understand."

"True. I'm big on nefarious enterprises. But we're not discussing anything but my ability to acquire information, are we?" He leaned forward. "You want to know who was behind Vasaro."

"And I'll find out."

"Not from me. Not now. I told you the truth. I didn't know anything about the attack except that it was going to happen."

Andreas studied him. Travis was staring at him boldly and he had spoken with seeming candor. But a man who made his living with his wits would have picked up certain skills and become a master of deception. Yet, dammit, Andreas's instincts were telling him that Travis *was* telling the truth. Disappointment surged through him.

"You wish I'd lied to you," Travis said. "Sorry."

"You still could be lying."

"Yes, I'm very good at it." Travis smiled. "But you haven't gotten to where you are in life without relying on your own judgment."

Andreas nodded. "Maybe you didn't know then about the person behind Vasaro, but you could have found out something since that night."

"I've been busy, and it wasn't high on my list of priorities."

"It's high on mine."

"I know. That's why I'm here."

"You're here because I told Danley to rope you in."

Travis smiled.

He was actually pretty tame.

Andreas had thought it an unusual description at the time, and looking at Travis now, it was even more off target. The man was perfectly at ease, but there was an alertness to him, an edge.

"Danley's a smart man," Travis said. "He might have run me down in a week or two. But I decided it would be to both our advantages to hurry things along."

"Why?"

"I needed to exit the scene for a while. You need more information."

"Which you tell me you don't have."

"Yet. That doesn't mean I can't get it if I work at it. It will just take time."

Andreas stiffened. "How much time?"

Travis shrugged. "As long as it takes. I don't see how you can lose. Danley hasn't learned anything yet, has he?"

"And what do you get out of it?"

"Protection. My position at present is a bit precarious. I need to be in a place that has absolute security for a minimum of a month."

"What am I protecting you from?"

"The aftershock of one of my 'nefarious enterprises.'"

"Which one?"

"Do you want me to find out who attacked Vasaro?"

"I could have Danley find out what you've been doing."

"Good luck."

Andreas was silent, thinking. "You do realize if I surround you with men for protection that they would also act as guards. I'd make sure they knew you were under suspicion. I wouldn't think twice about crushing you like a cockroach if I find out that you had anything to do with Vasaro."

"I understand."

"Good."

"You agree?"

"Oh, yes." Andreas smiled. "I know just the place—the gatehouse of an old manor in Virginia, plenty of security. And if any bastards make any move on it, you'd be the first to get your throat cut."

"Really? Now, I wonder why they would attack . . ." His eyes narrowed. "Cassie. So that's where you've hidden her. I suppose I should be honored you trust me enough to send me there."

"I don't trust you. I don't know what you're up to. But you saved her life and I don't believe you'd harm her. When you handed me Cassie at

Vasaro, I had a gut feeling about you. After all she'd gone through, she wasn't afraid of you. You may be a complete son of a bitch, but you risked your neck to protect her. I think you'd do it again." He paused. "And if you are lying to me about anything else, you'll be the—"

"First to get my throat cut," Travis finished. "I'll keep that in mind. When do I go?"

"Tomorrow night. About this time. Danley will find you a hotel for now." Andreas pushed back his chair and stood up. "I'll take you when I visit Cassie."

"How is she doing?"

"Bad." His mouth tightened. "So bad that my so-called sense of honor wouldn't stop me from burning those bastards at the stake when I catch up with them. I'll tell Danley you're ready to go."

"Not yet." He took out his telephone. "I have a few calls to make."

"You can make them at the hotel."

He shook his head. "I'm sure this room is thoroughly clean of bugs, and I need that privacy." He smiled. "It's not as if you told me the location where you're taking me. There must be thousands of old houses in Virginia."

"Yes, there are. Who are you going to call?"

"A friend. I don't like the idea of disappearing

from view with no one knowing you're responsible. I feel the need for a little insurance."

"But you say I'm such an honorable man."

"I could be mistaken. Tell Danley I won't be
more than five minutes."

"Call whomever you please." Andreas started
for the door. "I'll make very sure we're not followed tomorrow night, Travis."

"I'd be pretty stupid to try anything like that,
wouldn't I?" He started to dial. "Just insurance.
Good night, Mr. President."

"Jessica!"

Melissa jerked up in bed, her heart pounding.

Her jaw felt sore and she knew she'd been
screaming.

Oh, God. Oh, God.

The T-shirt she slept in was soaking wet with
sweat, but she was ice cold. She swung her legs
to the side of the bed and buried her head in her
hands.

As soon as she stopped shaking, she'd phone
Jessica and then everything would be fine. No,
she couldn't keep running to Jessica. She had to
be strong.

*Emerald eyes staring at the blood pooling on the
floor.*

She jumped up, went into the bathroom, and drank a glass of water in four gulps. After wrapping herself up in her terry robe, she turned on all the lights in the apartment, then snuggled down in the worn armchair by the window.

It was going to be all right. She was still cold, but her heartbeat was steadying. She could make it. Only three more nights until she'd be home with Jessica.

Blood pooling on the floor . . .

Don't scream. Don't scream.

Emerald eyes . . .

Don't scream.

"Nice house." As they drove through the gates, Travis studied the columned brick building set back from the road. "Shades of Tara."

"What do you know about Tara?" Andreas asked. "From the report Danley gave me on you, you've never spent much time in the U.S."

"My father always considered himself an American even though he chose to live abroad. He found it much easier to conduct business outside this country."

"Smuggling?"

Travis smiled. "Don't be crass. He was a romantic. Until the day he died, he thought of himself as a pirate."

"But you never considered yourself anything but a criminal."

"He chose his 'career' as a young man, he loved the excitement. I grew up with the reality of the underbelly of the game."

"Not the excitement?"

"Oh, yes. After all, I'm my father's son." His gaze was on the manor. "That's where Cassie is? Who's taking care of her?"

"Two nurses and her doctor, Jessica Riley."

"But no progress?"

"Not yet." Andreas turned to look at him. "Do you care?"

"Is that so strange? Let's just say I have a vested interest. I don't like to leave a job half done."

"Stay away from my daughter. I don't want her reminded of anything connected to that night."

"If she had to be reminded, you wouldn't be needing a doctor."

"You heard me." The limousine drew to a stop at the gatehouse. "Stay away from Cassie. I'm going to tell Dr. Riley exactly who you are and what you're doing here. And I'll give her orders that you're not permitted near my daughter."

Travis threw up his hands. "Whatever you say. I'm perfectly content to stay in my own little world." He got out of the limousine. "One last item of business. I know it's tempting to have my calls monitored, but I'd consider that a deal breaker. Besides, I'll be calling only one person. Jan Van Beck in Amsterdam. He'll be my go-between with any and all sources, and if he tells me your people are acting even a little bit intrusive, the deal's off."

"Why are you telling me about Van Beck?"

"You think I'm betraying him." He shook his head. "I'm making sure he's protected."

Andreas was silent a moment. "Your phone won't be tapped."

"Thank you. Then I'll be in touch."

"No, I'll be in touch." Andreas motioned for his driver to go on. "You can bet on it."

Travis watched the car move up the curved driveway. There were lights on in the upper floor of the manor. Cassie's room? Not his business. He turned and opened the door of the gatehouse. As long as he kept away from Cassie and was able to throw Andreas tidbits of information, he'd be permitted to stay here in safety. That was all that was important.

The gatehouse consisted of a living room, kitchen, and bedroom and was comfortably furnished. He spent the first thirty minutes checking for bugs and found five. There were more sophisticated means of surveillance, but they required a truckload of equipment, and he doubted the Secret Service agents would try them once they learned the bugs had been destroyed. The advantage of surveillance lay in the subject not knowing he was being monitored.

He did a final check on the books in the built-in shelves on either side of the fireplace and found two more bugs. He smiled as he realized one had been tucked behind a book by Dr. Jessica Riley, *Into the Light*. Not very clever. A book written by the owner of Juniper would automatically attract attention.

He sat in a chair, took out his digital phone, and called Van Beck. "I'm settled. Is everything set up?"

"In place."

"Then start negotiations."

"You're safe?"

"Stop being a mother hen, Jan. You're the one who's dealing with the bad guys. I'm surrounded by America's Finest."

"And that's supposed to make me feel better?"

"I'm safe, Jan."

"See that you stay that way."

"I'll call you tomorrow." He hung up and leaned back in the chair. Everything was set. He'd done the best he could. Would it be enough?

At least he had Jan doing the negotiations in Amsterdam. He could count the people he trusted on one hand. How long had it been since he'd accepted anyone at face value? Not since he'd been Cassie's age. He hadn't yet learned cynicism or that greed had a dazzling way of blinding a man. During those days when Jan and his father had taken him on their trips to Algiers, life had been full of excitement.

He went over to the window and looked up at the lighted window in the manor. He had a fleeting memory of Cassie's face that night at Vasaro. She'd never accept anything at face value again. She'd been torn away from childhood.

It wasn't his business. She was being cared for by experts, by this Dr. Riley. Just because he was plagued by the nagging feeling of leaving something unfinished was no reason to endanger his position here.

He turned away from the window. He'd take a shower and then hit the sack.

He stopped in the bedroom doorway, went back to the bookcase, and picked up Jessica Riley's book. It didn't mean anything. He often read himself to sleep. Besides, he made a good part of his living dealing in information, and it never hurt to know everything about his situation.

It had nothing to do with Cassie Andreas.

4

"You understand?" Andreas demanded.

"You've made yourself more than clear," Jessica said as she walked him out. "No contact with the gentleman in the gatehouse."

"I don't think you'd consider him a gentleman."

"According to you, he saved Cassie's life. That qualification is hard to dismiss."

"A single action doesn't eliminate the instability of a lifetime."

"I deal with instability all the time. It's how I make my living."

"Well, you have no cause to deal with this particular instability." Andreas walked down the front steps. "Ignore Travis. He won't be here long. You have your hands full." He looked back at Cassie's window. "No nightmare tonight. That's good, isn't it?"

"It's always good. They tear her apart." And Cassie's nightmares were becoming more violent. The aftereffect was that she went even deeper into withdrawal. But Jessica wasn't about to mention that to her father. He had little enough hope. "Will you be here tomorrow night?"

He shook his head. "I have to go to Japan for trade talks. I'll be gone almost two weeks, but my wife will be calling every day for a report. You know how to get in touch with me."

Jessica watched the car move slowly down the driveway before her gaze switched to the gatehouse. A light was burning in the bedroom at the back of the house. Evidently, the unstable Mr. Travis was still awake.

His arrival was an interesting development. Interesting and perhaps . . . promising. She might be able to use Michael Travis.

God knows, she'd use anything or anyone to stop Cassie from descending any deeper into the darkness.

★   ★   ★

"I'm here." Melissa took the front steps two at a time to envelop Jessica in a bear hug. "Roll out the red carpet. Strike up the band."

"I think that line's from *Hello, Dolly!* and you're no Barbra Streisand." She gave her sister a fierce hug in return. "But I'm glad to see you anyway. Good trip?"

"Until I got to the front gates." She stepped back and looked down at Jessica. "Have you shrunk? I'm too old to have grown an inch."

"You're just annoying enough to do it. Why couldn't I be the one to take after Dad?"

"It comes in handy on the basketball court. But you're more the southern belle clinging— Who is that?" Melissa had caught sight of the runner at the far end of the driveway.

"Our guest. He's staying at the gatehouse. He takes a run every morning."

"Really?" Melissa gave a low whistle. "You didn't tell me about him. Sexy."

Was he sexy? Jessica had studied him. Michael Travis was not really good-looking. He had a great body—tall, slim, and muscular—but his features were irregular. His nose was too big, his mouth too wide, and his dark eyes set deep. But she knew why Melissa had made the comment. He exuded an energy that was almost electric, and it was difficult not to keep looking at him.

The first time Jessica had seen him two days ago she had experienced . . . what? Surprise?

Melissa grinned. "You think so too."

"He's too old for you. He must be in his mid-thirties."

"For Pete's sake, I'm twenty-six. You keep thinking of me as a baby. I just may pay a visit to the gatehouse." She glanced slyly at Jessica. "Unless you have dibs on him."

"I've never said two words to him."

"Then you've been hanging out too much with children."

"The President says he's off limits."

"Great. Forbidden fruit always tastes better."

"You didn't ask why he was living in the gatehouse."

"I thought you didn't want to have your gigolo in the house with the kid. The gatehouse is much more private."

"Mellie."

She giggled. "Lighten up." She picked up her suitcase and carried it into the house. "I'll just take this to the dreaded blue room. Put on some coffee, will you? I need some caffeine after going through that gauntlet at the gate. Any minute I expected them to ask me to submit to a strip search. Now, if it had been your guy at the gatehouse . . ." Before Jessica could answer, she was running up the stairs.

Jessica felt a surge of relief as she headed for the kitchen. Melissa seemed perfectly normal. No apparent tension. Good spirits. The usual half-teasing, half-mischievous attitude. If anything, her demeanor was even more vivacious than customary. She was practically glowing.

"Want me to make some sandwiches?" Melissa breezed into the kitchen. "I'm hungry."

"There's ham and cheese in the refrigerator." She poured coffee into two cups. "I'll do it."

"Nope, I need to move. I'm charged."

Melissa was always charged, Jessica thought. She was constantly moving, talking, laughing. She had once said that she had to make up for those lost years, and Jessica could believe it. She had never seen anyone more alive than Melissa.

Except for the man in the gatehouse.

Strange that comparison had popped into her mind. They were nothing alike. Melissa had the eye-catching beauty their mother had possessed. High cheekbones, shining chestnut-colored hair, and blue eyes that tilted up at the corners. Her only similarities to Travis were their tall, athletic bodies and that air of feverish energy.

Feverish.

Michael Travis was not feverish; his every movement seemed controlled and deliberate. And the word didn't usually describe Melissa.

Yet there was a restless, fevered air about Melissa today.

"What are you looking at?" Melissa was gazing at her over her shoulder. "Do I have a smudge?"

"I don't know. Do you?"

"Oh, nuts, you're in analytical mode." She put the sandwich down in front of Jessica and sat across from her. "I'm fine. I just wanted to see you. Is that such a surprise?"

"Not if it's the truth."

"Why shouldn't it be the truth? How's the kid?"

"Not good. The nightmares are getting worse." It was clear Melissa wasn't going to confide in her. She'd have to back away and try later. "I'm worried about her."

"You have a right to be."

Jessica stiffened. "Why do you say that?"

"You know why. I've been there. I've told you before how close I came to not coming back. The nightmares drove me deeper and deeper until I—"

"But you came back."

"You pulled me back. You kept at me until I took the first step. There were times I hated you for making me return. I never realized how much you sacrificed and worked to heal me."

She smiled luminously. "Have I ever told you how much I love you, Jessica?"

"Shut up. You'd have done the same for me."

"I'd do anything for you," she said quietly. "Just give me the chance."

"Okay." She got to her feet. "You wash the dishes while I go check on Cassie."

"I've embarrassed you." She finished her coffee. "Sorry. I had to say it. Too many people go through life and never say the words. When I came back, I wanted to run around and tell everyone not to take anything for granted, that any minute they might go away and never come back."

"But you didn't."

"You wouldn't let me. It was okay for you to be the one who loves and serves, but you never wanted me to . . ." She shrugged. "But that's okay. It just took me a little while to get up the gumption to handle you."

"And now you have?"

"I hope so." She took her plate and went over to the sink. "Go and check on the kid."

"Why this sudden outpouring?"

"It was time." She put the dishes in the dishwasher. "Do you think the President's ban on the hunk in the gatehouse includes me?"

"Yes, I do."

"Pity."

Jessica was smiling as she went upstairs. It was difficult not to smile when she was around Mellie. Her joie de vivre was nearly palpable. It was a pleasure to be in the same room, on the same planet with her.

Her smile faded as she reached Cassie's room. Come back, sweetheart. See what joy life can bring.

The scream tore through the night like a knife blade.

Jessica had been expecting it. The nightmares had occurred the last three nights in a row.

"It's okay, Cassie." She gathered the little girl close. "I'm here. You're safe."

She kept on screaming.

"Wake up, baby."

She kept on screaming.

Oh, God.

"Cassie."

The screams didn't stop.

"Shall I prepare a sedative?" Teresa asked.

Jessica didn't want to use a sedative. She had tried it with Mellie, who had told her later that at times it had frozen her in the nightmare, tearing her apart. If Jessica increased the trauma, it might drive Cassie deeper into withdrawal. "Not yet."

"Cassie." She rocked her back and forth. "Wake up, Cassie."

Five minutes later Cassie was still screaming. Then, suddenly, she went limp.

That frightened Jessica even more.

The child was lying still, but her eyes were open.

"Cassie?"

She checked her heart and vital signs. Rapid pulse, but in no danger—this time.

What was she thinking? This whole episode had been fraught with danger.

"I thought we'd lost her," Teresa whispered.

Lost her mind or her life? Jessica had been afraid of both.

"You have to do something," Teresa said.

"I *know* that."

A half hour passed and Cassie's color gradually returned.

"Go and get some air," Teresa said. "You're paler than that child. I'll watch her."

"Just for a few minutes." Jessica stood up and arched her back to ease the tension. "Call me if there's any change."

She stopped in the hall and leaned back against the door.

"Is she okay?" Larry Fike asked. "She scared me to death."

"Me too. But she's resting now."

"All that screaming and sobbing . . ."

She nodded and started down the hall. *Sobbing?* Cassie hadn't been sobbing.

But there was sobbing, low, broken, barely audible. She could hear it and it wasn't coming from Cassie's room.

The blue room.

She moved slowly to the door. "Mellie?"

No answer.

She knocked and opened the door. "Mellie, are you—"

"I'm okay. Go away."

"The hell I will." In the darkness she could see Melissa in the big bed. "What's the matter?"

"What do you think? I'm pissed because you won't let me go after the hunk in the gate-house."

"If it means that much to you, I'll serve him up on a silver platter." She moved across the room and sat down on the bed. "Now you don't have any excuse, so tell me the truth."

"I hate this stupid blue room."

"Mellie."

She launched herself into Jessica's arms. "We're hurting so bad," she whispered. "We almost died, Jessica."

"What?"

"They keep coming after us and we can't get away. And there's so much blood. . . . We have to go deeper and deeper in the tunnel, but we still can't escape. There's only one way to escape."

Jessica froze. "Mellie. What are you saying?"

"What you don't want to hear. We're going to die, Jessica. We can't go on, we can't get away any other—"

"Mellie, shut up, you're scaring me to death." She reached over and turned on the lamp. "You're talking crazy."

Melissa didn't lift her head.

"You were just dreaming, right?"

"Yes . . . we were dreaming."

"Why do you keep saying *we*?"

"I think you know." She sat up and brushed hair out of her eyes. Her lips were trembling as she tried to smile. "After all, it's happened before."

Jessica moistened her lips. "Cassie?"

"She's a strong little girl. She had no trouble pulling me into the tunnel with her. Not like Donny Benjamin. He tried, but I was able to stay outside his little cave, even though he was so desperately lonely and I wanted to go in and keep him company." She took a deep breath. "If I'd gone in, he might never have come back.

But he did come back. You brought him back. Just like you brought me back." She paused. "Only you brought something else back with me, didn't you?"

"You think you joined minds with Cassie?"

"I know I did." She wiped her wet cheeks with the back of her hand. "You don't want to believe it, like you didn't want to believe it about Donny. It scares you."

"Hell, yes. Doesn't it scare you?"

"Not most of the time. Tonight it did. I want to live."

"And Cassie doesn't?"

"When the nightmares are going on, she's scared and confused and wants only to get away. There's just one place safer and further away than her tunnel."

"Mellie."

"I'm sorry. I know this upsets you." She got out of bed and moved toward the bathroom. "I'm going to wash my face. Then, maybe, we'll go downstairs, get a glass of lemonade, and sit on the front porch and forget all this. Okay?"

How could she forget it? Jessica thought. When she'd been treating Donny Benjamin, she had been able to dismiss the idea that Melissa was able to join minds with the little boy. She had chalked it up to imagination and the fact that Melissa had only recently been brought back herself. After all, Jessica had talked with Melissa about Donny and his progress. Just as she had discussed Cassie with her sister.

But the dreams of Donny had not been laced with terror and sorrow. Melissa had just talked calmly and sympathetically about the boy and then retreated when she faced Jessica's bewilderment and distress.

"Stop fretting," Melissa said as she came out of the bathroom. "That's not why I came home. If you hadn't barged into my private sanctum and caught me at a weak moment, you'd never have had to face my little hallucinations."

"But you don't think they're hallucinations."

"Sure I do. If they're anything else, you'll worry yourself into a nervous breakdown. After six years in never-never land, it would be weird if I didn't have a few hallucinations."

"You're lying."

"Maybe." She headed for the door. "But not about wanting that glass of lemonade. Coming?"

"Nice night. I like this. I remember doing this when we were kids." The swing moved slowly. "Do you sit out here much, Jessica?"

"I don't have time." Jessica sipped her lemonade. "If I'm not working with a particular patient, I'm usually at the learning clinic for autistic children."

"So you've told me. Now, that's major depressing. Compared with working with the autistic, your six years with me must have been a party."

"There are certain similarities in treatment, and we've made breakthroughs."

"And you spend your life looking for them." Melissa was silent for a moment. "Was it me? Was I the one to blame?"

"Blame? I don't know what you're talking about."

"I remember how you were when I was a kid, before Mom and Dad died." She smiled. "Miss Popularity, a cheerleader. Everyone's best friend. With a healthy dose of selfishness thrown in."

"I was young."

"You're still young, and there's nothing wrong with selfishness. I think you've forgotten that." She sipped her lemonade. "And I probably am to blame. You were saddled with taking care of a zombie and you turned into Saint Jessica."

"Don't be silly. Was it your fault you were in that car with Mom and Dad when they died? Life happens, and we just have to face it and choose our path."

Melissa lifted her glass. "Like I said, Saint

Jessica. In your place, I'd have been kicking and screaming and would have tossed me into a home."

"No, you wouldn't. You just like to talk tough. You'd have done the same thing."

"Good God, you mean I'd have turned into Saint Melissa?" She shook her head. "Nah, it doesn't have the same ring."

"Well, you've decided to study medicine. That's not exactly the most selfish career you could have picked."

"You think I'm following in your footsteps?"

"I think you're more generous and caring than you admit."

"Did it ever occur to you that I want to go to med school because I'm looking for answers?"

"That's why we all study."

"No, I want *my* answers. I want to know why I resigned from the world for six years." She looked down into her glass. "And I want to know about Donny Benjamin."

"Mellie, you were in a highly charged state and your imagination was working overtime."

"And you don't want to think your little sister is wacko."

"You're not wacko. If you'd actually thought you'd developed some sort of psychic power, you'd have enrolled in classes in psychic research."

"Oh, I've read enough books on ESP to fill a library. But I didn't want to find answers there. Believe me, I'd much rather discover some simple physical reason for what's happening to me."

"You're right. Donny Benjamin was an isolated incident and perfectly explainable."

"And Cassie?"

"The same explanation. I discussed both cases with you and you're highly sensitive to suggestion in that area."

"In the area of never-never land?"

"Whatever you want to call it. It's still perfectly reasonable that you—"

"Stop." Melissa was laughing. "The one thing I've come to realize is that what happened to me has nothing to do with reason. It's wonderful of you to make excuses to keep me out of the nuthouse, but I am what I am."

"And that is?"

"A freak." She held up a hand to stop Jessica's protests. "A nice freak, an intelligent and charismatic freak. But definitely a freak. And stop looking at me as if you want to put me to bed and soothe my fevered brow. I know you wrote this terrific book about me and the way we fought back to normalcy, but you screwed up on one point. I'm not normal."

"You most certainly are."

"I don't even know what that is. Not many people I know are completely normal. You're not normal, you're Saint Jessica." She stood up. "I'm going to bed. I've worried you enough for one night."

"Yes, you have."

"But you're already trying to find a solution. Or should I say cure?"

"Why haven't you talked to me like this before? Why tonight?"

"I was going to slide out of it again because I love you and I want you to respect me. But I was thinking about Cassie as I was sitting here. I may be selfish, but I can't hide what I am if it means Cassie dying." She soberly met her sister's gaze. "Next time, it will be worse. You have to find a way to break the stream. Find a way to enter something new into the mix. Anything to jar her out of the dream."

"How the hell can I—"

"I don't know. You're the shrink." She headed for the front door. "Just do it."

"Mellie."

She looked over her shoulder.

"Is that why you came home? Were you having dreams about Cassie?"

"No." She looked away as she opened the door. "I had no dreams about—with Cassie before tonight."

★   ★   ★

"You should have stayed away longer," Teresa said when Jessica walked into the room. "You needed it."

"How is she?"

"No different." Teresa stood up. "I'm going to go down and have a cup of coffee and then I'm coming back and sending you to bed. You're beginning to look like one of your own patients."

"I'm okay." It was a lie. She was definitely not okay. She was exhausted and so scared, she felt sick to her stomach. She wasn't sure if she was more frightened for Cassie or Melissa. The child was lost, but her sister, who she'd thought was whole again, might be spiraling downward.

Yet Melissa had been perfectly coherent. But how many patients had Jessica treated who'd seemed absolutely sane except when in the middle of an episode?

Melissa was sane. She was just . . .

What?

She leaned back in the chair with a sigh. She didn't need this additional worry. That any kind of mental joining had occurred was completely unacceptable. It offended logic. Whatever had happened tonight was as simple as the premise she'd offered Melissa.

She covered Cassie's hand with her own. "You've got to come back soon. The nightmares are hurting you. I thought we could wait, but it's . . . Come out of the tunnel, baby. You'll be so much happier, I promise. You'll see your mama and daddy and they'll be—"

Tunnel? Where had that come from?

She stiffened. Melissa had said Cassie was in the tunnel. It would have been more reasonable for her to see Cassie in the mental forest where she'd spent those six years. But that wasn't what she'd said.

She's a strong little girl. She had no trouble pulling me into the tunnel with her.

A chill went through her. Melissa's imagination or perhaps . . . ?

She wouldn't believe anything so outlandish. She had to use reason when dealing with Cassie . . . and Melissa. She didn't know if Cassie's frail body could withstand another night like tonight.

Next time, it will be worse. You have to find a way to break the stream.

Jesus.

5

"Karlstadt won't deal with anyone but you," Van Beck said as soon as Travis picked up the phone. "He wants to see the merchandise."

"You showed him the sample?"

"He says a raindrop does not make an ocean."

"More poetic than I'd expect from Karlstadt."

"He wants you here."

"Tell him I respect his wishes, but it's possible to drown in an ocean and I'm not willing to run the risk until I have an attractive offer."

"And what do you consider attractive?"

"Twenty-five million has a certain ring."

Van Beck snorted. "You're dreaming, Michael."

"No, they'll pay it. It's cheap for the price. Go

for it." He changed the subject. "Have you made contact with anyone who has information about the attack on Vasaro?"

"I'm going to pay a visit to Henri Claron in Lyon. I've heard he may know something. But he's being very quiet, and you know Henri is seldom quiet."

"On the contrary."

"And I've uncovered an interesting fact. Henri's wife, Danielle, grew up in the same village as Jeanne Beaujolis, Cassie Andreas's nanny."

"That is interesting."

"But, as I said, Henri's not being very forthcoming."

"Scared?"

"I've offered a considerable amount of money. It would take something big to scare him away from a payday that substantial. I'll let you know." He hung up.

Dammit. Travis slipped his phone back in his pocket and strode restlessly over to the window. Not exactly the progress for which he'd been hoping. He'd been here over a week and he was still at square one.

Well, square one was better than being in a wooden box six feet under. He was just not accustomed to being cooped up. There were only so many hours he could spend on the computer or reading. The only book he'd found really ab-

sorbing was the one by Jessica Riley. It was intriguing to delve into the past and minds of
Jessica Riley and her sister, Melissa. It made the
glimpses he caught of them on the property
even more interesting. He felt as if he'd gotten
to know them with an intimacy with which he
knew few people. Most people didn't open their
minds and their feelings to even their closest
friends, but Jessica had written with a clarity that
was poignantly touching. Her story of her fight
to help her sister through trauma when their
parents had burned to death before the child's
eyes had no trace of ego, only boundless affec-
tion in every word.

Through the rain he could see that the lights
in the upstairs bedroom were on again at the big
house. That was the third night this week. It
seemed Cassie was not doing well. Poor kid.

And poor Jessica Riley. If he could read between the lines of her book, she was probably
suffering almost as much as her patient.

None of his business. How many times had he
told himself that since he'd arrived at Juniper?
From sheer boredom he was being drawn into
speculation, and speculation was seldom enough
for him. He liked to be in control. If he wasn't
careful, he'd be abandoning his nice, safe position as observer and diving in and trying to sort
out the situation. It was clear he needed to get

back to his own life and forget about Cassie Andreas and the people around her.

Cassie screamed again.

"Baby, no." Jessica rocked her back and forth. "Please. Wake up. You can't go on like—"

Cassie's mouth stretched wide and she screamed. Over and over.

Pulse rapid. Skin clammy.

"Hypodermic?" Teresa asked.

"I gave her a shot during the last episode, and it hardly fazed her. If I give her too much now, it could kill her."

But what would work? she wondered frantically. This fit had been going on for over twenty minutes. It was Cassie's worst attack yet, and she couldn't let the child—

"Take care of her," she told Teresa. She jumped to her feet and ran out of the room, past Cassie's guard and down the hall. She threw open Melissa's door. "Cassie's bad. I don't know what you can do, but if there's a chance to—"

Melissa didn't answer.

Jessica turned on the lamp.

Melissa was lying with her eyes open.

"Mellie?"

Rapid pulse. Clammy skin.

"Shit."

Tears were running down Jessica's cheeks as she ran out of the room. What the hell could she do? Everything was crazy. Nothing made sense. There was no reason for that lovely child to die.

And Melissa. Oh, God, Melissa.

Sweet Jesus, what could she do? There was nothing—

You have to find a way to break the stream. Find a way to enter something new into the mix.

She was running down the stairs and out in the rain.

Break the stream.

Find something new.

She knew where to find a new element. She had known since the night Andreas had forbidden her to have anything to do with Michael Travis.

Screw it. She couldn't stand by and let this horror happen.

She pounded on the door of the gatehouse. "Open the door, dammit."

Travis opened it. "What the hell—"

"Come on." She grabbed his arm. "I need you. Now."

"What's happened?"

"Don't ask questions. Just come." She pulled him out. "I'm Jessica Riley and—"

"I know who you are. What I don't know is what you're doing here."

"I'll explain later. Just come with me."

"I'm coming." He ran beside her up the driveway. "The kid?"

"Yes. I think she could die." Jessica tried to steady her voice. "She's having a nightmare and I can't wake her." They reached the manor and she pulled him inside the foyer. "You've got to help."

"I'm no doctor."

"Don't argue. Just do what I say." She heard the screams as she ran up the staircase. Relief poured through her. If Cassie was screaming, she was still alive.

Larry Fike met her at the top of the steps, his gaze on Travis. "He can't come in, Dr. Riley. I have my orders."

"He *is* coming in," she said fiercely. "You can search him. You can come into the bedroom and stand beside him. But he's coming in. I need him."

"I have my orders."

"And are you going to explain to the President why you kept me from having the means to save his daughter's life?"

"I have my—" He stopped, his gaze on Cassie's door. "Spread-eagle and put your hands on the wall, Travis."

She watched impatiently as Fike frisked Travis. "Hurry. Please, she's—"

Fike motioned for Travis to go into the bed-room but followed him immediately.

Jessica flew over to the bed. "How is she, Teresa?"

"Maybe a little worse." She looked at Travis. "What's he doing here?"

"I'm asking the same question," Travis said. "What am I doing here?"

"I don't know. I had to do something—"

Another scream.

Travis jumped and then took a step forward. "Can't you stop that? It's got to be bad for her to—"

"If I could stop it, I wouldn't need you." She took a deep breath and tried to think. "She's having a nightmare and I can't jar her out of it. I think it's about Vasaro and she's trying to get away from something. But she can't escape it so the nightmare keeps going on and on. We have to have something to break the pattern."

"Me?"

"You saved her life at Vasaro. You may have to do it again tonight."

"She's that bad?"

"I don't know. The nightmare has to stop."

"You're damn right it does." Travis sat down on the bed. He gathered Cassie's hands in his. He was silent for an instant and then said,

"You're safe, Cassie. I'm here. It's over. Remember, we're going to go into the kitchen and wait for your mom and dad."

Cassie screamed.

"You're safe. I'm here. He's gone. They're all gone."

She screamed.

"Listen to me, Cassie." His voice was low, urgent. His gaze fastened on her face. Jessica could almost feel his will grappling with the child's terror. "It's over. You're safe. He's gone."

Cassie's scream broke off.

"No one can hurt you. He can't hurt anyone. You're safe."

Cassie was staring at him.

"He's gone. They're all gone. You're safe."

She drew a deep breath.

Minutes passed. Finally she closed her eyes.

Thank you, God. Jessica stepped forward and took Cassie's pulse. It was steadying.

"Is she okay?" Travis asked.

"For now. She's in a deep sleep."

"Will she have another nightmare?"

"Not likely. She's never had two in one night." She turned to Teresa. "Please keep an eye on her."

"I will." Teresa stared at Travis. "I'd keep him around."

Jessica nodded tiredly. "I'll be back soon."
Mellie. She had to check on Mellie. She left
the room, hurried down the hall to the blue
room.

"Mellie?"

No answer.

She crossed to the bed. Melissa also appeared
to be in a deep sleep. She took her pulse. Almost
normal.

Melissa's lids slowly opened. "Bad . . . time.
You almost . . . lost us."

"How do you feel?"

"Like we've been hit . . . by a truck." She was
looking over Jessica's shoulder. "Thank . . . you."

Jessica turned her head to see Michael Travis
standing a few feet away.

"For what?" he said.

"Later . . . sleepy . . ." Her lids fluttered closed
again. "Thank . . ."

"Good idea. Go to sleep." Jessica pulled the
sheet up around her sister's shoulders. "I'll check
on you in a few hours."

"Don't . . . have . . . to. We're . . . fine."

"I'll do it anyway." Jessica motioned for Travis
to follow her. "Good night, Mellie."

Melissa didn't answer. She was asleep.

In the hallway Jessica turned to Travis. "Why
did you follow me?"

"What else was I to do? Evidently, you had no

more use for me with the little girl, and that Secret Service man was staring a hole in me."

"You had no right to barge into my sister's bedroom."

He shrugged. "You left the door open, and when I saw you were taking her pulse, I thought you might need me."

"I didn't need you. Mellie . . . was just . . . tired."

"Oh?"

"Thank you, everything's fine now. You can go."

He shook his head. "I'm wet to the skin and I'm not going out in that storm until I dry off and have a cup of hot coffee." He started down the staircase. "If you'll point me to the kitchen? You needn't come with me. I'm used to fending for myself."

She could see that he was. His manner was as casual as if this were his home. But that he was also very wet was true. She'd been so upset, she'd not even noticed. "I'm sorry." She hurried down the stairs. "Are you cold? I guess I should have let you get an umbrella at the gatehouse, but my mind was on other things."

"I don't think you even realized it was raining." He followed her into the kitchen. "And you're as wet as I am. Or didn't you realize that either?"

She hadn't. "I'll get us a couple of towels after I put on the coffee."

"I'll get them. Tell me where they are."

"The armoire in the powder room down the hall to the left."

"Right."

Jessica had put the coffee on and set cups on the table by the time he came back.

"Nice house." He tossed her a big white towel and started drying his hair with the one in his hand. "It's not often you see antique armoires in a powder room. It must be like living in another age."

"Sometimes." She wiped her face and neck before dabbing at her hair. "Particularly when the electricity goes out." She tossed the towel aside. "Do you take cream or sugar?"

Travis shook his head. "Does the power go out often?"

"No, my parents had the place rewired when I was a kid, but it still has its quirky moments." She poured the coffee. "The President said you lived in Europe, so you must be familiar with ancient houses."

"Only in the slums." He sat down and cradled his cup in his hands. "The houses I grew up in usually fell down before they had a chance of becoming historic landmarks. When I became an adult, I usually preferred modern houses with all the conveniences because I was moving fast and hard." His eyes twinkled. "And I didn't have time to fix quirky electricity."

"Who does? It's a choice you make." She sat down across from him. "I want to thank you for helping me with Cassie. I know I must have seemed like a crazy woman when I came pounding on your door."

"It was definitely unexpected."

"But you came with me anyway. I'll always be grateful. I was terrified."

"I could see it." He sipped his coffee. "Tell me about Cassie."

"Everyone in the world knows that she's suffering from post-traumatic stress syndrome."

"But everyone doesn't know about those nightmares. Does she talk about them?"

"She doesn't talk, period."

"Then how do you know she's dreaming about Vasaro?"

She glanced down to her cup. "It's logical, isn't it?"

"Yes."

"And you were able to bring her out of it because you were at Vasaro."

"Also very logical. Why did you think she'd react to me?"

"You were a new element. It shook up the structure of the dream. When the President first told me about you, I had an idea you could prove useful."

He smiled mockingly. "I'm glad to have been of service. However, I don't think Andreas would agree I was the right candidate for the job."

"You're the only candidate Cassie will accept. He'd agree to anything to help his daughter."

"Then if you want to use me again, you'd better get on the horn and tell him so. I'd make a bet the Secret Service guys will be reporting in."

"What?"

"Call him and tell him you need me. He can't be any more stubborn than that Secret Service man you were ready to take on to get me into Cassie's room."

She had been so tired and numb, she hadn't thought past this one episode. But evidently Michael Travis had already been considering the next step. "I might not need you."

"Do you want to take that chance?"

No, she didn't. "It might not work a second time."

"And then again, it might."

Her gaze narrowed on his face. "Why are you so willing to help me?"

"Why do you think? My kind, generous spirit?"

"I don't know anything about you except what Andreas told me."

"That should be enough. Though it may be a little unfair, since I've made a study of you since I arrived at Juniper."

"What?"

He chuckled. "Don't worry. I'm no Peeping Tom. I read your book. It was very revealing."

"Oh."

"I didn't have anything else to do. It's been a very boring week. This is the most exciting thing that's happened to me since I left Amsterdam."

"You sound exhilarated. I'm glad what happened to Cassie furnished you with amusement."

"Amusement? No, but I have to admit that helping the kid did bring me a certain rush. I'm sorry if that offends you, but it's the nature of this particular beast. I can see you believe I should be as profound and selfless as you obviously are, but you won't find that in me. I don't get involved."

"Then why are you offering to help me?"

"I have a passion for disrupting the status quo. It interests me to change what most people think of as set in stone."

"How very . . . cool."

"You mean cold." He smiled. "I'm not cold, Dr. Riley. And changing the status quo isn't always bad. You had no objection to my doing that with Cassie."

And he hadn't been cold when he'd been talking to Cassie. His passion and forcefulness had jerked Cassie out of that deadly nightmare.

"Many things aren't black or white." He was reading her expression. "I promise I won't hurt your Cassie."

"She's not mine."

"Isn't she?"

He saw too much. "I want her well."

"And, unlike me, you do get involved."

"Most people do." Jessica studied him. Strength. Intelligence. A hint of recklessness. What else lay behind that face? "Why do you want to help Cassie? It isn't only boredom."

He chuckled. "You drew me into the situation as a pawn. I forgot to tell you that I also have a passion for control."

She stiffened. "I'm the one in control of Cassie. No one else."

"Cassie's in control of Cassie." His smile faded. "You need me, but you're not going to get me as a pawn."

"You couldn't stand aside and let that little girl die."

"You don't know that. I'm a wild card to you.

I could be anything. Do you want to take a chance?"

He knew she couldn't, damn him.

Travis shook his head. "I'm not going to move quickly. We'll start out with me being humbly at your beck and call. I just want an understanding."

She thought about it and then nodded jerkily.

"Good." He finished his coffee and stood up. "Now I'll get back to the gatehouse and you get on the phone to Andreas. Okay?"

"I'll think about it."

"Up to you. It will be harder if he calls you after hearing from the guards here." He waved and moved toward the door. "See you."

She sat there for a long time. She wasn't accustomed to taking orders, and Travis's suggestion had been dangerously close to an order. It seemed he had spoken truthfully when he said he liked control.

He wouldn't get it. She had no intention of yielding one iota of supervision over Cassie's treatment. From the moment he had sat down on Cassie's bed, she had seen a change in him. The challenge had seemed to electrify him, every cell in his body had taken on a force. She might need his determination but not his domination.

But, annoyingly, Travis had been right about

calling Andreas. She'd been tempted to ignore his suggestion just because he'd made it, but that would be counterproductive. Call Andreas, get it over with, then sit down and consider how she could use Michael Travis.

It was still raining, but Travis hardly felt the drops as he ran back to the gatehouse. He was still charged with the explosive energy of the battle with Cassie . . . and Jessica Riley.

Fascinating.

The struggle with Cassie and then the interesting interchange he'd witnessed between Jessica and her sister, Melissa. Pieces of a puzzle were coming to light that he found very interesting.

And dangerous.

Maybe he hadn't gotten his fill of walking on a tightrope after all.

6

Andreas was silent when Jessica finished.

When he did speak, his voice was thick. "You think she could have died?"

"I wouldn't have brought Travis to the house if I hadn't thought there was a strong possibility."

"Christ." Another silence. "What the hell is happening to her?"

"That's what I'm trying to find out."

"I want to be with her. I hate being thousands of miles away."

"You couldn't help her, sir."

"But Travis did."

"I don't believe there's any doubt he saved her life." She paused. "I may need to use him again."

"I didn't want him around her. I thought it would make the nightmares worse."

"They couldn't be worse."

Another silence. "Then use him. Use anyone or anything you have to. I'll send word he's to put himself at your disposal."

Travis would love that. "Thank you, sir. I'm sure that will help."

"She's getting worse." His voice was uneven. "Why can't we do something? Why are we just spinning our wheels while she—"

She couldn't bear the pain in his words. "I know how you feel. I wonder . . . if you'd consider taking her back to Vasaro."

"No! Absolutely not. I may be desperate, but I'm not crazy."

"I think it might—"

"No."

She heaved a sigh. She hadn't thought he'd accept the idea, but she'd had to try. It was radical, even dangerous, but she was as desperate as Andreas. "I wish you'd consider it."

"I'd consider getting a new doctor for my daughter first." He said something to someone in the background and then came back on the line. "I have to go. There's a damn reception at the royal palace. I want to hear better news from you the next time you call or I'll fly home and find someone who can help Cassie." He hung up.

The threat didn't bother Jessica. She knew he was just in agony over a seemingly hopeless situation. If she'd believed someone else could do a better job with Cassie, she'd go and hire him herself.

But he was right—lately they'd just been spinning their wheels, trying to maintain the status quo.

I have a passion for disrupting the status quo.

Maybe bringing Travis more fully into the equation might be a good step.

And maybe not. At any rate, something had to change. Cassie couldn't go on like this. Jessica had to explore every possibility to bring Cassie back.

She wearily started up the stairs. Time to check on Cassie and then get some sleep.

She stopped at the door of the blue room.

Every possibility.

Melissa.

Melissa was as exhausted as Cassie. Because the two had been joined?

The idea was wild, outrageous, frightening, a complete violation of logic.

Every possibility.

Not now. She had to give herself time to adjust to the idea.

Tomorrow . . .

★   ★   ★

"What's that wonderful smell?" Melissa asked as she came into the kitchen. "Lord, I'm hungry."

"Huevos rancheros." Jessica glanced over her shoulder. "But you've blown it. I was going to give you breakfast in bed."

"You know I can't stand lolling in bed." She went to the refrigerator and took out the orange juice carton. "How's Cassie?"

Jessica put two sausages on the plate with the eggs. "You tell me."

Melissa's smile faded. "I have no idea. And if I made a guess, you wouldn't believe me."

"I don't know what to believe." She poured the juice and sat down at the table. "Eat."

"You don't have to tell me twice." Melissa sat down and started to eat. "Wonderful. Tomorrow I'll make breakfast."

"You don't cook."

"Sure I do. I've learned to do a lot of things since I went away to school. Living on your own is very empowering." She took a drink of juice. "I would have learned sooner, but you seemed to enjoy being in charge and doing things for me."

"It was just that I'm accustomed to—"

"I know." Melissa grinned. "And I'll always be baby sister who got lost in the briar patch. It's fine with me. Whatever makes you happy."

Jessica felt a ripple of shock. Melissa's tone was almost indulgent. "I never meant to treat you—"

"You treat me just great." She took another bite. "And you make a fab breakfast. Now, how is Cassie?"

"Good. Not as good as you, but as normal as she gets these days." She leaned back in her chair and looked at Melissa. "I thought you both might die last night."

"I know you did." She reached for her juice. "I knew you were scared when you came into my room that first time, but I couldn't do anything to help you. I was pretty wasted."

"Help me? You were the one who—" She drew a deep breath. "What happened to you last night?"

Melissa looked down into her glass. "What do you want me to say? If you need lies, I'll tell you lies. I'm not sure you're ready for the truth."

"I have to be ready for whatever you tell me. I don't know if you remember, but I came to you asking for help."

"I only remember you being scared. I was somewhat involved at the time." She shifted her glance to Jessica's face. "Since you came to me, then you must have believed me on some level."

"I don't know what to believe. But Andreas told me once he'd beg help from a whirling dervish if it would get his daughter well. I'd do the same just to keep her alive."

"I'm not a whirling dervish, and I don't even know what I can do. I hoped I'd have more control, but it was like being sucked into a tornado. She just carried me along with her." She shuddered. "If Travis hadn't come . . ."

"You knew he was here?"

"How could I help it? He was as strong as Cassie. He put himself between her and the monsters."

"Monsters?"

"She sees them as monsters. They have eyes but no faces."

"The attackers at Vasaro wore ski masks."

Melissa nodded. "That would account for it."

"Tell me what it's like."

"Terror. Sorrow. We're in a long, dark tunnel and we were happy there, but the monsters have found a way to get in. They're chasing us and we know they'll catch us if we don't find . . ."

"Find what?"

"I don't know. Her thinking is all garbled by the fear. Whatever it is she's looking for, she can't find it. And there's only one other way to escape them."

"The hell there is. She can come back to us."

"We don't see that as an option."

"Half the time you say *her* and half the time you say *we*. You're not joined to her any longer, are you?"

Melissa shook her head. "But the link was very strong and so is the memory. I'll try not to— You're looking at me as if I'm crazy."

"Why should I accuse you of being nuts? I'm the doctor and I'm the one who's accepting all this as if it were perfectly normal."

"No, you're not. You're taking everything with a grain of salt and trying to find a reasonable explanation for it. It's not your nature to do anything else." She smiled. "Right?"

"I care about you." Jessica reached over and covered Mellie's hand with her own. "It scares me that you might—"

"The only thing you should be scared about is if we can't stop what's happening to Cassie . . . and me. I'm not nuts. I'm just riding that tornado and hoping something will make it go away." She squeezed Jessica's hand. "Toward the end, after Travis came, I was feeling stronger and I began to think instead of feel. Maybe if I can gain some control, I'll be able to stop the tornado."

"God, I hope so."

"But I have to have Michael Travis, Jessica. I'm not strong enough to fight for Cassie by myself. He has to stand between."

"You're talking as if he's some kind of medium."

"I don't know why he's able to help Cassie. You brought him to Cassie because I told you to find something to break the flow. It worked. *He* worked. We may be able to do without him later but not now. Get him, Jessica."

"Oh, I got him. It wasn't difficult. He finds the situation very interesting and he's bored at the moment." She made a face. "But he's not going to be easy to handle."

"I could tell." She got to her feet. "Now I need to go for a run before I hit the books." She brushed a kiss across Jessica's forehead. "Poor Jessica. I know it's hard for you. But everything will be okay."

Melissa was treating her as if she were a child. Well, she felt as confused as a child. Everything Melissa had said was out of her realm of belief, yet she had no option but to go along with her. "Just one more question. What would have happened to you if I hadn't brought Travis last night?"

She didn't speak for a moment. "I don't know. I'm not sure how it works. But I don't think I could have broken free at the end."

"The end?"

She moved quickly toward the door. "If Cassie had died, she would have taken me with her."

★ ★ ★

Melissa knocked on the door of the gatehouse. "The sun is shining and all's right with the world. Come out and play, Michael Travis."

Travis threw open the door. "I beg your pardon?"

"In case you don't recognize me as the rag of a woman you saw in my bedroom last night, I'm Melissa Riley."

"Oh, I recognize you."

"Then go change and come out and run with me. You usually run about this time, don't you?"

"Yes."

"I'll wait." She came into the house and dropped onto the sofa. "This is a nice place. Jessica and I used to play here when we were kids. Hurry, will you? I have to get back and study."

He smiled. "I'll try not to keep you waiting." He disappeared into the bedroom.

Mellie glanced around. Open laptop on the dining table, books piled on the coffee table. But other than that, he was very neat. It was what she'd expected. Everything organized.

She leaned forward and checked out the book titles. She smiled. Smart. Very smart.

She moved to the window and looked up at the manor. How many times had he stood here and stared at the lights in Cassie's window?

"Ready." He came out of the bedroom wearing shorts and an Oxford University T-shirt. "Unless you've changed your mind, Ms. Riley?"

He didn't know what to think of her. That was okay. It put her one step ahead. "No way. And call me Melissa or Mellie like Jessica does." She jumped to her feet and trotted outside. The sun struck her face like a blessing, and she stopped and closed her eyes. "Isn't it beautiful today? And smell that grass. I love mornings after a rain. It just sort of . . . fills me until I overflow."

"Your cup runneth over?"

"Yep." Her eyes flicked open and she jumped down the steps. "Race you to the pond in back of the house."

She beat him by four yards. She leaned against the willow tree and tried to get her breath. "Did you let me win?"

"What makes you think that?"

"You're in good shape and I've seen you run."

"You're in pretty good shape yourself."

She chuckled. "From another man I'd take that as a pass."

"Why not from me?"

"Because you're not interested in sex at the moment. You're wondering what the hell I'm up to."

"Am I going to find out?"

She nodded. "When I get my breath." She sank down on the ground. "What do you think I'm up to?"

"I'm supposed to talk until you get your breath?"

"Good guess."

"Let's see." He dropped down a few feet away. "It's difficult to assess motivations, since I've never met you before. From what I've observed at a distance, you and your sister seem very close. Did she send you with a message?"

"Jessica delivers her own messages. I deliver mine."

"And what is your message?"

She stared him directly in the eyes. "Don't you dare do anything to hurt my sister."

His brows lifted. "I have no intention of harming her."

"I believe you. However, action doesn't always follow intent. It gets sidetracked when personal gain becomes involved. You don't care anything about Jessica. I doubt if you care about Cassie. It's hard to tell."

"Is it? But you must know I helped her last night."

"No one knows better." She paused. "As I think you're aware."

He looked at her inquiringly.

"You had three books on parapsychology on the coffee table. One I left when I came down for a visit. I read it in the gatehouse because I didn't want Jessica to see it around the manor. I've never read the other two. Where did you get them in the middle of the night?"

"I sent one of the Secret Service men at the gate to an all-night bookstore in D.C. They were very obliging as long as I didn't leave the property. I spent several hours scanning them." He smiled. "And since I didn't get any sleep, I wasn't going to take my usual morning run."

"Am I supposed to feel sorry for you?"

"Heaven forbid. You have enough problems."

Her gaze narrowed on his face. "Then I assume you found what you wanted in those books?"

"I overheard what you told your sister in the bedroom last night. That was enough to pique my interest. So I hit the Internet and then hunkered down with a few books."

"And you found out I was a freak."

"But not the only one. Not even the first one."

"What?"

"Did you think you were the only case who came back with a little baggage on the side? Professor Hans Dedrick discovered four cases similar to your own. One in Greece, one in Switzerland, and two in China."

"Dedrick?"

"*Trauma, Memory, and the Way Back.* It was written in 1999. You didn't read it?"

She shook her head in bewilderment. "And I even combed through the libraries trying to find something, anything . . ."

"It was published by a university press in Great Britain. As you've noted, I'm an expert at retrieving information. I'll let you borrow it if you like."

"I'll get my own copy as soon as I get back to school. Did Jessica mention anything about me?"

"Not a syllable. It's natural that she'd be very protective. She's spent a good many years caring for you. Your talent is somewhat 'unusual,' and she wouldn't want you to be misunderstood."

Jesus, he was clever. He had watched and listened and put the puzzle pieces of their lives and relationship together. "And do you understand?"

"Do you mean believe? Perhaps. I spent a lot of my early years in the East, and I've seen stranger things. It certainly doesn't make me uneasy."

Melissa studied him. "No, it only interests you. Jessica told me you dealt in information, and I can see how you'd be good at that. You

gather and dig and analyze. . . . You find it exciting, don't you?"

"Yes. Since I've been cursed with boundless
curiosity, it's definitely an addiction."

"And dealing with Cassie is a quick fix for a
few weeks of boredom?"

"I'm not quite so callous. I wouldn't use that
nice kid just to relieve the monotony. I help her,
she helps me." He chuckled. "Though I didn't
realize until you appeared on the scene how intriguing the next few weeks may prove to be.
When did you realize you had this bizarre talent? Your sister didn't mention anything about it
in her book."

"She didn't know about it. She was so happy
she'd brought me back that I didn't want to
spoil anything for her. I wouldn't have told her
about it if we hadn't run into this problem with
Cassie. She's not like you. It makes her damn
uneasy."

"I can see why. She impressed me as being a
very solemn, pragmatic lady."

"She's had to be pragmatic. It's not as if she
doesn't have a great sense of humor. She didn't
have much chance to—"

"Okay, okay. I didn't mean to insult her. She
seems to be a very caring woman." He changed
the subject. "You didn't answer me. When did

you realize you were broadcasting on a different wavelength?"

"About five months after I came back. It scared the hell out of me." She stood up. "Now, take your curiosity and stuff it. That's all you're going to get out of me."

"You can never tell. I haven't even started yet." He got to his feet. "Let's be perfectly clear. You're warning me to stay away from your sister and Cassie?"

"Where did you get that idea? Cassie needs you."

"And do you need me, Melissa?" he asked softly.

"Yes, but I'm working on it." She bent down and retied her left running shoe. "So don't get used to the idea. You're going to be replaced." She straightened. "Jessica is the most decent human being on the face of the earth. I won't have her hurt." She held up a hand as he started to speak. "I don't care that you don't intend to do it. Right now the most important thing in her life is getting Cassie well. If Cassie dies, she'll be devastated. So you're going to make sure she doesn't die. You're not going to walk away if you see something more interesting on the horizon. You're going to stay until Cassie's on the road to recovery if it takes years."

"Are you quite finished telling me what I'm going to do?"

"No, you have to promise to protect Jessica. The President put you here because you needed to be kept safe. I don't want any of the flak surrounding you to impact her."

"Is that all?"

"For now."

"Good. Then I'll race you back to the gatehouse." He looked back over his shoulder. "And this time you won't win, Melissa."

He hadn't promised anything, but she hadn't really counted on it. It was enough that he knew what she expected of him. "It won't bother me." She started after him. "I'll just work on it."

I'll just work on it.

Travis stood in the doorway and watched Melissa race up the drive. That single sentence seemed to sum up Melissa Riley. Courage in adversity and a determination to have her own way no matter what it took. On the other hand, maybe that sentence didn't encompass her entire personality. He'd never seen anyone with such glowing vitality. In her book Jessica had talked about the first months after Melissa had come back. Not only had her sister displayed a superior intelligence, she had also shown an insatiable thirst for life, which Jessica had attributed to the desire to make up for lost time. She'd said she expected the effect to dwindle after a few years.

Well, those few years had passed and he had an idea Jessica had been wrong. Melissa Riley was a firecracker and more complex than any of them might be able to imagine. Jessica had bargained and handled him with reason and maturity. Melissa hadn't tried to bargain. She'd analyzed his character and then thrown down a challenge . . . and a threat.

How phenomenally well she'd read him in such a brief encounter.

Interesting . . .

"What were you doing down by the pond with Travis?" Jessica's voice was disapproving. "Not a good idea, Mellie."

"He's not off limits anymore." Melissa grinned over her shoulder as she started up the stairs. "And he's more interesting than I first thought. He's very bright, and intelligence is mega-sexy."

"The President may have said he's not off limits, but I didn't. For God's sake, he's a criminal."

"And you want me to find a lawyer or a doctor or maybe a computer executive. What about a banker?"

"Sounds good to me."

Melissa smiled. "Okay, I'll look for one the minute I go back to school."

"I'm not joking, Mellie."

"I know you're not. You think I need a stabilizing influence. You're probably right. Stop worrying, I didn't ask him to go to bed with me. We just took a little run together."

Jessica moistened her lips. "I didn't think you— I wouldn't ask you to tell—"

"But I'll tell you anyway." Her smile faded. "I'd never do anything to cause you concern. If you don't want me to go running with Travis, it stops right here."

"And you think I'm a nosy bitch."

"I think you love and care about me. And not running with him is no great loss. Our little jog couldn't have been more casual."

"It didn't look casual. It looked damned intense."

And it had felt intense. For the few minutes they were running together, Melissa had been aware of a weird sense of intimacy. And when they had been talking at the pond, she had almost felt the sparks, the undercurrent, that lay beneath every word. It had been . . . exciting. *He* had been exciting.

Well, danger was always exciting, but Travis could become an enemy in a heartbeat.

So? Playing games with the enemy was stimulating too.

Still, that didn't make it the best option to choose in this circumstance. She started back up the stairs. "Nah, it's definitely the banker for me, Jessica."

Amsterdam

"Something very interesting is happening," Provlif told Deschamps over the phone.

"You found Cassie Andreas?"

"No, but while my CIA contact was nosing around trying to locate her, he stumbled on another bit of information. Andreas sent *Air Force One* on a hush-hush trip to Amsterdam a few weeks ago."

"Carrying his daughter?"

"No, it was a retrieval. They picked up Michael Travis and brought him to Andrews Air Force Base."

"Travis?" Deschamps was puzzled. It didn't fit

with the information he'd gathered. "The CIA captured him?"

"They picked him up and delivered him to the President. They left together for an unknown destination."

"You're sure?"

"My source in the CIA is impeccable."

"Then why can't they tell you where the girl is?"

"The CIA and the Secret Service seldom confide in each other."

"Find them."

"Whatever you say. As you know, I've been concentrating on finding Cassie Andreas only since you told me that's what you wanted me to do."

"I wanted you to do what was needed. Get the child. Find Travis."

A pause. "And kill him?"

"No. I want to do it myself. Besides, he's going to prove more valuable alive for a while." He hung up.

Travis and Andreas. Travis was *not* being held against his will. What in hell was happening? Since he had been here, he had stumbled on intriguing and profitable possibilities he hadn't expected. But now the picture was becoming more puzzling.

Also more promising?

He'd always believed a clever man was one who let others win the prize and then plucked it from their grasp. Travis was moving, manipulating, and obviously shifting into high gear with Andreas. . . .

A gift for me, Travis?

7

"Get up here," Jessica said when Travis picked up the phone two nights later. "Now."

"I'll be right there."

She was waiting on the porch when Travis arrived a short time later. "How long has it been going on?" he asked.

"Fifteen minutes."

"Why didn't you call me sooner?"

"I wanted to give her a chance to come out of it by herself."

He followed her into the house. "And eliminate the need for my services."

"Of course."

"I understand. But that fifteen-minute delay might not be healthy for Cassie."

"And are you healthy for her?"

"I'm the best game in town." They climbed the stairs, and Travis nodded at Fike as they reached Cassie's room. "Good evening. Same drill?"

"Sorry."

"I didn't expect anything else." He leaned against the wall while Fike searched him. "At this rate, we're going to become very intimate friends." He opened the door. "Has she been screaming like that since it started?"

Fike nodded. "Poor kid. I've never heard anything like this before. Sometimes she scares me to death."

"Stop talking and go help her, Travis," Jessica said curtly. "If you can."

Travis sat down on the bed. "I'll do my best." He gathered Cassie's hands in his. "Listen to me, Cassie. It's Michael. I'm here and nothing's going to harm you. You don't have to run away."

Cassie screamed.

"I stopped them before. I can do it again. Just let me help you and we'll find a way. . . ."

Thank God.

Michael was there in the darkness of the tunnel. Melissa couldn't see him, but she could feel him. Which meant Cassie could feel him too.

*Or maybe she could see him. Melissa was so fright-
ened, she couldn't tell.*

*The monsters. Sweet Jesus, the monsters. They
were going to catch us and blow our heads to bits.*

Run.

Run.

Run.

Find it.

Run.

Find it before they got close enough to—

Run.

*It hurt to breathe. Their hearts were going to burst.
No, slow down.*

*Michael was here. The monsters couldn't touch
them as long as he stood between.*

What was he saying?

It didn't matter.

He was here.

*Cassie's grip on Melissa was loosening. She was
floating free. . . .*

She could feel Cassie's desperation. "Come back.
Miss you," *the little girl told her.*

*The call was as alluring as a siren's song. Don't
yield. Stay clear.*

"You're part of me," *Cassie said.*

"No."

"Lonely."

"Then come back with me."

She felt Cassie's ripple of fear. "Bad."

"Not anymore."

"Lonely. Safe now. No monsters. Together we'll find it. Come back."

Melissa was lonely too. Why not stay and let herself be— She was drifting closer to Cassie. She made a tremendous effort and jerked herself free. "No, I'm going away. Good-bye, Cassie."

"Lonely . . ."

"Melissa."

She opened her eyes to see Jessica's face above her. She was so tired, she could barely speak. "Hi. It's . . . okay, isn't it?"

Jessica nodded. "Cassie's sleeping?"

"Not yet. But she will be soon. The nightmare's over." She reached out and took Jessica's hand. "Don't look so worried. We're both fine. Where's Travis?"

"Outside in the hall." She paused. "He . . . helped?"

"I know you'd like me to say no, but we couldn't have made it without him." Her eyes closed. "And you didn't have to leave him out in the hall. He . . . knows about me."

Jessica stiffened. "What does he know?"

"That I'm a freak."

"You told him?"

"He figured it out for himself. He's very comfortable with it. Not like you. Poor Jessica . . ."

"Poor Mellie."

"No, I'm learning. . . . It's not like I thought. There's so much more going on with Cassie. I had a weird feeling she's hiding something."

"What?"

"I don't know, but things may not be what I thought. And she's so lonely, Jessica. It hurts me that she's so lonely."

"You said Donny was lonely."

"Not like this."

"Weren't you lonely when you were in your forest?"

"No, I had you, I knew you were there. Maybe out of sight, but you never left me."

"Cassie has people who love her."

"But she's afraid to let them in. She's afraid if she lets anyone into her tunnel, the monsters will get in." Her grip tightened. "The monsters are terrible, terrible creatures. We can't let them in."

"Cassie can't let them in."

Melissa tried to smile. "I did it again? The monsters frighten me as much as they do her, and it kind of throws me back."

"We have to get Cassie to let us in so we can bring her back."

Melissa nodded. "It's just that . . ."

"The monsters?"

"Think of your worst childhood nightmare and multiply it a hundred times and you'll realize how Cassie feels." She closed her eyes. "Good night, Jessica. I don't want to talk anymore. Go hash this out with Travis. He's probably listening at the door. I'll see you in the morning." She heard a chuckle from the other side of the door and called, "Good night, Travis. You did very well tonight."

"Eavesdropping is exceptionally rude," Jessica told Travis.

"She didn't mind."

"But I did. If I'd wanted you in the room, I'd have invited you."

"And if I'd waited for invitations in my line of work, I'd be a pauper. You don't gather information by standing politely to one side. I wanted to know what was happening with Melissa, so I listened." He took her elbow. "Come on. I'll make you coffee."

"I don't want coffee." She bit her lip. "I want to talk about Mellie. I'm sure what's happening is only temporary. She's not really . . ."

"You want me to promise I won't call the local funny farm and tell them to bring the straitjacket for your sister?"

"There's nothing wrong with her."

"I believe that." He looked at her. "Do you?"

"Of course I do." She rubbed her temple. "I'm not taking this very well. This psychic stuff's not my cup of tea."

"Then let me handle it."

"The hell I will. Mellie's my sister. All I want from you is for you to not hurt her."

"That sounds very familiar," he murmured. "You two aren't as different as I first thought. Never fear. I'm not going to use anything I hear in this house to hurt Melissa."

She gazed at him suspiciously.

"Why should I? It's nothing to me."

She nodded slowly. "That's right, none of us is important to you."

"I can't let you be important." He smiled. "But that doesn't mean I don't admire you both. I think I'm even starting to like you."

"Amazing."

"Yes, it is. So can I make you coffee? We can both use it, and since I'm going to be around, we might as well call a truce."

She stared at him without speaking. His principles were questionable and he was different from anyone she'd ever known. There was a blunt honesty about him she found oddly comforting. "You have truces only when there's war.

If you keep helping Cassie, there's no war." She started down the stairs. "One cup of coffee."

Go to sleep, Melissa told herself. It was all right now. Cassie had drifted off.

It had gone better than the last time. After Travis had come, she had been able to step out of Cassie and see her with a little detachment. Not much, but she'd take anything she could get.

And Cassie had been forced to recognize Melissa as a separate entity, which was real progress. But the impression of something that wasn't quite right, that wasn't as it seemed to be, still bothered her.

And what was Cassie searching for?

Together we'll find it.

She should have asked Cassie what she was trying to find. The chance had slid right past her because it had been such a struggle to leave.

Next time . . .

"May I come in?" Travis asked from the doorway. "If you're too tired, I'll go away."

"I'm tired." She turned on the lamp. "But I'm probably too charged to sleep, so you might as well come in. Sit down, Travis, and tell me what you want from me."

He smiled. "Maybe I don't want anything. Maybe this is purely a social call." He sat down in the chair beside her bed. "After all, we did share a rather unique experience tonight."

"You wouldn't have crept up here after you left Jessica if you'd wanted to socialize."

"You make me sound like a cat burglar."

"Have you ever been one?"

He didn't answer the question. "It's true Jessica doesn't know I'm here. I didn't want to upset her. She's pretty protective of you."

"So why are you here?"

"I thought we should get to know each other." He chuckled as she raised her brows. "No, not in the carnal sense. I have no intention of taking advantage of you when you're—"

"Rode hard and put away wet?"

"Good God, what a ghastly image."

"It's how I feel at the moment. Cassie's not easy." She propped a second pillow beneath her head. "Okay, you don't want to screw me. And I doubt if you're going to tell me anything about yourself, so the getting-to-know part is aimed at me. Right?"

"Right."

"Why?"

"We've already established how curious I am."

She could see the curiosity in his face. His expression was alert, searching. "Didn't you find out enough about me from Jessica's book?"

"From her point of view. But information can always be slanted."

"Jessica is intimidatingly honest."

"We don't always see things the same way. Didn't you ever want to give your viewpoint?"

She should probably tell him to go away. She was none of his business. But she suddenly realized she didn't want him to leave. "What do you want to know?"

"What do you want to tell me?"

"Look, don't pull that bull on me. I'm a psych major."

He laughed. "Sorry. You grew up here at Juniper?"

She nodded. "It's a great place for a kid to grow up. I was the baby of the family and my parents and Jessica spoiled me rotten. She was my idol and I was a real pain in the ass to her." She looked away from him. "And then, after the accident, I was an albatross around her neck."

"I'm not asking you to talk about the accident."

"But the accident is the dividing line. It's like looking at before and after pictures. I can talk about the accident. Jessica says it's good for me to keep it out in the open. I think she's scared that if I repress it, I'll explode or something."

"How old were you?"

"Fourteen. My mother and father and I were driving home from one of his favorite restaurants in Georgetown. I was in the backseat." She moistened her lips. "A car ran us off the road and down an incline. There was an explosion. I couldn't get the door open. I knew my father was dead, but my mother was screaming in the front seat. She was on fire. And the smell of burning flesh . . ."

"That's enough."

"I finally managed to get out. I opened the passenger door and pulled Mama out and started beating at the fire. But I couldn't get it out and she was screaming. . . ." She swallowed. "And then she stopped screaming."

"And then you went away to your forest."

"Yeah, it seemed the thing to do at the time." She drew a deep breath. "I was a selfish bitch. I should have been there for Jessica instead of becoming the burden of the century."

"I'd say you had cause." His hand tightened around hers. "And I'd bet Jessica agrees."

She hadn't realized he had taken her hand. She should move it.

What the hell. She didn't want to move it. His grasp felt warm and strong and gave her a sense of security. It was odd that a stranger would give her this feeling of safety. "Anyway, when I came back, I tried to get off Jessica's welfare roll. I went to high school, took special tutoring, and then entered the university."

"I would have thought you'd travel or just have a good time for a while."

"I had a good time. I ran, I played tennis, I learned to fly a plane. I made good friends." She smiled. "I always have a good time. That's what life's about on the outside. Enjoying every moment. But Jessica needed to know I was a stable, solid citizen. I can't tell you how disappointed she is about this Cassie development." She met his eyes. "So do you think you know me well enough now, Travis?"

He shook his head. "I have an idea I've just scratched the surface." He released her hand and stood up. "But it's been interesting. I didn't think you'd be this frank with me."

"Being enigmatic is too complicated for me. I'll leave that to you." She settled back down in bed. "Now turn out the light and let me go to sleep."

"I'm on my way." He switched off the lamp and moved toward the door. "Good night, Melissa."

"Travis."

"Yes."

"Why *did* you come back up here?"

"Why do you think?"

"You think being father confessor is going to draw us closer together and give me confidence in you?"

"You believe I'm that Machiavellian?"

"If you'd be as frank with me as I was with you, I'd find out."

"Well, you dismissed one of the most interesting reasons."

"What?"

"I never said I didn't *want* to screw you. I just said it wasn't my intention."

She burst out in laughter. "Flatter the lady and dodge the question. Jesus, you *are* Machiavellian. Get out of here, Travis."

She was still smiling as he left. He was utterly impossible . . . and much too stimulating. She could feel the blood tingling through her body, and her mind was humming and wide awake. It was entirely possible that he'd come here because he'd wanted to allay her suspicions for some reason.

It was also possible that he'd wanted to open the door to a sexual encounter. His last remark had been provocative as well as amusing, and if she'd responded differently, he might have turned around and come back.

The idea was too intriguing. What kind of

lover would Travis be? She shied away from the thought even as she felt her body ready. She'd already promised herself that she wouldn't worry Jessica, and she wasn't about to sneak around behind her back.

So concentrate on how safe she'd felt when he'd been holding her hand. That's a nice, platonic thought. If Travis wanted to be buddies, that was fine. It was sex that disturbed the mind as well as the senses, and she had enough disturbances in her life just then.

Travis quietly let himself out of the manor and went down the porch steps. It had been a fascinating evening, and not the least interesting facet had been the time spent with Melissa Riley. She had thought the visit had been planned, but she was wrong. It had been pure impulse, and he was not an impulsive man.

Curiosity?

Yes, he was curious, and he'd been rewarded more richly than he'd expected. She was probably the most frank, open person he'd ever met.

And her full-bodied laugh had been as sensual as a hand stroking him.

Jan had once said a man should listen to a woman laugh to determine how good she'd be in bed.

Well, he'd probably never know how good Melissa Riley was in bed. Since her sister was so protective, it would be courting trouble to move in that direction.

But some things were worth a good deal of trouble.

Forget it. He'd once mentally compared Melissa Riley to a firecracker and he didn't need to set off any more rockets than he had already. The situation was explosive enough.

8

"Karlstadt says he'll give you twenty million," Jan Van Beck said. "Not a dollar more."

"If he'll go twenty, he'll go twenty-five. Keep pushing."

"You can say that, but Karlstadt doesn't push easily."

"Then you'll earn your thirty percent."

"His people aren't above taking me out to the country and trying to squeeze your whereabouts out of me."

"Isn't it lucky you don't know?"

"Lucky for you."

"What did you find out from Henri Claron?"

"Nothing definite. I'm still working on him."

"He knows something?"

"Oh, yes. Henri's not a good actor and he's a frightened man. Almost as frightened as his wife. She kept looking at me as if I were torturing Henri."

"If he's that nervous, I'm surprised he hasn't been erased."

"He could have taken out insurance." He switched subjects. "Karlstadt's getting very edgy. He's heard about the Russians, and thinks you may be dealing with them too."

"A little worry never hurt anyone."

"Yes, it has, and this time it may be me."

"I promise I won't leave you hanging out on a limb."

"If he goes to twenty-five million, you'd better be prepared to wrap this up in a hurry."

"Then work on Henri Claron."

"What does one have to do with the other?"

"Everything. It all has to come together to get me back to Amsterdam. Come on, Jan, you can do it."

"I'm dealing with Karlstadt. I don't have time. Maybe I can find someone else to put the squeeze on Henri." He sighed. "I'll do my best, Michael."

"One more thing. Can you do some snooping on the Wind Dancer?"

"What? I will *not* help you steal that statue, Michael."

"I don't want to steal it. I just want to know about security and if it's going on tour anytime soon."

"That sounds pretty suspicious to me. Forget it. I have too much on my plate."

"Well, maybe later." Travis put away his phone and moved over to stand at the window. Karlstadt wasn't the only one on edge. He'd never seen Jan this disturbed, and the Dutchman wasn't one to go off the deep end without cause. Maybe he shouldn't have mentioned the Wind Dancer. It had just occurred to him that since he had found Cassie at the foot of the statue, it might be an avenue worth exploring. Ordinarily, Jan would have agreed with only a few complaints, but his refusal had been curt. It was obvious that he was very worried.

There was still time though. As long as they were bargaining, Jan was safe. Karlstadt would be dangerous only after the deal was made. At that point Travis would have to move with lightning speed to avoid Karlstadt suspecting a stall.

No lights in Cassie's room tonight. He'd been there three nights already this week. Jessica had started calling him when the episodes began, and they had been able to cut the last one to under fifteen minutes.

What would happen to Cassie Andreas when he left?

And how the hell would he manage to get away from here if he didn't get the information about Vasaro from Henri Claron? There was no way Andreas would consider letting him go. He'd made plans before he arrived here, but it was time to refine them.

He didn't want to leave with Cassie on his conscience. But would he do it if it came down to a choice?

It didn't have to come to a choice. Find a way to get the kid to come back to normalcy and the problem was solved. Andreas might even be so grateful, he'd forget about finding who led the attack on Vasaro. The best of all possible solutions if—

The phone rang.

"Get here right away," Jessica said tersely. "It's started."

He glanced at the house. He'd been so absorbed, he hadn't noticed the lights had come on. "Right away."

"Don't leave," Cassie pleaded. "The monsters don't stay long anymore, Melissa."

"They wouldn't show up at all if you'd come back and let Jessica help you."

"Scared. Nicer here."

"No, it's not. It's wonderful outside. Remember? I'll show you so many beautiful things."

"Scared. Beautiful in here. I could show you—but I can't find it."

"What can't you find?"

Cassie's agitation was growing. "Can't find it. It's here but I can't find it."

"What?"

"It was supposed to be here."

Melissa was afraid if she persisted, she'd jar Cassie back into the nightmare state. Could she flow back into the child and find out what she was thinking? It was risky. The last few times it had been easier to separate from her, but she didn't know what would happen if she gave Cassie what she wanted.

What the hell?

She edged closer, then closer still. She could feel Cassie's agitation like huge waves.

Closer.

Find.

Find what?

A tongue of thought darted out and touched Melissa. Oh, God.

"No!" She tore free in panic and spiraled away into the darkness. Get away. Get away. Get away.

"Come back! Lonely . . ."

★　★　★

Melissa's heart was going to jump out of her chest. Wake up. Get control. Jessica and Travis would come in soon wanting to know if there was anything she could tell them about the episode.

Lie. She had to lie. She couldn't talk about that horror. Breathe deep and try to calm down. Tell them how well everything had gone. Cassie and she were growing closer even when separated. In time she had hopes of being able to persuade Cassie to come back. They'd be glad to hear that, so glad that maybe they'd mistake her anguish for the usual tiredness.

If not, she'd have to lie.

Travis showed up at the front door of the manor at four the next afternoon. "We need to talk," he told Jessica. "Where's Melissa?"

"In her room, studying. What's wrong?"

"Time's wasting. We need to find a way to get Cassie well."

"What do you think we've been doing?"

"It's not moving fast enough." He went to the bottom of the stairs and yelled, "Melissa!"

"Do you know how little studying she's been able to get done since she got here?"

"She's bright enough to make it up. Hell, she's bright enough to run rings around most of us."

He started up the stairs. "She didn't hear me. I forgot about those solid oak doors. Come on. We'll go to her."

"And do what?" She followed him. "We're making progress. You heard Mellie last night."

"Yeah, bubbling with enthusiasm." He knocked on the door of the blue room. "See how polite I'm being?"

Melissa opened the door. "I'm studying."

"Later." He went inside and sat down in a chair. "Will you go get all the stuff you told me Andreas sent with Cassie, Jessica?"

"I'm surprised you couched that as a request. But you forgot to say please." Jessica left the room.

"Jessica doesn't like orders." Melissa sat down on the bed and crossed her legs. "You're lucky she's going along with you. What are you up to, Travis?"

"Cassie. We need to do some brainstorming. We're moving too slow."

Her gaze narrowed on his face. "What's happening?"

"Don't you want Cassie well as soon as possible?"

"What's happening?"

He smiled. "Let's just say I can't wait years for Cassie to come back to us, and you told me I had to stay until she was well."

"Something's going on with you."

"And something's going on with you. Last night it was clear you were hiding something."

She stiffened. "Jessica didn't notice."

"Because she wants to believe you. Do you want to talk to me about it?"

She didn't answer.

"Then don't give me the third degree, Melissa."

"Here they are." Jessica carried four photo albums and several notebooks into the room. "But I've gone through all of these before."

"I've no intention of covering old ground." He was flipping through one album. "Tell me what you've done with these."

"Nothing much. I selected certain photographs to show her and test responses."

"The result?"

"Nothing from any family members. One photograph . . ." She turned the pages until she found the picture. "Cassie and the statue of the Wind Dancer. I thought there was some . . . flicker."

"I found her with the Wind Dancer at Vasaro. That's the only photograph she recognized?"

"I don't know. It's the only one I sensed. . . ." She shrugged helplessly. "It's hard to tell."

"Then you could have been mistaken," Melissa said. "How could anyone tell what

Cassie's feeling? Was there a muscle response or any change in expression?"

"Maybe. A little. It's just . . . an impression."

"But you could have been wrong." She reached over and turned the page. "What other pictures did you show her?"

Travis flipped the page back. "Let's stay with the Wind Dancer for a while, shall we?"

Melissa's lips tightened. "Why? It's only a statue."

"But a remarkable piece of art. It's recognized as one of the most valuable treasures in the world. The Andreas family claims there were historical references that indicate the statue was in the hands of Alexander the Great during his first campaign in Persia, that it once belonged to Charlemagne and was passed down to several famous historical figures through the ages. There are legends that men and nations rose and fell because of the statue's presence on the scene."

"Idiotic."

"Most legends are." He smiled. "But that doesn't stop them from being fascinating, and I'm sure the stories increased the value of the statue. We're a culture intrigued by fairy tales."

"I'm not. What's your point?"

"I don't know if there is one. I know only that Cassie must have run from her bedroom straight to the Wind Dancer that night."

"That's ridiculous." Melissa got up from the bed. "Everyone knows she ran to her nanny for protection." She crossed her arms over her chest and glared at him. "It's stupid to assume she'd run to an inanimate object at a moment like that."

"I'm not sure." Jessica frowned. "Her father said she was terribly fond of it. She'd make up stories about the statue and play in the library where he kept it."

"It's dumb," Melissa said fiercely. "The statue has nothing to do with any of this."

"How do you know?" Travis gazed at her with speculation. "Did she confide in you in one of your nightmare trysts?"

"I'm just being logical. Neither of you seems to know the meaning of the—" She strode toward the bathroom. "Excuse me."

Jessica blinked as the door slammed behind Melissa. "Well, no one can say my sister doesn't have decided opinions."

"Have you ever discussed the Wind Dancer with her?"

"Only casually. Naturally, I told her the circumstances of Cassie's trauma." She shook her head. "I'm sure she didn't mean to blow up. She's been under a good deal of stress lately, and she didn't want her study time interrupted."

"She didn't hurt my feelings." He leaned back.

"Have you ever considered going back to Vasaro and re-creating the scene there?"

"Not if there's any other way. Too traumatic. The cure could be worse than the illness."

"But you've considered it?"

"I've considered every step imaginable. Even if I wanted to take Cassie to Vasaro, her father absolutely refuses to allow it."

"Oh, that could be a problem." He thought for a moment. "What about the Wind Dancer? That's part of the picture."

"Andreas lent it to the Museum d'Andreas in Paris."

"I'm checking to see if the statue is going on tour anytime in the near future."

"You are?" She looked at him in surprise. "Then you do believe there's a connection."

"I don't know. I'm grabbing at straws, but if we could take her to Paris and arrange for her to—"

"The President is not going to permit her to go anywhere until the people who attacked Vasaro are found." She stared meaningfully at him. "Isn't that your job?"

"I'm working on it." He smiled as he recalled that that was the phrase Melissa had used. "Maybe we can ask Melissa to broach the subject of the Wind Dancer during the next episode with Cassie."

"After that reaction?"

"Persuade her." He stood up. "The clock's ticking. If we don't make a breakthrough soon, we may be forced to take radical action."

"Radical? Things are going just fine. I don't intend to rock the boat."

He gave her a sober glance. "Rock it, Jessica."

She was going to throw up.

No, she could stop it, Melissa told herself. It wasn't as if it hadn't happened before. Just don't think about it and do the usual things. She bent over the washbasin and splashed cold water in her face.

But it hadn't happened before. Not like this. Dreams were dreams. This was reality.

Damn him. She should have known Travis would dig and probe until he came up with a lead. It wouldn't do him any good. She would stop him and it would go no further.

Emerald eyes staring . . .

Sweet Jesus . . .

She rushed to the toilet and threw up.

"You look pale." Jessica frowned worriedly as she watched Melissa come down the stairs. "Are you okay?"

"I'm fine." Melissa smiled. "I've probably been hitting the books too hard. I've been cooped up in that room all day. If you're feeling sorry for me, you could get me a lemonade and come and keep me company on the porch. I need some air before I go back to the grind."

"I could use a glass myself." She headed for the kitchen. "Go on out. I'll be with you in a minute."

Melissa settled on the swing and sent it moving gently. It was a hot, muggy night, and she could hear the frogs croaking in the pond behind the house. Summer sounds. Life sounds. Wonderful . . .

"Daydreaming?" Jessica handed her a glass and sat down beside her. "You look a lot better."

Melissa laughed. "I'm not sure that's a compliment. It's dark out here."

"There's moonlight."

Melissa looked up at the sky. "Yes, there is."

Silence.

"Mellie, why did you blow up this afternoon?" Jessica asked hesitantly.

"I was waiting for that question. I worried you, didn't I? You thought I was irrational, and considering the fact that you're not sure how well balanced I am anyway, it—"

"That's not true. I know there's nothing

wrong with you. I just wondered why you got so upset."

"I'm sure you gave Travis all kinds of excuses for my lapse."

"Of course I did. Maybe a couple of them might even have merit." She sipped her lemonade. "We never kept secrets from each other. Talk to me, Mellie."

It wasn't true. She had kept so many secrets from Jessica since she had come back from the other place, but she was glad Jessica had never been aware of that lack of trust. "You wouldn't believe me if I told you I was really—" She shook her head. "Okay, I don't want Travis to get too interested in the Wind Dancer."

"Why not?"

"He's like a steamroller. Once he sets his sights on something, he won't stop."

"That's not always a bad trait."

"It can be. Sometimes people get swept along into places they shouldn't be in. All it takes is one push and it sets things toppling . . . like dominoes."

"And what does that have to do with the Wind Dancer?"

"That's what Cassie is trying to find in the tunnel."

Jessica went still. "You're sure?"

"Oh, yes."

"But that's a good thing to know. We can build on that. Maybe Travis's idea about using the Wind Dancer isn't too bad if we can figure out a way to—"

"No." Melissa tried to temper the sharpness of her tone. "You don't understand. It's not . . . it's a bad . . . feeling. Delving into it might hurt Cassie."

"She's afraid of it?"

She didn't answer directly. "You don't want to open that can of worms."

"I know you're concerned for Cassie, but you don't understand all the psychological ramifications of her condition. You'll have to trust me to work it out."

"Forget about the statue."

"I can't forget anything that might help Cassie. You can't either, Mellie. We have to work together."

"Half the time you don't even believe what I tell you about Cassie's nightmares."

"So I have a few problems in that area. But I do believe what you say about Cassie trying to find the Wind Dancer, because when I showed her the photograph, she—"

"You told me you didn't actually see a reaction." She smiled sardonically. "What are you? Some kind of spook like me?"

"Not fair. I've never called you a spook." She

paused. "The Wind Dancer is the only lead we have. We have to pursue it, Mellie. I want you to promise me that you won't reject Cassie if she opens up the subject."

Melissa was silent.

"Please." Jessica sighed. "We have to help Cassie, and I don't know which way to turn."

What difference did it make? Melissa thought wearily. The dominoes were falling and she couldn't stop them by pretending they didn't exist. "I won't encourage it, but I won't reject it. Is that enough?"

"That's enough." Jessica leaned forward and kissed her cheek. "Thank you." She stood up. "Now I've got to check on Cassie and then go to bed. Are you coming in?"

"Pretty soon."

"Don't study too late."

"I won't." She leaned back on the swing. "Have a good night."

"Let's hope we all do." Jessica went into the house.

The conversation had been a complete bust, Melissa thought in despair. She had hoped that if she introduced a hint of a threat to Cassie, Jessica would veer away from the Wind Dancer. She hadn't counted on Jessica's total obsession with bringing Cassie back. If Melissa had just left the subject alone, maybe Jessica's interest would not have been piqued.

Or maybe it wouldn't have mattered. Fate?

To hell with fate. That was defeatist thinking. Travis certainly wouldn't rely on a whim to shape his destiny. He was already trying to find a way to have his cake and eat it too. Now, thanks to Melissa's own clumsiness, she might have driven Jessica into his camp. In her heart Jessica would always consider Melissa the dependent child she had been all those years ago.

The lights were on at the gatehouse. They often stayed on most of the night. She had learned in the past several days that Travis seldom got more than four hours' sleep a night and that he was a great reader. Was he delving into that pile of books she'd seen delivered yesterday afternoon? Insatiable curiosity and a thirst for knowledge could be dangerous qualities in an enemy.

It was the first time she had acknowledged to herself that Travis could be an adversary. She had been wary of him, but she hadn't believed he offered any challenge she couldn't meet. In a weird way, she had felt a kind of bond with him. Crazy. It was probably a carryover of Cassie's trust in him and view of him as a savior. But she had enjoyed their battles of wits and admired his sharpness and intuitiveness.

She didn't admire them now. His intuitiveness was striking too close to home. He had brought the Wind Dancer out of the darkness into the light.

She could handle it. Crush down the panic. If she wasn't strong enough, she would concentrate, learn, and develop.

She only hoped she had enough time.

9

Lyon

"Don't answer it," Danielle Claron said.

The doorbell rang again. Henri started for the door.

"Don't be a fool," she told him.

"If it's Van Beck, I'd be a fool not to answer it. We've already discussed this, Danielle. We need to leave Lyon, and I've no intention of leaving it a pauper."

"You'd rather leave it in a hearse?"

"Haven't I always taken care of you? During these last ten years you've never lacked food on the table, but now we have a chance to live the way we deserve to."

"I'm the one who gave you that chance. And I'm telling you that you shouldn't—"

The bell rang again.

"Very well, answer it. But be careful."
Danielle moistened her lips. "We should never
have gotten caught up in this. We didn't need
that extra money."

"You never complained before. This is no different, only bigger. Now leave me to bargain."

She moved toward the bedroom. "Believe
me, I've no desire to be here."

"That's good. You're too transparent. I saw Van
Beck watching you when he was—" He suddenly tensed as he looked through the peephole.
It wasn't Van Beck. This man was tall, fair-haired,
powerfully built, and only in his late thirties.

"Yes?"

"Monsieur Claron?" The man smiled. "My
name is Jacques Lebrett. I've been sent by Jan
Van Beck. I have something for you."

"Why didn't he come himself?"

"He's a busy man. I believe he told you he
might send someone?"

Van Beck had mentioned the possibility, but
Claron was still uneasy. "Tell Van Beck if he
wants to have the—"

"He's involved in some very delicate negotiations." Lebrett flipped open his briefcase and
held it up so that it was visible through the
peephole. "But he's not too busy to furnish you
with suitable funds for your information."

Money. Stacks and stacks of francs. He'd never seen so much.

"Can we talk, Monsieur Claron?"

So much money . . .

Henri unlocked and threw open the door. "Come in."

"Thank you." The man smiled. "I'm sure we can come to terms."

The wife had escaped.

No problem. Edward Deschamps had disabled the car in the driveway and the house was miles from the road. Henri Claron had died too easily, but tracking his wife down would be a challenge. He had needed this kill. He had been on the hunt for Travis too long, and that made him edgy. When the need for removing the Clarons had become clear, he had eagerly leapt at the chance.

Deschamps washed the bloody knife, carefully wiped his fingerprints from the sink, then did a pass around the house. Not that these precautions would do much good. Forensic tests made it very difficult for a man to do his job these days. Yet he still did as he'd been taught as a boy. Habits were hard to break.

He left the house and scanned the yard and

surrounding woods. Which way would she go? The fields that eventually led to the highway?

No, the woods. She'd think she could hide in the trees.

But he would find her. This was the game in which he excelled. He'd known that Claron would open the door. Money was always the key. Several authentic bills on top and paper below and the man had thought he was rich. What a fool.

He went down the steps into the farmyard, flicked his lighter, and lit the taper he'd brought with him. He tossed the taper on the gasoline-soaked boards of the porch.

The house exploded in flames.

"Henri Claron is dead," Van Beck said.

"What?" Travis's hand tightened on his phone. "How?"

"His house burned to the ground, but the police think he was dead before the fire started. They haven't found his wife yet."

"She escaped?"

"Maybe. But if she did, she dug a hole and isn't going to come out."

"If she's alive, I need to know where she is. You said she was as nervous as her husband.

There's a good chance she knew what he knew. Or maybe more."

"You think she's going to risk getting her throat cut after what happened to Henri?"

"Sometimes fear or revenge is a greater spur than money. Try to find her, Jan."

"I've already started." He paused. "Yesterday I found two bugs in my apartment. They weren't there three days ago, when I made my last check."

Travis stiffened. "Karlstadt?"

"Perhaps. Or possibly CIA. But the bugs were Chinese. I wouldn't think they'd be regular CIA issue."

Travis didn't like it. Events were taking a nasty turn and the pressure was mounting.

"What about the negotiations with Karlstadt?"

"He's up to twenty-three. You wouldn't consider taking him up on it?"

"I'll think about it."

"Good. I've got a bad feeling about this Claron development. I find it curious that he was murdered before I could complete our transaction. It makes me wonder if there's a wild card out there and closer than I'm comfortable with." He didn't speak for a moment. "And I think someone's been following me."

"CIA?"

"Oh, them too. Two men, green Porsche. I had them spotted three days after you left Amsterdam. But I have a hunch there's someone else."

"Did you see anyone?"

"No, but I've got that tingling in the back of my neck."

"Indisputable proof."

"Enough for me. As you know, it's saved my life any number of times. Things are getting too tense. I think I'll take my cut and set sail on a long, long cruise. Call me when you make up your mind. Good-bye, Michael."

"Wait." Twenty-three million was enough, and he didn't like the way the situation was shaping up for Jan. "Take the offer."

"Good." Jan gave a sigh of relief. "Karlstadt will want delivery at once, you know."

"Stall him."

"It's like trying to stall a cobra that's set to strike. He hates having to bargain for—"

"We don't have a choice. I'm having a few problems with my situation here."

"Four days tops. I'm warning you, Karlstadt will explode."

"I'll call you."

Jan suddenly chuckled. "I didn't think you'd give in to Karlstadt. Are you getting soft, Michael?"

"Maybe. You keep telling me what a tough customer Karlstadt is."

"Oh, I don't think you're afraid of Karlstadt. I believe you may be worried about me. I approve."

"Why should I worry about you? You've got that magical tingling neck to keep you safe." He hung up.

Four days.

How the hell was he going to find a way to leave here in four days? The barriers were monumental. Cassie. Andreas. The Secret Service.

And Jessica and Melissa Riley. The two women might be the most formidable obstacles of all.

Well, obstacles were meant to be overcome. An idea had already occurred to him as to how to finagle his departure, but he'd been trying to think of some other way.

It was nasty. Very nasty.

But so was the situation in Amsterdam, and that was his real life, not this hiatus here at Juniper. Jan was no fool, and if he thought there was danger, then the threat existed. His life might be on the line. It was Travis's part of the deal to grab the money and get them both safely away from the Russians and Karlstadt, and that was what he had to do.

It was ironic Jan had accused him of going soft. He'd change his mind if he knew how Travis was planning to get away from here.

Nasty . . .

The sun was going down when Jessica opened the door to Travis.

"May I speak to you?" he asked.

She frowned in puzzlement. "Come in. Is something wrong?"

"Nothing that can't be solved. I'd rather not come into the house. Why don't we go for a walk down to the pond?"

"I have to get back to Cassie. I'm only taking my dinner break."

"I'll try not to be long."

She hesitated. "Fifteen minutes." She followed him down the front steps. "I wanted to speak to you too. I had a talk with Mellie last night. She told me the Wind Dancer was what Cassie was searching for in the tunnel. She seems to have an idea pursuing that lead will be bad for Cassie."

"And what do you think?"

"I think we have to grab any straw we can to help her. I made Mellie promise not to try to steer Cassie away from the statue."

"I imagine she had a few problems with that," he murmured.

"She agreed." She glanced at him. "You don't seem surprised."

"I think we both knew your sister's reaction was a little extreme."

"Then why didn't you follow up?"

"Why should I? I knew you'd do it and you would have only resented my accusing her of anything."

"Yes, I would have." She stopped as they reached the pond. "She didn't mean any harm. She was only concerned for Cassie."

"And that's your concern too."

"Of course."

"You love your sister very much, don't you?"

"That's no secret."

"And you wouldn't want anything bad to happen to her."

She went still. "My God, are you threatening Mellie?"

"Yes, I suppose I am." He turned to look at her. "I have to leave here soon. I've got to get back to Amsterdam. I'd like to take you, Melissa, and Cassie with me. It's the only way I can think of to salve my conscience at leaving." His lips twisted. "And I admit the package deal will make getting out of here easier."

Panic shot through her. "You *can't* leave."

"I can't do anything else."

"The hell you can't. Andreas won't let you."

"I'm going, Jessica."

"Cassie will die."

"Not if you come with me."

"And Mellie."

"She's been getting stronger. She might survive even if Cassie doesn't."

"You son of a bitch." She brought her trembling hand to her lips. "It's crazy. For God's sake, you're talking about kidnapping Cassie. They'll find you, lock you up, and throw away the key."

"Not if we find a way to heal her."

"We? You think I'll become involved in this criminal madness?"

"Do you have a choice? You're crazy about Cassie and Melissa. You wouldn't want anything to happen to them."

"Nothing will happen to them." She glared at him. "You're staying and we're going to go on just the way we have been."

"Not quite."

"What do you mean?"

"If Cassie has a nightmare, I won't come to help her."

"What?" She stared at him in disbelief. "You have to come."

He shook his head.

"You may be a bastard, but you couldn't refuse to help Cassie when she suffers."

"It's your call and your responsibility. I've told you I'm willing to help her . . . on my terms."

"You're bluffing. You're not that cold."

"When I have to be, I'm colder than you could ever imagine." He stared directly into her eyes. "Am I bluffing, Jessica?"

Oh, God, she was afraid he wasn't. His face was without expression, but his eyes . . . She had gotten to know him over the past weeks; he wasn't capable of letting Cassie go through a nightmare without helping. "You're bluffing."

"I'm sorry. I hoped to make it easy for all of us. I wouldn't mention this to Melissa. It will only worry her. After all, you're rolling the dice for her well-being too."

"I'll do what I like."

"No, you'll do what's best for the people you care about. That's what I'm banking on."

Her hands clenched as she watched him walk away. Damn him. Damn him.

He was bluffing. He had to be bluffing.

The next night the lights came on in Cassie's room.

The phone in the gatehouse rang.

"Get over here," Jessica said. "Now."

"Nightmare?"

"Yes."

He hung up the phone.

Don't call back.

Don't go to the manor.

Don't think of that little girl.

He went back to the window.

And waited.

Thirty minutes later he saw Jessica running down the driveway. He opened the door and waited for her.

"You son of a bitch." Tears were streaming down her cheeks. "You bastard." She grabbed his arm. "You come with me."

"No."

"You've got to come—"

"I don't have to do anything. I do what I choose to do."

"I'll have Fike come down and drag you up there."

"And I'll sit in the chair by her bed and not say a word."

"You couldn't—" She stared at him in disbelief. "You could. My God, you're going to let Mellie and Cassie . . ." She turned and ran back up the driveway to the house.

Jesus, he felt sick.

Don't give in. You've gone this far. If you give in tonight, you'll have to do it again tomorrow or the night after.

Five minutes.

Ten minutes.

The phone rang.

"All right, you bastard." Jessica's voice was shaking. "I'll do anything you want. Just get up here."

"I'll be right there." He started up the driveway at a dead run.

Christ, it had been even more ugly than he'd imagined it could be.

"What happened, Jessica?" Melissa's voice was weak. "It went on for so long. . . ."

Jessica didn't answer as she took her pulse. "How do you feel?"

"Like hell. He didn't come. . . . It took so long. . . ."

"Your heartbeat's still a little erratic, but it's coming back to normal now." She drew Melissa's coverlet up around her shoulders. "And Cassie's fine too."

"She wasn't fine. She's grown to depend on him. I tried to break away and talk to her, but she wouldn't . . . accept me. When I'm part of her, I'm part of the terror . . . not the salvation." She moistened her lips. "He's . . . the one she identifies as the savior."

"Some savior." She brushed the hair back

from Melissa's forehead. "Are you going to be okay if I leave you and go back to Cassie?"

"Sure. Where was he, Jessica?"

"He got here a little late."

"Bad . . ." Her eyes closed. "So bad. We were so scared. He should have come sooner."

"It was bad." Jessica moved toward the door. "But it won't happen again. He'll be here right away next time."

"Good. We . . . couldn't breathe and our heart hurt. . . ."

"It won't happen again," Jessica repeated, and closed the door behind her.

Son of a bitch. She blinked her stinging eyes and started down the hall toward Cassie's room.

Fike straightened away from the wall. "Gee, I hoped the little girl was getting better. This was the worst I've ever heard her."

"She's better now."

"Mr. Travis is still in there with her. He usually helps, doesn't he?"

"Usually."

"He told me you almost lost her this time. I'm crossing my fingers that she comes around."

"Thank you, Larry. I'm sure she will." She opened the door and went into the bedroom.

Travis was sitting on Cassie's bed and glanced up at her. "How's Melissa?"

"How do you think she is?"

He squeezed Cassie's hands. "Good night, sweetheart. I'll see you soon." He got up and moved out of Cassie's hearing. "Melissa's probably tired and very weak. Right?"

"You couldn't expect her to be anything else." Her hands clenched into fists. "You could have killed them."

"You wouldn't let that happen."

"That's what you counted on. You gambled on me giving in to keep them from suffering and maybe dying. How could you do that?"

"It was necessary."

"The hell it was."

"Think what you like. We all have our own agendas."

"Then why did you muscle into ours?"

"You invited me in. And can you honestly say that you weren't glad to have my help? When I didn't come tonight, I just returned the situation to the way it was."

"To get your own way."

"To get my own way." He gazed directly into her eyes. "I hope you won't force me to do it again. Because I *will* do it, Jessica."

"I know you will." She folded her arms across her chest to stop them from shaking. "And as soon as I can find a way to do without your help, I'm going to hang you out to dry. I hope they send you to prison for the next hundred years."

"You'd better be darned sure Cassie is cured first. You wouldn't want me to be out of her reach. Did you tell Melissa anything?"

"No, only that it wouldn't happen again. She'll not be satisfied with that answer when she's stronger."

"Then you'll have to stave her off. Melissa's fully capable of throwing a wrench into my plans, and that would be bad for all of us."

"I'm not going to lie to her."

"Would you rather we leave her here, where you can't keep an eye on her? I don't know if she'd still be connected to Cassie at a distance, but I wouldn't want to chance not being able to monitor her." He paused. "But perhaps you would."

"You asshole."

"I didn't think so." He started for the door. "Handle it any way you have to."

"Wait."

He looked back over his shoulder.

"You're not going to do this to us without paying. I'll cooperate with you, but I want your promise that if we get out of here, you're not going to drop us in Amsterdam."

"I told you I wouldn't do that."

"And I want another promise. I want you to arrange to take Cassie to the Wind Dancer and make sure she has some time with it."

"That won't be easy. And why should I? I've already won, Jessica."

"Because you owe it to us, you bastard."

He was silent a moment. "Good point. Okay, you have my promise. Just be aware if we're caught at the museum, they could shoot me or take me off to jail. Either way, it will be bad for everyone."

"It would almost be worth it."

He shook his head. "You don't mean that."

He was right. She didn't mean it. There was no way she would sacrifice Cassie and Melissa just to punish Travis. She gazed at him in despair. "This is so crazy. Change your mind. You can't get away from here."

"Yes, I can. But you're not going to like the way I do it."

She stiffened. "What do you mean?"

"If I tell you, you'll argue and then worry about it until it happens."

"Are you going to kill someone?"

"Not if they don't try to kill me. I'll give you the game plan right before we start moving." He left the room.

Dear God, what was she getting into? If they didn't get shot, they'd be hunted like criminals.

They *would* be criminals, and she couldn't see Jonathan Andreas being lenient where his daughter was concerned.

And if the escape didn't work, it would all be for nothing. She'd end up in prison and Cassie and Melissa might be lost.

The escape had to be successful. The stakes were too high. Would Travis keep his promise to help cure Cassie? She'd have to worry about that later. As she'd have to worry about his plan to escape from Juniper.

Jesus, she hoped no one got hurt.

10

The phone at the gatehouse rang at 12:17 A.M. two nights later.

"Get up here right away. She's having an episode," Jessica said when Travis picked up the phone. "And no games tonight, Travis."

"All the games are over. I'll be right there."

Larry Fike was frowning with concern as he watched Travis come down the hall a couple of minutes later. "It sounds like a bad one again. Good luck."

Travis nodded grimly. "We'll need it."

Cassie's scream tore through the room as he opened the door.

"How long?" Travis asked as he crossed to the child's bed.

"Ten minutes," Jessica said. "Thank God, you came right away."

He took Cassie's hands. "Come here, Jessica."

Jessica stepped closer. "What?"

He didn't look at her as he said in an undertone, "Find an excuse to send Teresa away."

She stared at him in bewilderment.

"Do it."

She turned to Teresa, who was standing by the door. "Go get me a hypodermic from the medicine chest downstairs."

"You think you'll need—"

"I hope not. I want to be prepared. Just get it."

Teresa hurried out of the room.

"How long will it take her?" Travis asked.

"I don't know. Last time I looked, there weren't any hypodermics in that chest. She'll look around and then go to the one on the third floor."

Cassie screamed.

"Do something. Talk to her."

Travis dropped Cassie's hands and stood up.

"What are you doing? *Talk* to her."

"We're leaving, Jessica."

She froze. "Not before you take care of her."

He opened his jacket, took out his laptop computer, and dropped it into Jessica's medical bag.

Cassie screamed.

"Talk to her. Can't you see she's hurting? She's screaming, dammit."

He turned to her and said quietly, "She has to scream, Jessica."

"What?"

"I can't help her. She has to scream."

"Is this some kind of power play? I told you that you'd won."

He closed the medical bag. "It's no power play."

"She's hurting. Mellie's hurting."

"Run out in the hall and tell Fike that you're having an emergency. Cassie's having a seizure and you need an ambulance to get her to the hospital. Give him this." He handed her a piece of paper. "It's the number of the emergency room at Shenandoah General, the closest hospital."

"Don't do this to Cassie."

"And tell Fike to notify the President."

"Talk to her."

"Not yet. The sooner you put her in the ambulance, the sooner I can help her." He gave her a push. "Go to Fike."

"Damn you." She was sobbing as she ran into the hall.

Cassie screamed. The cry held all the agony and fear a child could feel.

He could stop it. God, how he wanted to stop it.

He walked to the window and stared blindly at the iron gate through which the ambulance would come.

He was wrapping Cassie in a blanket when Jessica came back into the room. "Fike?" he asked.

"He called the hospital. He's on the line with Andreas now. The ambulance should be here within ten minutes."

"Go get your sister and bring her down to the ambulance."

"How am I supposed to get her on her feet? She's probably in as much shock as Cassie."

"That's your problem." He picked up Cassie. "I've got enough on my plate."

"It's not going to work. You may get out of the gates, but there'll be a truckload of Secret Service at the hospital."

"It will work," he said as he passed Jessica. "Get Melissa downstairs."

Fike was outside in the hall. "Can I help?" He flinched as Cassie screamed again. "Christ, that poor kid."

Travis nodded. "You can make sure there's security at the hospital." He started down the hall.

"And a carful of your guys to follow the ambulance."

"We've already taken care of the hospital." Fike ran down the stairs ahead of Travis. "And you can bet I'll be in that car following the kid."

"Good."

"What are you trying to do?" Jessica whispered, stunned.

"This way they think of us as a team." He heard the distant wail of a siren. "There's the ambulance. Get Melissa."

Cassie was already being placed in the ambulance when Jessica half led, half carried Melissa down the front steps.

"Jesus," Fike murmured when he saw Melissa's dazed, tear-stained face. "What's wrong with—"

"You know how close she and Cassie have grown." Jessica pushed Melissa into the ambulance. "She wants to go to the hospital with her." She turned to Teresa as she climbed in after Melissa. "I'll call you from the emergency room."

The EMT slammed the door shut and ran around to the passenger seat. The siren wailed as the ambulance tore down the driveway with the Secret Service car following.

Jessica whirled on Travis. "Now help her," she said fiercely.

"I've every intention of doing that." Travis knelt beside Cassie, gathered her hands in his, and began to talk to her.

Within five minutes she started quieting and Jessica felt the tension ebbing out of her. No matter what happened to the rest of them, Cassie and Melissa were easing.

Travis checked his watch. He broke off in midsentence, got up, and looked out the back window at the Secret Service car behind them. "Too close," he muttered.

Even as he spoke, the ambulance took on more speed. Jessica fell sideways as the vehicle screeched around the curve in the road.

Bluff on one side. Steep slope on the other.

Travis glanced out the back window. At least two hundred yards separated them from the car now. The ambulance tore up the hill. A gentler slope ahead led to a stand of trees.

"Come on. Come on," he murmured. "Now."

The highway behind them exploded. Fifty yards of concrete jettisoned into the sky. The escort car swerved to avoid the yawning hole torn in the tarmac, then whipped off the road and down the steep incline.

The ambulance careened down the gentler slope and into the trees.

"Hold on to your sister." Travis had Cassie in a secure grip as the ambulance bumped over the rough ground.

Jessica grabbed Melissa.

The ambulance screeched to a halt and the back door flew open.

"I was getting worried," Travis said as he straightened away from Cassie. "You ran it too close, Galen."

"I'm hurt. It wasn't easy setting up those charges and diverting the traffic. I'm not used to having to worry about innocent bystanders." A man in jeans and T-shirt began to roll the gurney out of the ambulance. "Is this the little girl who may cause me to lose my head?"

"You can bet on it if you don't lift off in two minutes." He jumped out of the vehicle and helped Melissa to the ground. "Those Secret Service agents are no slouches. I figure we have a four-minute lead."

Galen's eyes were on Melissa. "What's wrong with her?"

"It's a long story. Bring Cassie." He picked Melissa up and carried her to the helicopter. "Come on, Jessica."

Jessica jumped out of the ambulance and ran

toward the helicopter. The ambulance driver and EMT were already climbing into the aircraft. The man Travis had called Galen placed Cassie gently in the helicopter and then boosted Jessica inside. He waved his arm at the pilot. "Go."

The helicopter lifted off and soared over the trees just as the Secret Service car tore into the clearing. Jessica tensed as she saw Fike jump out and pull his gun.

"Don't worry," Travis said. "No one's going to get trigger-happy when they know the President's daughter is on board."

He was right. No shots were fired, and in seconds they were out of range.

Cassie screamed.

Galen jumped. "Holy shit."

"She's back in the nightmare. I didn't have time to get her entirely out of it." Travis crawled over to Cassie. "How much time do we have?"

"Ten minutes until we land at the airport and transfer planes." Galen grimaced as Cassie screamed again. "Do something, will you? The kid sounds terrible."

"I'm doing it. I hope ten minutes are enough." He began to talk to Cassie.

Jessica cradled Mellie in her arms and watched him. Gentleness. Strength. Determination. How could he change from moment to moment? She had wanted to kill him in Cassie's bedroom tonight. She still wanted to kill him. He was doing only what he had to do, and he'd done it at his convenience.

"Wonders never cease, do they?" Galen was also watching Travis. "He's actually reaching her. What's his secret?"

"He got a head start at Vasaro."

Galen nodded. "Yeah, that's right. I remember when he came out of that study with her. I told him we should go, but he wouldn't leave the kid. I had the devil of a time getting him out later."

"You were at Vasaro that night?"

"Sure." He grinned. "You may have heard Travis was the hero, but it was really me. I was just too modest to stay around and take the bows." His smile faded. "Don't worry, we'll get you away safely. I've got it all set up."

"Why shouldn't I worry? I don't even know what happened tonight. How did you know we'd sent for an ambulance?"

"When Travis knew Andreas was going to stash him somewhere, he called me and told me to be ready to set up a technical van."

She frowned in confusion. "To intercept the call to the hospital?"

"Oh, that came later. He wanted me to trace his location at Juniper from his phone signal.

And he wasn't sure the Secret Service boys would obey the President's orders not to listen to his calls. He wanted my guys to occasionally interrupt their satellite signal monitor when he said a code word to Van Beck. Of course, not all the time, or it would have tipped them off."

"Van Beck?"

"Never mind, I'm probably throwing too much at you."

"Yes, you are. And all this technical mumbo jumbo will be for nothing." She shook her head. "Andreas will set every law enforcement agency in the country after us."

"I admit it's quite a challenge."

She looked at him in astonishment.

"Okay, maybe a little bit more than I'd usually take on." He shrugged. "But Travis promised me he'd make it right."

"He's going to make kidnapping the daughter of the President right?"

He made a face. "Don't remind me. As long as I take one step at a time, I'm okay. When he first told me about his plan, I wanted to break his neck. I told Travis the last time I saw him that I didn't like living on the edge anymore."

"But you're doing this for him. Why?"

"I owe him." He shrugged. "Even so, if it was an ordinary job, I'd have told him to find someone else. This one means something to him."

"Money?"

"Sure, but there's something else thrown into the pot." Then he added, "Besides, I like him. God knows why. He's not an easy man to like. You have to beat down too many walls to get to him."

"Then I wouldn't bother." She glanced away from Travis. "What airport are we going to?"

"A private field north of Baltimore. We'll transfer to the jet there and by morning we should be in Antwerp. We drive from there to Amsterdam." He grimaced. "I told him that's the first place they'll look for him. He said it was necessary."

She shook her head in wonder. "You talk as if flitting around the world is going to be so easy. I don't even have my passport with me."

"That's okay. I have all kinds of documents for you. Part of the service. Of course, you'll have to get used to a new name. I think it's Mary or Marilyn or something like that. You won't have to use it very often. We sort of skirt around immigration. Piece of cake."

False documents. Illegal entry. Piece of cake? The casualness with which he spoke made her think that for him criminal activity was a simple fact of life. To her it was a new and frightening world. "That's hard for me to believe."

"You'll see." His gaze went to Melissa. "She's

looking better. Her color's coming back. Is she on drugs?"

"No."

"Sick?"

"No." Her grasp tightened around Melissa's shoulders. "She's going to be fine."

Melissa woke up as they were getting her out of the helicopter.

"Jessica . . ." She looked around dazedly. "What the devil . . . ?"

"It's okay."

"No, it's not. Nothing's been right all night. Broken. All broken . . ."

"Can you walk?"

"I'll try . . . but slow. I'm groggy . . . and my knees are like rubber."

"Slow isn't possible." Galen picked her up and started at a run for the small private jet. "Just hold on and we'll get there."

Melissa frowned up at him. "Who are you?"

"Sean Galen."

"It's okay, Mellie." Jessica was running beside him. "I'll explain later."

"You'll have to." Her eyes closed. "I'm too tired to think now. Where's Travis?"

"With Cassie."

"Good."

Her eyes suddenly flicked open and she stared up at Galen. "No. Don't do it."

He looked down at her.

"Don't . . ." Her eyes closed again. "Don't let him, Jessica. . . ."

She was asleep.

Galen ran up the stairs to the jet and deposited Melissa on a leather couch. He nodded at the privacy curtain that divided the plane into two compartments. "Travis is up front with the kid. Sit down and fasten your seat belts." He headed for the cockpit. "We're out of here."

"Wait."

He looked back at Jessica.

"I'm calling Andreas."

He stopped short. "You'd better talk to Travis about that."

"I don't care what Travis says. I'm calling Andreas and telling him Cassie's safe." She added dryly, "Don't worry, I won't blow the whistle."

"He won't believe you, but I suppose it can't hurt. Make it less than two minutes. I'll tell Travis." He disappeared behind the curtain.

She drew a deep breath and then dialed Andreas.

"You *bitch*."

"I can understand how you would think that."

"How much money were you paid to take my daughter?"

"It wasn't money. I had no choice. I was afraid for Cassie and I didn't see any other way out."

"You said she was getting better."

"She *was* getting better, but it was only temporary and—"

Travis was standing in the curtained doorway, and he made a motion to cut the call short.

"I have to go. I just want to tell you that none of us intends to harm your daughter."

"What do you want from me?"

"Nothing."

"I want to talk to Travis. Put that bastard on."

"He wants me to hang up."

"Tell him if he so much as touches her, we'll catch him and crucify him. And that goes for you too."

"I'd probably feel the same way. You have to do what you have to do. But Cassie's safe and we'll try to keep her safe." She hung up and looked at Travis. "I had to do it. I couldn't let him go through that hell."

"I'm not arguing. My only priority was to get you off the line before the call could be traced." He turned back. "Fasten your seat belt."

★ ★ ★

Tokyo

Andreas whirled on Keller. "Did you get the location?"

The Secret Service man shook his head. "She hung up too soon. If we'd just had thirty seconds more . . ."

Andreas's hand clenched until the knuckles turned white. "What the hell is all this Star Wars technology for if you can't do a simple trace? If you can't find a child who—" He had to stop and wait until he could speak again. "You promised me she'd be safe at Juniper. Now, you find my Cassie, damn you."

"Yes, sir, I've already notified Danley."

"Have they picked up Travis's contact in Amsterdam?"

He shook his head. "They were in Van Beck's flat five minutes after we knew what Travis had done. He'd already slipped away."

"Then tell Danley to locate him."

"Danley's boarding a plane in D.C. in twenty minutes. Should we notify the media about the kidnapping?"

"God, no. If the whole world knows Cassie's out there and vulnerable, she could be targeted by other groups. And how the hell do we know Travis won't call back with a demand? I only talked

to that bitch of a shrink. We're not sure of anything, and until we are, you make damn sure no
one knows Cassie's missing. *You* find her."

"If Travis heads for Amsterdam, there's a good
chance we'll need international help."

"Circulate pictures of Travis and Jessica Riley
to every police department in Europe. Tell them
the U.S. government would be very grateful for
their cooperation in apprehending them. Make
up some story. Call them . . . terrorists or anything else you can think of. Just don't mention
Cassie."

"Yes, Mr. President."

"I'm going to return to Washington. Make
some excuse and call the Vice President to re-
place me here. Tell them I've got the flu or
something."

"Yes, sir."

"And, Keller."

"Yes, sir?"

"Make sure my wife doesn't find out." His
voice was uneven. "Until you bring my daughter back, she's not to know that Cassie's not safe
at Juniper."

11

Melissa didn't wake again until they were over the Atlantic.

Vibration. Throb of engines. A plane . . .

Plane?

Jessica. Where was Jessica? She jerked upright.

"Shh. It's okay." Jessica was suddenly beside her. "Everything's fine, Mellie."

"I don't think so." She slowly sat up. It *was* a plane and she was lying on a leather couch. "I have an idea nothing's fine. Cassie?"

"She's sleeping in the front. Travis is with her. I wanted to stay with you."

"Is she well?" She tried to remember. "There was an ambulance. . . ."

"Travis arranged that."

"And this plane?"

"Travis and his friend Sean Galen."

"Where are we going?"

"Amsterdam. By way of Antwerp."

"Amster—" Melissa drew a deep breath and said slowly, "I believe you have a few things to tell me. I go to sleep at Juniper and I wake up on my way to Amsterdam?"

"Would you like a cup of coffee?"

"No, I'd like to know every single thing that I've obviously not been privy to."

Jessica sighed. "Okay, I just thought you might need the caffeine before I throw all this at you." For the next several minutes she detailed the dilemma with which Travis had confronted her.

Melissa started swearing. "I can't believe it. I asked you what the problem was the other night, and you lied to me."

"Not really. I just didn't tell you everything. Okay, I lied to you."

"Why?"

"It was my decision whether or not to give in to Travis, and you would have complicated things."

"*Your* decision? I'm pretty deeply involved in this. I think I should have been allowed to put in my two cents' worth."

"Cassie's my patient."

"And you still think of me as a patient too. Which leaves you in charge, right? Well, I'm not a patient and I won't be treated like one. I'm not sick or off my noggin and I can pull my own weight."

"You didn't look like you were pulling your own weight tonight."

"That was a low blow."

"You deserved it. You may not be my patient, but as long as you have this connection with Cassie, you're as much in danger as she is. Do you think I'm going to let anything bad happen to you because I'm afraid of hurting your feelings?"

Melissa stared at her for a moment and then said grudgingly, "Dammit, you could have let me be right this one time, Saint Jessica. I'm all full of righteous indignation and you pull the carpet out from under me." She shook her head. "But you still should have told me. Together we could have found a way to pull the plug on Travis. His whole scheme is absolutely insane."

"Do you think I don't know that? I couldn't see any way out. We need him."

She couldn't argue about that, Melissa realized in frustration. "Why Amsterdam?"

"Travis has business there." She hesitated. "I didn't tell you, but I got him to promise me . . . the Wind Dancer."

Melissa froze. "What?"

"I pressured him into promising he'd find a way to bring Cassie and the statue together."

"No."

"Yes." She looked down at Melissa's hands clenched on the coverlet. "I knew this would upset you, but you're wrong. I believe this is a chance to help her. I'm not sure I can trust Travis to keep his word, but I'm going to try to hold him to it. I won't go through all this madness and not get something out of it."

Melissa could feel the muscles of her stomach twist. "Christ, how can I convince you what a mistake you're making?" she whispered.

"You can't convince me. My patient. My decision." Jessica squeezed her hand. "I'm afraid this time you'll just have to come along for the ride." She got to her feet. "Now I think I'll make coffee and sandwiches. If you want to get out of that nightshirt, there's a change of clothes and a toothbrush in the bathroom. They're in an overnight case neatly labeled with your name." She headed down the aisle toward the back of the plane. "Galen seems to have provided for everything."

Galen. A memory came back to Melissa of the man who had carried her to the jet. Dark hair, dark eyes, quick, strong . . .

And dangerous, very dangerous.

She had gotten those same vibes from Travis.

He was probably even more dangerous than Galen. Certainly more dangerous to her, because he was the one who had promised Jessica the Wind Dancer. She had to talk to Travis, tell him to forget about the damn statue.

Emerald eyes . . .

Not now. Block that memory. She was upset and shaking, and she needed to be clearheaded when she dealt with Travis.

Jesus, the Wind Dancer. As if this situation weren't bad enough . . .

She got up and headed for the bathroom.

"I want to speak to you."

Travis looked up from his notebook. "How do you feel, Melissa?"

"Mad as hell." She glanced at Cassie. Her eyes were closed and she was probably asleep. Better not to take a chance. "We need to talk. Privately."

"That doesn't surprise me." He stood up and moved down the aisle. "We can keep an eye on her from here."

"Your concern is touching considering what you put her through."

"I couldn't see any other way. I know it must have been hard for her . . . and you."

"You don't know jack." Her voice was shaking. "We trusted you and you weren't there for us. And if that wasn't bad enough, you pulled Jessica into this stupidity. If she doesn't get thrown into jail, she's bound to lose her license. I could kill you."

"I'll make it turn out right for Jessica."

"And Cassie? Jessica told me you've promised her the Wind Dancer. You can't do that. The Wind Dancer's bad news."

"If Cassie's afraid of being with the statue, maybe she just needs to face her fears."

"It's bad news."

He studied her face. "If Cassie's looking for the statue, she can't have bad feelings toward it, can she?"

She didn't answer. "If it's in the Museum d'Andreas, how are you going to get hold of it? There has to be all kinds of security surrounding it." She shrugged. "Why am I worrying? You won't be able to keep your word to Jessica. We'll probably get caught in Amsterdam."

"That's a favorable option to you?"

"Yes. Why are we going to Amsterdam anyway? Isn't it the first place they'll look for you?"

"Yes. But I have business there. I have to see my friend."

"You have a friend? He must not have known you for long."

"All my life. He and my father were partners.

He helped raise me." He smiled. "He says he likes me, but I suppose he just doesn't want to admit he did a bad job with me."

"More than likely." She stared directly into his eyes. "I'm not letting you get away with this, Travis. I won't be dependent on a son of a bitch like you, and I won't let Cassie be either. And when I find a way to get out from under you, I'll call Andreas and have him pick you up so quick, it will make your head swim."

"I may be a son of a bitch, but at least I'm not abandoning you. I could have left you all and flown off in the helicopter by myself. It would have taken a hell of a lot of heat off me."

"I'm surprised you didn't."

"I made Jessica a promise." He grimaced. "And you may not believe me, but I couldn't live with myself if the kid had been hurt by all this."

"You're right, I don't believe you." Melissa walked away from him. So much for calm and persuasion. She shouldn't have lost her temper. She might have had a shot at changing his mind. So do what you told him you'd do. Find a way to break free. Cassie was the tether that held them all together. Cut the tether and they'd all be able to go their own way.

How to do it?

She had made a little progress separating herself from Cassie during the last four nightmares, but it was very slow. She hadn't been worried because she'd thought she had time.

Her time was running out. How soon after they arrived in Amsterdam would Travis turn his attention to the Wind Dancer? He shouldn't be able to do anything about the statue, but, dammit, he shouldn't have been able to get them away from Juniper either. The odds had been stacked sky-high against him.

"Well, did you finish venting your wrath on my poor friend?"

Melissa looked behind her and tensed. He was taller than she remembered, but those eyes were unmistakable. "You're Sean Galen."

"I have that honor." She noticed the faintest British accent as he continued. "I'm flattered you were aware of my sparkling persona. I should have known that even through the deepest drug haze I remain unforgettable."

"Who said I was drugged? Jessica?"

"No, but the signs were pretty clear."

"I wasn't drugged." She sat down on the couch. "And that makes you pretty lame at reading signs, doesn't it? How did you know I was arguing with Travis? I didn't see you."

"I was in the cockpit and I opened the door as you were ripping into him. Since my discretion is legendary, I stayed put until you marched off. Could I get you a cup of coffee from the galley?"

"No, I want to rest."

"You look very rested now."

"But we've already established you're lousy at reading signs."

"Ouch." He made a face. "Since I can't admit to being wrong, I suppose I've got to believe you're trying to get rid of me."

"I suppose you do."

He tilted his head inquiringly. "Why? Most people line up for the pleasure of my company."

"Before you shoot them?"

His smile faded. "Now, that came out of left field. And I thought we were getting along so well. Why did you say that?"

She looked away from him. "You're a friend of Travis's. Jessica said you were at Vasaro and helped him with the escape from Juniper. I can do the math." She leaned back on the couch. "If you don't mind, I want to rest."

"I'll go away." He squatted down beside her. "Just one question."

"You shouldn't have any questions. I'm sure you overheard my entire conversation with Travis while you were practicing your legendary discretion."

"Yes, it was very interesting. I intend to quiz Travis on the details later. But this question has nothing to do with him." His gaze narrowed on her face. "When I was carrying you to the plane, you looked up at me and said, 'Don't do it. Don't let him, Jessica.' What did you mean by that?"

"How should I know? I was out of my head." Face him down. "After all, you can't expect someone on drugs to be coherent."

"Stung." He stood up. "Serves me right. Never ask intimate questions of a stranger."

"That question wasn't intimate."

"Wasn't it?" He smiled. "It felt intimate. Never mind, we'll get back to it later."

She watched him walk away from her. Her first impression had been correct. Galen was a very dangerous man, and the less she had to do with him, the better. Forget about him.

Think about Cassie instead.

Break the tether.

How?

There had to be a way to wrest control of those nightmares from Cassie. The girl was strong, but her loneliness was heartbreakingly evident each time—

My God.

Why take on Cassie at the worst possible moment? Don't wait to be pulled into the nightmares; try to invade a gentler dream or sleep state.

She was crazy. She'd never tried anything like that before, and the prospect scared her. She sure as hell didn't have any idea if it was possible. But if Cassie could pull Melissa from deep sleep into her tunnel, why shouldn't she be able to go there herself?

Because maybe there were rules about this kind of thing?

Rules were made to be broken.

So go for it. There was no time like the present, since Cassie was sleeping.

Melissa closed her eyes. How the hell did you go about something like this?

Concentrate . . .

Amsterdam

"I want the delivery in the morning, Van Beck." Karlstadt looked out at the canal. "And there won't be any tricks."

"I stand by my reputation. You know I've never been accused of cheating a client."

"I don't like your idea of the transfer taking place in the park. For God's sake, that place even has a playground. There will be too many people around. I'll come to your flat in the morning at nine."

"Travis likes the idea of people being around. It's easier to become lost in a crowd. It will be in the park or nowhere. I told you how it's to be done, and that's the way it will be done."

Karlstadt's lips thinned. "Then you'd better not disappear until I have the merchandise verified."

"I'm sure you intend to have us followed until you finish the verification." He paused. "Oh, did I forget to tell you that you'll receive only half tomorrow? The other half will be sent to you in Johannesburg."

"What?"

"Merely a safety precaution. Naturally, you'll transfer half the money tonight to the Swiss account number I gave you. We'll wait for the other half tomorrow at the park."

"And what if you decide to take the first half and leave me in the lurch?"

"That's the chance you take. However, we both know Travis has never broken his word in a deal, and he'd be a fool to cheat you. He knows you'd never give up searching for him, and he likes civilized pleasures too well to want to hide in a third-world country. The only question you have to ask yourself is: Does Travis have the merchandise?" He smiled. "And I'm sure you've verified that information."

"He has it." Karlstadt's voice was harsh. "The Russians wouldn't be after him if he didn't."

"Aren't you lucky to be dealing with Travis instead of those unreasonable Russians?" He turned away. "I'll see you in the morning, Mr. Karlstadt, and I'll check the Swiss account tonight."

"Van Beck."

"Yes?"

"I've been hearing troublesome rumors in the last few hours about your Mr. Travis. Rumors about U.S. Secret Service and CIA involvement."

He'd been hearing them too, but he'd hoped Karlstadt wasn't that deep in the loop. "I'm sure they're completely untrue."

"I don't care what Travis has done to irritate the Americans. I just want you to know it must not interfere with the deal. I would find that very annoying."

"He wouldn't allow that to happen." He paused. "Good night, Mr. Karlstadt." He walked rapidly from the bridge and down the street. He could feel Karlstadt's gaze on him, but he didn't look back. Karlstadt enjoyed his little games of intimidation and would have been entirely too pleased if he knew Van Beck was uneasy.

And there was no doubt he was uneasy. There

were too many strings to this deal Travis had
handed him. He could handle Karlstadt, but the
business with Henri Claron was making him
nervous. He was getting too old to keep all these
balls the air.

He looked up at the sky. Travis should be only
hours away by now, and soon he could turn the
whole business over to him. Travis was young
and as sharp as Van Beck had been when he'd
worked with Travis's father. God, that seemed a
long time ago.

Only a few more hours . . .

"You're here."

*Melissa could feel Cassie's delight and excitement
envelop her in the swirling darkness. "I seem to be.
Though it took me long enough to get here. It takes a
while to get the knack."*

"Are you going to stay?"

"No, I'm just visiting."

"Oh." Disappointment. "Lonely."

*"We've gone through that. You don't have to be
lonely."*

*"Not if you stay." A pause. "We're not . . . to-
gether. We need to be together."*

*"No, we don't. We're friends and we can stay apart
and still be friends."*

"Better together."

Melissa could feel the effort the child was making to draw her closer, to absorb her. Jesus, she was strong. "Stop that or I'll have to go away."

"You're going to go anyway." Sorrow. "You told me so."

"But I'll come back if you don't make it sad for me."

"Together isn't sad." But the effort to merge ebbed and then stopped.

"For me it is. I want to be your friend, like your mama and daddy."

"Gone."

"They don't have to be gone."

"They can't come into the tunnel."

"But you can come out."

"Gone." Melissa could feel Cassie's panic, like the fluttering of a captured bird. "They can't come in."

And Cassie wouldn't face coming out. But she could become accustomed to the idea. Jessica thought constant reminders helped and used them in therapy.

"Together." The strongest pull yet from Cassie.

It took several exhausting minutes for Melissa to fight her off. When she finally broke free, she felt limp. "That's it. I warned you. Good-bye, Cassie."

"No." Sorrow. Panic. "Stay. Won't do it again."

"Maybe I'll stay for a little while. But it's boring in this tunnel. No trees, no lakes. Nothing pretty . . ."

"Safe."

"Boring."

"Not if we find the Wind Dancer. He'll make everything— What's wrong? You're scared." Panic. "Are the monsters coming?"

"No." Melissa tried to close out her fear. "No monsters. And we don't need the Wind Dancer. Would you like me to tell you about my home, Juniper? You saw only the one room, but there's so much more. There's a pond and willow trees and an arbor where purple clematis climb. . . ."

"Mellie." Jessica was shaking her, Melissa realized drowsily. "Wake up. We'll be landing in a few minutes."

That jarred her wide awake. She sat up and opened her eyes. "Amsterdam?"

"No, Antwerp. Some small airport in the backwoods that Galen said is used by drug traffickers."

"Wonderful. Just the kind of people I always wanted to associate with."

"He arranged to have a van waiting for us to drive to Amsterdam." Jessica was frowning as she studied her. "You were sleeping awfully hard. I had trouble waking you."

It didn't surprise her. She had been totally exhausted when she finally managed to leave Cassie. She still felt drained. "It's been a rough night." She got up and headed for the bathroom. Why hadn't she told Jessica that she'd reached Cassie? She had always hated keeping things from Jessica, but lately she seemed to be doing nothing else. Later, maybe. She hadn't really accomplished anything, and Jessica was having enough problems with Melissa's involvement in Cassie's nightmares. Melissa could imagine how she'd freak if she told her about the casual visit to Cassie in a normal sleep state.

Casual? She'd have to work up to casual. Just controlling the bond with Cassie had been a gigantic effort.

Travis and Sean Galen were waiting when she left the bathroom.

"Sit down," Travis said. "We're on the final approach."

"Where's Jessica?" She sat down and fastened her seat belt.

"Up front with Cassie. She wanted to be there in case the kid woke up and showed any signs of anxiety."

As if Jessica could tell if Cassie was anxious, she thought sadly. The only thing Melissa had gotten a gut feeling about was the Wind Dancer. For her sister, it was like working blind. "Okay, so tell me how you're going to work this, Travis. I trust you do have a plan to keep us from getting shot on sight."

"No, I left that up to Galen. If you get shot, blame him."

"The hell I will." She leaned back in the seat. "Galen?"

"I've arranged to stash the three of you in a small farmhouse outside Amsterdam. I've contacted a few of the guys I use when I'm in Holland and they'll meet us and act as escort. We stay at the farmhouse and protect you while Travis goes and conducts his business."

"How long will that take, Travis?"

"If it takes more than eight hours, then we're all in trouble. The CIA won't be spinning its wheels. I wouldn't be surprised if they'd staked out every airport in Holland."

"More trouble," Melissa corrected him. "Then what happens?"

"I see what I can do about prying the Wind Dancer from the Museum d'Andreas."

"There's no way."

"Galen?" Travis asked.

"Difficult," Galen murmured. "It will take money. Lots of money. You actually want to steal it?"

"Borrowing would do. I'd need at least four hours to give Cassie a chance to respond to the statue."

"Forget it. It won't work," Melissa said flatly.

"I'm aware of how you feel." Travis studied her. "I just can't figure out why."

"I told you why."

He smiled. "As I said, I can't figure out why. But I'm sure it will come to me."

12

5:20 A.M.

The stone farmhouse was set a few miles back from the road and surrounded by trees. The interior consisted of a huge kitchen, a bathroom, and two small bedrooms, all spartanly furnished but spotlessly clean.

"Carry Cassie into that first bedroom," Jessica said. "After I get her settled, I need to fix her something to eat."

"I'll do it." Melissa headed for the kitchen.

Travis put Cassie on the bed and looked down at her. As usual, he couldn't be sure whether she was asleep or awake. "Hi," he said softly. "This all must seem pretty scary to you, but it's going to work out. I promise."

"Don't promise what you can't deliver." Jessica had come back from the bathroom with a basin and a washcloth. "Particularly since she seems to be low on your agenda."

"I'll deliver." Christ, he hoped he was telling the truth.

When he went back into the kitchen, Galen was just coming in the front door. "Secure?"

"As far as I can tell. I have a couple of my guys scouring the area to be sure, and we weren't followed from the airport." He sat down at the table. "I'd keep to that eight-hour limit if I were you. You're too hot for it to be safe to stay in one place for long. Get moving."

"That's what I'm doing."

He dialed Jan Van Beck as he walked toward the rental car Galen's men had brought to the airport. "I'm on my way to the park," he said when Jan picked up. "Any problems?"

"No, I slipped away from the apartment the minute Galen notified me that your departure was imminent and went to the new flat. You're the one with problems. Even Karlstadt heard about them. The rumor is that you took something you shouldn't have. What have you been up to, Michael?"

"Things got complicated."

"I remember you saying that as a boy. And I always told you that it was you who did the complicating. Always keep it simple."

He certainly had done the complicating at

Juniper, Travis thought ruefully. Jessica may have drawn him to Cassie, but he hadn't had to dive in with both feet. "The Swiss account transfer?"

"It went through. I told Karlstadt only a portion of the merchandise would be delivered this morning and that the rest would be sent to him in Johannesburg. Just in case he decided to cut our throats at the park."

"Smart."

"Of course. I'm looking forward to my cruise, and death would definitely interfere with it. You wouldn't care to come with me? It would be like the old days."

"I might join you later. I'm going to be a little busy for a while."

Van Beck sighed. "I can see how you might. Remember, keep it simple."

He chuckled. "I'll do my best. Start packing. I'll meet you at the park by eight at the latest." He hung up.

"How is she doing?" Melissa asked Jessica as she came out of the bedroom.

"I can't see any change." Jessica sat down in the chair across from Galen. "I don't think there's been any harm done by the trip." She wearily rubbed her temple. "But what do I know? Sometimes I think I don't do these kids any good at all. How can I, when I can't—"

"Bull." Melissa set a bowl of soup in front of Jessica. "You're just tired. Of course you did them good. You brought me back, didn't you? And what about Donny, and Eliza Whitcomb and Pat Bellings and Darren Jenk—"

"Okay, okay," Jessica interrupted and held up a hand. "I get the point. I'm wonderful."

"You're darn tooting." She hesitated. "But I've been wondering if you're being a little too patient with Cassie."

"What do you mean?"

"She's not like the other kids you've treated. She's so strong. . . . Maybe she needs to be met with strength."

"You were strong too." Jessica frowned, troubled. "Do you think I was too patient with you?"

"No, of course not. You did everything exactly right. I was just wondering . . . Remember, I told you I thought she was hiding something? Do you suppose she's using the monsters as an excuse to stay in the tunnel?"

"That's a pretty complicated fantasy. She's seven years old, Mellie."

"You told me her father said she had a wonderful imagination. Put that together with an immensely strong will, and you might— Oh, I don't know. Just think about it. Now eat that soup before you go back to Cassie." She glanced at Galen. "Do you want a bowl?"

He shook his head and rose to his feet. "I'm going to take a look around the perimeter and make a few phone calls. As soon as Travis gets through with his little business with Van Beck, he's going to hop on me to get you access to the Wind Dancer. I always like to be ahead of the game."

"Fine." Jessica began to eat. "It's the only good I can see coming out of this mess. I want a chance to help Cassie before they catch us and line us up before a firing squad."

"Don't be a pessimist." Galen smiled. "If Travis didn't have my invaluable services, you might have to worry, but I've the reputation of a miracle worker."

"God knows we need a miracle," Jessica murmured as he left.

"No, we need to make a deal with Andreas and put an end to this craziness," Melissa said. "He could force Travis to help Cassie."

Jessica shook her head. "I told you what happened when I called his bluff. I won't risk you or Cassie again."

"The bastard." She was silent a moment. "You don't have to worry about me. I think I'm getting ahold of this thing."

"There's still Cassie."

Her lips tightened. "And you won't risk her."

"You wouldn't either."

"Wouldn't I? Sometimes you have to do things you don't want to do." She moved toward the door. "You finish that soup. I'm going to talk to Galen. I hope to hell his phone calls have come up with zilch."

Galen was leaning against a tree a few yards from the porch. He switched off his phone as she came out of the house. "I was expecting you."

"Why?"

"You're not one to sit around when you're not happy about something."

"How do you know?"

"My impeccable intuition. Which at the moment is telling me that you want to grill me about my progress."

"Consider yourself grilled."

"Promising. If Travis can come up with the cash. A million dollars is not to be sneezed at."

"For the Wind Dancer?"

"No way. For the privilege of spending four hours in privacy with the statue."

"A million dollars for that short a time? He'll never go for it."

"You hope."

"It wouldn't help Cassie."

"Shock value?"

"It wouldn't help." Her hands clenched into fists. "And I don't want it happening. Don't give Travis the proposal."

"I beg your pardon?"

"I don't know what he's paying you, but I'll pay you more."

"You have that kind of money?"

"My parents left a comfortable inheritance. I have a trust fund."

"And you'd use it to bribe me?"

"I'll pay you anything if you'll forget about the Wind Dancer. If I don't have enough money, I'll find it."

He shook his head.

"If you don't want money, name your price. I'll do anything you want."

He tilted his head. "Are you offering me sexual favors?"

"I would if I thought it would do any good. But you're not attracted to me. We're too much alike."

"Are we?"

"Yes. You must have sensed it too. It would be like making love to your sister."

He laughed. "And I'm definitely not into incest."

She tried to keep desperation out of her voice. "Tell me what you want and I'll do it. I'm not dumb and I have terrific motivation. That can get most things done."

His smile faded. "If we're so much alike, then you should know I wouldn't betray a friend. I have old-fashioned principles."

She had known the chances were slim, but she'd had to try. "I mean it. I'll do anything. Think about it. There must be something you want done that no one else is willing to do. It's not often you get an offer like that."

"It's hard not thinking about it." His gaze narrowed on her face. "I can see I'm going to have to keep my eye on you. You're entirely too single-minded on this issue. You just might decide to make a call to Andreas."

Jesus, he was sharp. "If you've talked to Travis, you know that's not an option."

"I'm not so sure. . . ." He shrugged. "Go back inside. I don't want to take the chance of anyone seeing you. People remember good-looking women. I have to check with my guys in the woods."

She smothered her despair as she watched him walk away. It had been a long shot, but she had been willing to try it. Okay, so it hadn't worked. She would just have to think of something else before Travis got back.

If he came back. The impression she had gotten was that Travis's "business" was not safe. His life had never been safe, and there was no reason to expect it to change now. It was possible he wouldn't come back. He could be killed or sent on the run. All her worry might be for nothing. He might abandon them if his life was on the line.

He wouldn't abandon them. As much as she resented and feared him, she knew he would keep his promise to Jessica. Christ, how she wished he wouldn't do it. The dominoes were falling faster, and she couldn't seem to stop them.

Stay away, Travis. Don't come back.

Please, don't come back.

"At last." Jan Van Beck gave Travis a bear hug. "It's about time you came and took over the reins. I'm too old for this."

Travis laughed as he returned the hug and then stepped back. "You weren't too old to chase after that pretty little Italian countess six months ago. Is she going with you on your cruise?"

"There's a possibility. She has a daughter, in case you're interested. I understand the woman even has a modicum of brains. Though I never understood why you make that a requisite. Stupidity is so much more relaxing." He started toward the playground a short distance away. "Where are the goods?"

"My jacket pocket." He fell into step with Jan. "You weren't followed?"

"Is the student questioning the teacher now? I'm never followed when I don't want to be." He glanced at Travis, whose gaze was scanning the surrounding trees. "You don't believe me. I'm insulted."

"Sorry. It's habit. I've had to be a bit cautious in the past several months."

"And now also, evidently. That fake mustache definitely does not suit you."

"I thought it wouldn't hurt. One of Galen's sources told him my picture was ordered to be circulated to every police officer in Amsterdam. Let's hope they haven't gotten around to it yet."

"Well, they won't expect you to be strolling in a place as public as this." He thought about it. "Maybe."

"Thanks for being so comforting. Is that the phone booth where we're supposed to leave the package for Karlstadt?"

Jan nodded. "The minute we're sure the money's in the waste can."

"Which waste can?"

"The red one by the front gate." He grinned. "The one being discreetly monitored by the bearded man by the cotton-candy stand. I told you Karlstadt would be anxious."

Travis glanced at the man Jan had indicated. Good-looking, blond hair, full face, beard. As he watched, the man casually folded his newspaper and strolled over to a bench by the gate. He frowned. "There's something familiar about him."

"How can you tell with that bush on his face? It's got to be as phony as your mustache."

"I don't know. It's just . . . something." He shrugged. "I may have run into him before if he's a hired gun."

"Possibly. Are you worried enough to walk away?"

Was he worried? He was always worried when an unexpected element appeared in a deal. Yet familiarity was not recognition. . . . "I guess not."

"Good," Jan said. "I want the deal done. I don't think Karlstadt's man will try to stop us as long as he sees us make the exchange. And Karlstadt knows you're holding back half of the goods."

"Let's get it over with and get you on that cruise." He waited until the crowd around the playground entrance had dispersed before strolling toward the red waste can, keeping one eye on the man by the stand. "A department store shopping bag?"

"Right. De Bijenkorf's."

The shopping bag was jammed to one side of the can, the top stuffed with newspaper. So far, so good. While Jan blocked him from view, he retrieved it and moved quickly toward the phone booth. "Come on, Jan. I can practically see you walking up that gangplank now. You've got it ma—"

A popping sound.

Silencer.

Shit.

He dove for the ground as he reached for his gun. "Down, Jan."

"Too . . . late." Jan was falling. "My . . . leg. Run, Michael."

The blond man was sprinting toward them with a gun drawn.

Another shot.

The bullet whistled by Travis's ear as he rolled over in the grass. He got off a shot.

The blond man faltered, blood sprouting high on his shoulder. But he was almost on top of Jan. He grabbed Jan's shirt, jerking him to a kneeling position, then pressed the gun to Jan's temple. "Throw down the gun and pitch me the money, Travis."

"Screw you. Let him go, or you'll have a bullet in your brain before you can press the trigger."

"Do what I say and I won't kill him. I'm actually grateful to Van Beck. He's been very helpful. Give me the money and I'll let him live." His finger tightened on the trigger. "Even though you've caused me no end of trouble, I'll even let you live for a while. Your usefulness isn't at an end yet."

"You're lying. You won't do it. There are witnesses all over the place."

"I dislike witnesses, but I'll make an exception. Look at my face."

The cold son of a bitch would kill him. He threw him the shopping bag. "I'm putting down the gun. Now back away from him."

"Very wise." He glanced over his shoulder as he heard a commotion at the gate. Several security guards were racing toward them. He smiled. "Never mind. I'd love to stretch this out, but it seems we're about to be interrupted. Next time."

He shot Jan in the head.

"*No!*"

Agony twisted through Travis as he watched Jan's blood and brains splatter on the grass. "*Jan!*"

Dead.

And the man who had done it was streaking down the path toward the street.

Travis grabbed his gun, leapt to his feet, and raced after him. He could hear the shouts of the security guards behind him.

Another shot. This one not muffled by a silencer.

Who was shooting?

It didn't matter. All that mattered was catching the man running ahead of him and killing the son of a bitch.

Stinging pain.

Something warm and wet running down his side.

Keep running.

The man had reached the street and was ducking into a small Volvo.

Travis lifted his gun but couldn't get a clear shot as the Volvo pulled away from the curb.

Gone. Rage tore through him as he watched the car screech around the corner.

Shouts behind Travis. Another shot.

Get away. Find the son of a bitch later.

He ran across the street, down the alley, and then around the corner. His car was parked four blocks away. Reach it. Get back to the farmhouse.

Streaks of pain ripped through him. Murder. Jan's head exploding.

Don't think about it yet.

Get back to the farmhouse.

Jan . . .

13

"Get me a first aid kit, Melissa." Galen flung open the door and helped Travis into the kitchen. "The stupid ass got himself shot. I knew I should have gone with him."

"Shot?" Melissa felt her heart jerk. "Bad?"

"A bullet wound is never good." Galen lowered Travis gently into a chair. "It only grazed his ribs, but he's lost some blood."

"Who did it?"

Travis shook his head. "I'm not sure. I have to think about it. Just get a bandage on me and give me something to clear my head."

"CIA?"

"This had nothing to do with Cassie."

"How do you know if—"

"Get him bandaged before you cross-examine him," Galen told her. "And women are supposed to be the gentler sex."

"Shut up. Go in the bedroom and get Jessica's medical bag, but don't wake her. She just got to sleep."

"She's a doctor. Maybe we should—"

"I can take care of this. I don't want her bothered."

"Heaven forbid," Travis murmured. "We wouldn't want your sister bothered."

"No, we wouldn't. You've put her through enough hell." She went to the sink and filled a basin of water. "Take off your shirt." She saw him struggling and said through her teeth, "Oh, stop it. You look like you're going to pass out. I'll help you." She put the basin on the table and carefully stripped the shirt off him. "I take it your 'business' didn't work out as you hoped."

"You could say that. Hurry, will you?"

"I'm hurrying. Do you think I like fussing over you?"

"Here's the bag." Galen set the leather satchel on the table and opened the latch. "May I help? I'm pretty good at first aid myself."

"I bet you are." Melissa deftly cleaned the long, jagged graze. "All those battle wounds . . ."

"What?"

"Nothing. Give me that antiseptic." She

glanced at Travis's face. "This is going to hurt." She didn't wait for a response but put the antiseptic on the open cut. He didn't flinch. He looked as if he didn't feel it. Her lips twisted. "Macho man."

"Yeah, that's me." Travis looked at Galen. "Get on the phone and find us another place. I wasn't followed here, but we need to make sure that the man who killed Jan isn't able to—"

"Jan's dead?" Galen interrupted. "Oh, God, I'm sorry, Travis."

"So am I." Travis looked at Melissa. "Are you through with me?"

"I wish." She finished bandaging the wound. "But that should hold you." She gave him three Tylenol. "You're not having enough pain for anything stronger."

"Oh, I'm having enough pain."

He wasn't talking about physical pain, she realized. She smothered the ripple of sympathy. "If your head's messed up, it's not because of that flesh wound."

He swallowed the Tylenol and said to Galen, "He knew we were coming and he knew about the delivery. He was either Karlstadt's man or someone else who had access to the information. He said Jan had been helpful. Jan found two bugs in his apartment last week. I thought maybe CIA, but . . ." He shook his head. "He could have been a rogue agent, but that doesn't smell right. I have to think about it. Just get us out of here."

"Paris?"

Travis shrugged. "Why not?"

"Right." Galen rose to his feet and took out his phone. He hesitated. "I really am sorry. I know he was like family to you." He strode out of the house.

Melissa barely heard those last words. "Paris? Why Paris?"

"You know why," Travis said wearily. "I made a promise and I want to get it over and done with."

She closed her eyes. "Shit."

"I agree with you." He put on his shirt. "I know you hoped I might be thrown off course by Jan's—" He stopped. "Death."

It hurt him to say the word. She could feel his raw pain. She *wouldn't* feel it, dammit. Her eyes opened and she glared at him. "I can't help it if your friend died. He must have been crazy or he'd never have thrown his lot in with you. You should have learned your lesson, but you haven't. You're going forward blindly, not caring who you hurt."

"I won't hurt anyone."

"Tell that to your friend Jan."

He flinched. "You would have had a ball

practicing medicine in the old days before they discovered anesthesia." He finished buttoning his shirt. "Now, if you don't mind, I think I'll go outside and find Galen. I need some air."

Her hands clenched as she watched him leave. She had caused him pain, but she would be damned if she'd show him the remorse she felt. He was tough enough to take almost anything, and she had to be just as tough.

She carried Jessica's medical bag back to the bedroom and put it on the chair by the nightstand. Jessica was curled up on the bed next to Cassie. She stood looking down at the troubled child and her sister, who was willing to give up everything to protect her patient. They were both sleeping deeply, and she felt a sudden surge of protectiveness toward them. Strange. Jessica had always been the caregiver, the safety net in a shaky world.

Not now. Jessica was beyond her depth. Hell, maybe Melissa was too, but she couldn't let that matter.

She had to dive in, try to keep them all afloat and hope they didn't drown.

She moved over to the other nightstand, opened Jessica's handbag, and began to search through it.

★ ★ ★

"You okay?" Galen asked as he walked toward Travis. "Shouldn't you be resting?"

"Because of this wound? I remember hearing about a time in Tanzania when you walked five miles with a machete stuck in your leg."

"Yeah, but not every man is a superman like me. And I always take R and R when I can get it." He checked his watch. "You have forty-five minutes before transport arrives. Go on back in the house and sit down."

"It's more restful out here."

Galen nodded. "I can see your point. She definitely doesn't want you going after the Wind Dancer."

"She'll have to get used to the idea." Travis leaned back against the doorjamb. "Have you been able to finalize it?"

"I had a man contact Paul Guilliame, the assistant curator of the museum. He's known to be open to bribes."

"The Wind Dancer is a little different."

"But Guilliame's frailty of character should hold us in good stead if the money's enough and the presentation is right." He smiled. "And my presentation is always right."

"There's something else I need you to do."

Galen gazed at him quizzically.

"I think I know the man who killed Jan. He certainly knew me. He wanted *me* dead, not Jan."

"You recognized his face?"

He shook his head. "The eyes were vaguely familiar. Green, slanted a little . . . but he had a fake beard."

"So what do you want from me?"

"Find someone to break into Interpol's computer banks for me. I need to look at mug shots."

"Unless you have a starting place, it could take you the next fifty years to go through that many records."

Travis knew that, but he had to begin somewhere. "Then it will take me fifty years. Just get me the hacker."

Galen nodded. "I can't promise to deliver him by the time we get to Paris, but I'll find someone."

"Good." It wasn't good. He couldn't see much good in anything right now. Jan . . .

"Do you want to talk about him?" Galen asked quietly. "Sometimes it helps."

Travis shook his head. "He's dead." His lips twisted. "There's nothing to say."

"It's not your fault. Jan's been in the business a long time. He knew what he was doing."

"I know that."

"But you're alive and your friend is dead." Galen shrugged. "Tough. But deal with it."

"I am. Just get me the hacker."

"Consider it done. I've just thought of a man

who might be able to do it. Stuart Thomas. He's a little weird, but there's nothing he doesn't know about computers." His phone rang and he answered it.

He listened for a moment and then hung up. "I think we've got Guilliame. He'll take the statue out of the display case to a room in the back on the pretext of having it cleaned. He says there will have to be guards at the door or it will look suspicious. He knows a couple who will look the other way for a price."

"And the price?"

"Total? It's gone up. Two million. Pretty high for four hours with a bloody statue. I can bargain."

"No time."

"You have the money?"

"I have something to barter with."

"Worth two million?"

"I think Guilliame will agree. Karlstadt did."

"You're going to use the merchandise you promised Karlstadt?" He gave a low whistle. "That could be dangerous."

"I'll worry about that later."

"You may have to worry about it sooner."

"Screw him. It could have been Karlstadt who killed Jan."

"But you're not sure."

"No, I'm not sure of anything right now." He met Galen's gaze and repeated, "Screw him."

"Far be it from me to interfere with a man bent on revenge. I've found reason usually goes out the window." He turned away. "We should be in Paris by midnight."

"Hire more men," Deschamps said as soon as Provlif picked up the phone. "And don't talk to me about money. I have all the money you could possibly want. Now find Cassie Andreas."

"She may not be here to find."

"What?"

"My CIA contact says there are rumors she's been taken by your old friend Travis." He launched into the explanation.

Deschamps was silent for a moment after Provlif finished. "Highly unlikely."

"The President flew back to Washington from Japan claiming he was ill. Andreas is healthy as a horse."

The more Deschamps thought about it, the more he was inclined to believe the rumor. Travis had never mentioned the child in his conversations with Van Beck, but Andreas could have trusted him enough to ask him to help his daughter. And Travis was sharp enough to have been able to pull off the escape. Excitement began to surge through him. Everything was coming full circle back to him. Travis, and now perhaps the child.

"Deschamps?"

"It could be true."

"Why would he take the kid?"

For the same reason Edward had wanted her? It was possible. Maybe Travis's interference at Vasaro had been merely a setup for a move of his own.

"I want Travis's phone number."

"I've been trying to get it."

"Try harder. You know damn well the CIA knows it if Travis was at this place in Virginia."

"I told you they weren't able to trace his calls."

"I don't want to trace them. But I may want to talk to him."

"I'll work on it."

"Do it. Then get on a plane and come back here. I may need you." He hung up and sat back in his chair. He wanted that phone number. He felt a strange need to be in contact with Travis. It had never happened before with any of his other targets, but Travis was different. Travis had humiliated him, and taking the money from him wasn't enough. And this new information showed Travis as still another danger. He was not only a threat, he was competition. Yes, he wanted to savor this kill, toy with Travis, show him he would always be one step ahead.

What would that next step be? If Travis was as hot as Provlif thought, he should be hiding out. But Edward had killed his friend and Travis was sentimental enough to want revenge. To do that he would have to identify and then locate Edward. The only lead Travis had was Henri Claron's death, and it was likely he would pursue it.

So, Lyon?

Perhaps.

Or perhaps not.

Travis had been robbed of the money he'd been expecting, and keeping Cassie Andreas hidden could be an expensive proposition. He might decide it was necessary to go forward toward his prime objective.

Edward would definitely have to go over everything he'd learned about Travis and then just follow his instincts. . . .

Paris

The modest apartment was on the outskirts of Paris near a small, very green park. It was also four blocks from the Museum d'Andreas.

"Nice." Galen put the suitcases down and glanced around the living room. "Old-fashioned, but very comfortable. Maybe a little too much blue. Blue may be a primary color, but I've always found it depressing."

"It's okay. We won't be here long enough to be depressed." Travis carried Cassie into the bedroom and put her down before turning to Jessica. "She hasn't had a nightmare since we left Juniper. That's good, right?"

"Do you want me to tell you kidnapping her is good therapy?" she asked dryly. "I won't do it, Travis."

"Well, it hasn't hurt her."

"Yet." Melissa came into the room, deposited a suitcase and Jessica's medical bag by the radiator under the window. Then she went into the adjoining bathroom and slammed the door.

Jessica made a face. "She's right, you know. I don't know what long-term effect this will all have on Cassie."

"I can't help that." He tried to keep the edge from his voice. "I'm doing the best I can." He went out into the living room to see Galen heading for the front door. "Where's Stuart Thomas?"

"In the apartment across the hall. He likes his privacy. Believe me, you don't want him too close. When he gets involved in a project, he thinks things like showering and brushing his teeth are a waste of time."

"And is he involved in this project?"

"On a small scale. If you'd asked him to break into top-secret Pentagon records, it would have been more interesting for him." He opened the door. "I'll go check on him."

"I'll go with you."

"No, you won't. You're too tense and I won't have Stuart upset. Besides, it's after midnight. Get some sleep. You can see him in the morning."

"I don't need—" He stopped as he met Galen's steady gaze. It would do no good. Galen had made up his mind and wouldn't budge. "Wake me if Thomas has a breakthrough."

"In the morning." The door shut behind him.

Damn Galen.

And thank God for Galen.

"When are you going to take Cassie to the Wind Dancer?" Melissa stood across the room.

"Two nights from now, after the museum closes. If all goes well."

"It won't go well." She walked to the window and stared out. "But you won't listen to me, will you?"

"I can't listen to you."

"You're hurt. Why don't you wait until you're better?"

"As you pointed out, this is hardly a scratch. Not worth the time it took you to bandage it. Isn't that right?"

She was silent a moment. "Yes. I wish he'd killed you instead of your friend."

"Well, you're out of luck."

"We may all be out of luck." She paused. "I want you to get me a gun."

He stiffened. "Why?"

"I want to be able to defend myself. I'm not going to depend on you." She smiled sardonically. "Don't worry, I'm not planning on shooting you, though it's tempting."

"Do you even know how to use a gun?"

"There were some rapes and assaults on campus a while back and my roommates and I got a little nervous. We took self-defense classes and I bought a Smith and Wesson .38 for the apartment. We all took lessons."

"Okay, I'll have Galen get you one tomorrow morning."

"Good." She started to go back to the bedroom but stopped and looked over her shoulder at him. He was surprised at the desperation in her expression. "I don't want you dead. I don't want anyone dead. Life is such a precious gift. Every minute should be treasured and—"

"Do you think Cassie is enjoying her life?

Jessica is doing whatever she can to make it better." He wearily shook his head. "And I guess I am too."

"Jessica doesn't understand. You don't understand." Her voice was filled with despair. "I can't let you do it."

Travis stared thoughtfully at the door after she'd shut it behind her. The intensity of Melissa's feelings was growing, and that could be dangerous.

Jesus, he didn't need this. All he wanted was to come through on his promise to Jessica and get on with finding Jan's killer.

Think about the man in the park. Go over every minute from the time he'd first seen him. He'd told Jan there was something familiar about him. What was familiar? Green eyes . . . But he hadn't been close enough to see those eyes when he'd made that remark to Jan.

He sat down on the couch. Think. Go over it. Make a connection.

Washington, D.C.

"Danley thinks he's located Travis, Mr. President," Keller said. "Well, not exactly located, but there was an incident in a park in

Amsterdam yesterday. Jan Van Beck was murdered."

"By Travis?"

"No, the assailant fled with Travis in pursuit. We believe Travis was wounded in the attack."

"Good," Andreas said. "I wish the bastard had been skewered on a spit."

"Not until we find your daughter," Keller said. "After that, we'll be glad to accommodate you, Mr. President. Danley thinks they've also located a company in Antwerp that rented the van to transport your daughter. The timing is right. We're getting closer, sir."

"Not close enough. I'm going to Amsterdam."

"That wouldn't be wise."

"I'm going. Get *Air Force One* ready. That plane was built so that the President could run the country from it during an emergency. It's going to be tested. Then get the doctor to say I've had a slight relapse and can't leave my room. I'll make an appearance on the balcony so that everyone will know I'm not on my deathbed."

"What about the First Lady?"

Chelsea. She had been suspicious from the moment he had stepped off the plane from Tokyo. She knew him so well, they were too close for any deception to fool her for long.

God, he didn't want to tell her about Cassie.

And he couldn't not tell her if he took off for Amsterdam.

He stood up. "I'll go see her. We leave in an hour, Keller."

"Yes, Mr. President."

A few minutes later Andreas was opening the door to their private suite. She was lying in bed, working on her laptop.

"Is that resting?"

"I'm flat on my ass, aren't I?" She gave him that radiant smile that had first captured his attention all those years ago. She was more beautiful now than she'd been that day.

His love, his partner, his best friend . . .

He came into the room. "I have something to tell you, Chelsea."

14

"Piece of cake," Stuart Thomas said. He stood up and gestured to the computer screen. "There you go, Mr. Travis. It's all yours."

Thomas's T-shirt was sweat stained and as unpleasant smelling as Galen had warned him, Travis realized. The idea of working in close contact with the kid was not appealing. "Why don't you go get a meal? I'll page you if I need you."

"You're not going to find him just by browsing. What's he supposed to have done?"

"Murder."

"What kind of murder? Crime of passion, burglary, mercy killing? You've got to narrow it down if you want results."

"Let me work at it."

Thomas hesitated. "Then will you give me my money? I usually get paid half upfront and half when you say you're through with me. I waived the first payment, since Galen is a good friend, but I really should have——"

"How much?"

"Five thousand."

"Wait here." He left Thomas and went to the apartment across the hall.

"Trouble?" Galen rose from a chair.

"More an inconvenience. Thomas wants to be paid and I have a cash flow problem. Five thousand?"

Galen shook his head. "I can get it by tonight."

"He wants it now. Never mind." He went to his duffel and drew out his laptop, then opened the disk drive and took out a pouch. "You'll have to use your powers of presentation and convince him to accept goods instead of cash." He poured out half the contents of the pouch onto the coffee table.

"Holy shit," Galen murmured. "Diamonds?"

Travis sorted through the gemstones. "Even the smallest of these will bring over five thousand dollars."

Galen was staring at the pile. "And you smuggled these in your laptop?"

"It seemed a pretty good place as long as I wasn't going to be frisked by airport security."

"So that's why you hitched a ride on *Air Force One*."

He nodded. "I wasn't about to risk losing these to customs after all I'd gone through to get them."

"Andreas won't be pleased you used his plane for your own ends."

"At this stage of the game, he'd agree that smuggling is the least of my sins." He picked up one of the stones. "I'm no expert, but I'd say this is pretty high quality."

"The best."

"Is that how you're going to pay off that curator at the museum?" Melissa had come into the room, her gaze on the diamonds glittering on the coffee table. "They're stolen, aren't they?"

"You might say that."

"And this is why your friend died?"

"You might say that too." He handed the first diamond he'd chosen to Galen. "Tell Thomas it's bonus time. Any appraiser in Paris will tell him that stone is worth twice what he asked me for."

"You can bet he'll be hotfooting it to the diamond exchange to check it."

"No problem. It will pass any test they can put it through." He separated the pile and gave one half to Galen. "For Guilliame. I'm sure he'll want to check the merchandise before tonight."

"This has got to be worth more than the price he asked, Travis."

"Just give them to Guilliame and let's get it over with." He scooped the rest of the diamonds back in the pouch and stuffed the pouch in his duffel. "But I want a guarantee of those four hours or I'll cut his heart out."

"What a true gentleman you are, Travis," Melissa said.

"I wasn't gently reared on a southern plantation. I was taught to smooth the way with sugar but always have the knife handy." He met her gaze. "You should appreciate that. You're very good with the knife, Melissa."

"I'm getting better."

"I believe I'll get out of here and go about my job," Galen said. "It's getting a little too chilly in here for me. I'll let you know if there's a problem, Travis."

"Right." His gaze never left Melissa. "I have enough problems."

"That you have."

"No wonder you haven't been worried about moving us around Europe like chess pieces," Melissa said after Galen had left. "Money can open doors, can't it?"

"The doors of the Museum d'Andreas, at least."

"What if I tell Jessica that you're using stolen money to help Cassie?"

"We both know it won't make any difference to her. She'd find a way to justify spending ill-gotten loot if it saved the kid." He smiled. "But it would make her worry and feel bad. So you won't tell her, will you?"

She didn't answer.

"Nice try, Melissa." He stood up. "Now I have to get back next door and do a little work. If you need anything, come and get me."

"Where's Travis?" Jessica asked when she came into the kitchen ten minutes later.

"Next door." Melissa forced a smile. "I just made iced tea. Would you like some?"

"Please."

"How's Cassie?"

"The same." She sat at the table and rubbed her temple. "Jesus, I hope this Wind Dancer thing works out."

"If you have any doubts, you shouldn't do it." Melissa put the glass down before Jessica. "We're making progress. I know it. If you'd let me try to be a little tougher with her, we might even hurry it along."

"You might know it, but I don't." Jessica took a sip. "I may be going along with you, but I still can't quite believe all this psychic connection stuff. It goes against my every instinct and training."

"I know it does. That's the problem." Melissa suddenly fell to her knees before her sister and buried her head in her lap. "Try to believe me, Jessica." Her voice was muffled. "I love you and I want only what's best. That's all I've ever wanted for you. I took so much away, let me try to give something back." Her arms tightened around Jessica's waist. "Let me help you. Listen to me. Please."

"Mellie?" Jessica lifted Melissa's chin and looked down at her. She touched her wet cheek. "You're crying. . . ."

Her lips twisted. "Just goes to show how unstable I am, right?"

"Not right." She grasped Melissa's shoulders and gave her a gentle shake. "And you took nothing from me that I wasn't willing to give. Everyone has a path to follow in life. Don't you realize that you helped me to find mine? I've never regretted one minute of those years I spent with you."

"I have."

"Then stop it." She grimaced. "And for God's sake, stop crying. You're choking me up."

"Sorry." She laid her head back in Jessica's lap.

"Just answer me one question. If I swear on my love for you that I'm right about the Wind Dancer, that it's a danger to Cassie, will you believe me?"

Silence.

"Oh, Jesus."

"I'm too firmly grounded in reality, Mellie. I know you think you're right, but my mind automatically searches for a reasonable explanation for everything that's happened. And reason tells me that exposing Cassie to an influence that's always been benign to her might open a door."

"It's a risk, such a terrible risk."

"A risk worth taking." She paused. "And I have to take it, Mellie."

"That's your final word?"

"Yes. But if you disapprove, you don't have to go with us."

"The hell I won't." Melissa sat back on her heels and wiped her eyes. "Where you go, I go." She stood up. "Drink your tea. I'll go wash my face and then I'll fix you some lunch."

2:45 P.M.

He was getting nowhere.

Travis leaned back in his chair and rubbed his

eyes. Flipping through the records on the computer screen was proving to be as tiring as it was
frustrating. He'd known there was little chance,
but he'd hoped he'd run across something that
might trigger a memory, anything. . . . Sometimes
something clicked, a flash of—

Nothing.

Well, what had he expected with what he had
to work with?

Green eyes, slightly tilted. Blond hair that
might or might not be his true color. A beard
that hid his features like a mask.

Mask . . .

He slowly sat upright in the chair.

Mask.

He hadn't recognized the man's face. He
hadn't thought the man was familiar until he'd
seen him walk from the cotton-candy stall to the
bench.

Mask.

"Christ."

"Have you got it?"

"Cool it. It takes time." Thomas didn't take his
gaze from the screen. "I've been working on it
for only a couple of hours."

"You said it would be easier if I could narrow
it down," Travis said. "I've narrowed it down."

"Six foot two or three, age between thirty-five and forty, Nordic coloring, nine-millimeter pistol weapon of choice." He flipped through more screens.

"And a terrorist background," Travis said.

"That's the key. If you'd told me that before, I could have been—"

"I didn't know before. How long? There can't be that many who fit the profile."

"You'd be surprised. It's a violent world we live in."

Another hour passed.

"Bingo." Thomas leaned forward. "Take a look. This may be your man."

Age thirty, but this record dated back ten years. Clean-shaven, pale brown hair slightly receding, but the eyes were right. Green. Slightly tilted at the corners.

Yes.

"Print it out."

Thomas pressed a button. "Nasty." He read the history. "Arson, theft, murder . . . IRA, Italian Sons of Liberty, Nazi skinheads. He doesn't seem wedded to a single cause, does he?"

"Not unusual. Mercenaries go where the money is." He took the mug shot off the printer. "I thought he may have terrorist affiliations since two of the dead at Vasaro had them."

"Vasaro?"

"Never mind." He grabbed a pencil and began shading in a beard. There was no doubt.

"It's him?" Thomas asked. "I did it?"

"You did it." He pushed back his chair. "You're a genius, Thomas."

"Genius should be rewarded." Thomas smiled slyly. "Don't you think I deserve a tip? Maybe another one of those pretty baubles?"

"Don't be greedy," Travis said absently, as he stared at the mug shot. "Can you get me a background and psychological profile?"

"The CIA probably has one. Give me thirty minutes."

It took forty-five minutes before he punched the button to print and then handed the two pages to Travis. "There you go."

"Thanks." He headed for the door.

Edward James Deschamps.

Gotcha.

15

"Edward Deschamps." Galen lifted his gaze from the rap sheet. "You're sure?"

Travis nodded. "As certain as I can be without seeing him again."

"And you think he's the leader of the team at Vasaro?"

"It adds up. He knew me and indicated I'd gotten in his way sometime in the past. He was familiar to me, but I didn't recognize the face. I must have remembered the way he moved."

"I was outside in the courtyard, so I didn't see him. How did he move?"

"Fairly distinctively. Fast, springy, on the balls of his feet, like a tennis player."

"Karlstadt had nothing to do with Jan's murder?"

Travis shook his head. "It's not likely. Vasaro happened before I became involved with Karlstadt and the diamonds. Besides, Deschamps went for the money first and not for the diamonds. The diamonds were Karlstadt's first priority."

"Then you now have the Russians, Deschamps, and Karlstadt after you?"

"You've forgotten the CIA and the Secret Service," Melissa said from the corner, where she was curled up in a chair. "I find that very encouraging. With those odds, someone is bound to catch up with you."

"You can hope," Travis said. "But maybe if you tell your sister Deschamps is back on the scene, she might change her mind about the Wind Dancer. She might not think the risk is worth it."

"I'll tell her." She rose to her feet. "But she won't change her mind, not unless there's a direct danger to Cassie."

"You're resigned at last?"

"Hell, no," she said fiercely. "I've accepted only the first step. That doesn't mean I won't fight every other step along the way."

"I'm sure you will. Then you intend to go with us?"

"You were hoping I wouldn't. Sorry. I wouldn't miss it."

Galen was frowning as he studied the mug shot. "I think I've run across him once. Somewhere in Portugal. Possible?"

"He didn't belong to a Portuguese group, but that doesn't mean he didn't operate there." Travis was reading the profile. "He's a U.S. citizen, but he's bounced around all over Europe. He's something of a gourmet. Snazzy dresser . . . has his suits tailored in Rome." He skipped over a few lines. "His mother divorced his father and brought Edward to Paris when he was six. She married Jean Detoile, the owner of an art gallery. Detoile had money and put the kid in a private boarding school. Excellent grades at first, very high IQ. Then, when he was twelve, his stepfather accused him of theft and turned him in to the police. He was in jail for two years."

He scanned the rest of the page. "When he came out, he worked the streets—drugs, con games, theft. Evidently, that didn't pay enough, because he turned hit man by the time he was twenty. He became an expert with surveillance equipment." He glanced up. "That would correspond with what Jan told me about the bugs in his apartment." His gaze shifted back to the report. "Then he graduated to terrorism. Worked with a number of groups and then formed his own. It didn't last long. He was essentially a loner and his team drifted away."

"What about his parents?"

"His mother died when he was in prison. His stepfather was murdered four years after Deschamps was released."

"By Deschamps?"

"Probably. It was never proven. Not one trace of evidence was found. But it was an extremely gory death." He paused. "It's interesting that he didn't kill his stepfather immediately upon his release. He waited and learned and then he moved. Cold-blooded son of a bitch."

"But evidently very bright."

"Not so bright. The only reason he had for killing Jan was to hurt me." He added softly, "That mistake is going to cost him."

"And you'll enjoy it," Melissa said.

"No doubt about it. Would you like to hear some more about Deschamps? I believe you'd think even I come out pretty good in comparison."

She headed for the bedroom. "It would take a mass murderer to make you look good to me."

Travis turned to Galen as the door closed behind her. "Do you have enough info here to find him?"

"If there was enough info here, the CIA or Interpol would have gotten him a long time ago." He took the report from Travis and scanned it. "He was picked up three times in

Paris at different periods in his career. He obviously likes it here. It's a place to start. I'll put
some feelers out right away. But don't hold your
breath."

12:35 A.M.

"It's almost time to go, baby," Jessica whispered. She wrapped the light blanket around
Cassie. "It's going to be exciting. You're going
to see an old friend." She turned to Melissa.
"Travis said we're leaving Paris right after we go
to the museum. He wants everything in the van.
Will you make sure I've cleaned everything out
of the bathroom while I get us a cup of coffee?"
She grimaced. "Though I don't know why I
should feel the need for a jolt of caffeine when
I'm so nervous."

Melissa shook her head. "You're never
nervous."

"I am tonight." Jessica went into the living
room, where Travis and Galen waited. "Almost
time?"

Travis nodded. "How's the little girl?"

"Awake."

"Keep her that way. Otherwise it's going to be
a very expensive nap. Where's Melissa?"

"Packing up." She walked to the kitchen and poured a cup of coffee. "Where are we going from here?"

"If this works with Cassie, I'll settle you and Melissa somewhere safe and let you negotiate terms with Andreas."

"Where is somewhere safe?"

"How do you like the Riviera?" Galen asked.

"I don't know. I've never been. But it doesn't sound like a place to hide."

"Which is usually the best place."

"We have to be on borrowed time anyway. I don't know why Andreas hasn't caught up with us yet."

"We've moved fast, and we've had Galen."

"And what about terms for you?"

Travis shook his head. "Andreas won't be inclined to make any deals with me."

"All done." Melissa came out of the bedroom, carrying the duffels. "Let's go and get it over with."

Poor Mellie. She was so pale and tense that Jessica's heart ached for her.

"I'll bring the van around to the back and make sure there's no one around." Galen moved toward the door. "If I don't phone you, bring Cassie down in five minutes."

Jessica handed Melissa the cup of coffee. "Drink it. You look like hell."

"I don't need it."

"Drink it, Mellie."

Melissa smiled faintly. "Yes, ma'am." She took a few swallows and handed the cup back to her. "Satisfied, Saint Jessica?"

"Yes." She turned to Travis. "How do we get Cassie into the museum without being seen? Carrying her around is sure to attract attention."

"We park the van in the alley and go in through the back entrance. Galen says the artifacts room is right down the hall."

"The guards?"

"Two, and they've been bribed. One at the back entrance and one at the door of the artifacts room. Inside the room is a door leading downstairs to a storage area in the basement. Galen is stationing one of his own men at that door just in case."

"Christ, I hope everything goes smoothly."

"Jessica . . ."

Jessica turned to Melissa. Her sister's eyes were glazed and she took a staggering step forward. "Jessica . . ."

"Catch her, Travis," Jessica said.

Travis sprang forward as Melissa's knees buckled and she started to fall.

Melissa's gaze clung to Jessica's face in horror. "No . . . Jessica."

"Shh." Jessica plumped the pillow on the couch. "Don't worry, Mellie."

"Dear God. You don't know what—" She slumped in Travis's arms, unconscious.

"What the hell?" Travis murmured.

"A sedative in the coffee," Jessica said. "Put her on the couch."

"You drugged her? Why?"

"This was going to be too hard on her. You saw how upset she was about the Wind Dancer. This way she'll wake up and it will all be over." She draped a throw over Melissa. "And there was a possibility she might have interfered. Cassie deserves this chance."

Travis gave a low whistle. "You're pretty damn tough."

"You knew she could be a problem. Are you saying you weren't tempted to do something like this?"

"I was tempted." He looked down at Melissa. "But I couldn't do it."

"Why not?"

"It seemed like dirty pool. A fighter like her deserves an even match." He brushed the hair from Melissa's forehead. "I like the shrew when she's not stabbing me with her little poison darts. I decided I'd rather have the problem than the solution."

"And I decided to not take the chance and protect both Mellie and Cassie." Jessica checked her wristwatch. "Time to take Cassie downstairs."

"How long will Melissa sleep?" He turned toward the bedroom. "She took only a couple of swallows."

"I didn't expect anything else. I gave her a hefty dose. Four to five hours." She brushed a loving kiss on Melissa's cheek and whispered, "It's for the best. Good night, Mellie."

12:45 A.M.

Paul Guilliame was a thin, graceful, dark-haired man in his late fifties. He was also extremely nervous.

"Come in. Come in." He nodded to the guard outside the artifacts room and gestured for them to enter with one fluttering hand. "I must be insane to do this. Four hours. No more."

"We're not pushing it. Just find a chair for the lady," Galen said. "And then go get a drink to steady your nerves."

"I'm not leaving the premises," Guilliame said. "And what's that child doing here? You never said anything about a—"

"The clock's ticking. If you want us out of here, leave us alone and don't interfere," Travis said. "Where's the Wind Dancer?"

"On the worktable opposite the sarcophagus."

Jessica's gaze had already fastened on the statue. "My God," she murmured. "I've seen pictures of it, but it's different seeing it in person. It's wonderful."

"Where do you want the chair?" Guilliame was carrying one from across the room.

"A few yards from the statue," Jessica said.

He put the chair where she'd indicated and hurried out of the room.

Jessica sat down and held out her arms. "Put Cassie on my lap, Travis."

"I can hold her."

"No."

"She trusts me."

"But I'm the one who's been trying to persuade her to come back. You've just been a security blanket. I want her to realize that everything's different now."

He placed Cassie on Jessica's lap, facing the Wind Dancer. "Now what?"

"We sit and we wait." She pulled Cassie closer. "Open your eyes, sweetheart. He's here. He's so beautiful, it almost makes my heart stop. I can see why you love him so much. Please open your eyes. . . ."

★   ★   ★

"He's here!" Cassie's cry of joy tore through the haze surrounding Melissa. *"I've found him. She keeps saying I have to open my eyes to see him, but I know he's here. You come and we'll see him together."*

Darkness. Haze. Lethargy.

"We can stay here. He'll keep us safe. She wants me to come out, but we don't have to. We'll go deeper. He took me away once. He can do it again. And he'll come with us. I know he will."

She should say something. But she couldn't think. Why couldn't she think? The mist was deep and heavy as molasses. *"What are you talking about?"*

"The Wind Dancer, silly."

Fear jolted through Melissa, tearing the fog. *"What?"*

"I told you. He's here. I've found him."

Her heart was starting to beat like a jackhammer. *"Where?"*

"Jessica brought me to him."

Jessica.

The coffee.

No!

"Melissa, come on. I've found him, but I don't want to leave you here. Come with me."

She had to open her eyes.

"Melissa."

"Don't go with him, Cassie."

Open your eyes. Open your eyes. Open your eyes.

Finally her heavy lids lifted. Blue curtains. The apartment. Hazy. Everything was hazy.

Sit up. Move.

Too hard.

Move.

It took her five minutes to sit up and another five to get to her feet.

One thing at a time. Get to the door.

What if she couldn't make it? She had to stop Jessica.

"Melissa, where are you?"

"I'm coming. Wait for me."

She fumbled in her pants pocket for the number she'd copied from Jessica's phone book. Now get to the phone.

Jesus, she couldn't see the numbers on the phone. It took her three tries before she dialed the number correctly.

"Hello," Andreas said.

"Cassie . . . Jessica. Museum d'Andreas."

"What? Who is this?"

"Melissa. Now. Go now." She hung up. They might not get there in time. They might not get there at all.

Take the purse; it had the gun Galen had given her. Get to the street. The museum was only four blocks away. She could do it.

One step at a time.

"Melissa, I'm going to open my eyes. I have to see him again. He's so beautiful."

Panic shot through Melissa. If Cassie saw those emerald-green eyes, then Melissa would see them. She didn't know if that would make any difference, but she couldn't chance it.

"No. Don't open your eyes. Wait for me."

"I'll try. Hurry."

One block.

She couldn't make it. Too tired.

"I can't wait any longer, Melissa."

"Yes, you can. You can do anything you want to do."

Two blocks.

She lurched and fell against the brick wall of the building next to her.

Straighten. Go on.

"I'm opening my eyes."

"No!"

"I have to do it."

And then Melissa saw it.

Emerald eyes staring out at the world with ancient wisdom. The statue was standing on a beat-up wooden worktable in a huge, cluttered room. A cat-walk. Paintings. Travis was standing to one side of the worktable beside an Egyptian sarcophagus.

"I told you." Cassie's excitement was swirling

around both of them like a cloud of static electricity
"He's here. He's here."

One more block. The museum was just up ahead.

The emerald eyes, but no pool of blood. It could be different. It had to be different.

She turned down the alley.

"Jessica is happy. She thinks because I opened my eyes that I'm coming back. She's talking to me, telling me the Wind Dancer would want me to do that."

"She's right, Cassie."

"How do you know? He took me away. It's safe here."

"But you can't see the Wind Dancer as you're do-ing now." Was she making sense? She was so scared, she couldn't think. All she could see were those emer-ald eyes.

But no pool of blood. No pool of blood. Make, it different. Please, no pool of blood.

She was climbing the stairs to the back door, holding on to the railing.

So hard. Such a long way to the top.

She leaned against the door to gather strength. Another minute and she'd be in the hall. It was okay. She'd made it and nothing had happened. She'd not even been stopped by the guards.

The guards.

Where were the guards?

She pushed open the door.

Blood. Staring eyes. Two bodies.

The guards.

"Why aren't you talking to me, Melissa?"

"Close your eyes, Cassie." She was lurching down the hall. Jesus, another body beside the door to the artifacts room. Blue suit, not a guard. Guilliame? *"Listen to me, I want you to close your eyes."*

"Why? Then I wouldn't be able to see— What was that sound?"

"What sound?"

"Popping. Heard it before. Heard it before." Melissa could hear the panic in her voice. *"Michael is running downstairs toward the other door. He's leaving me."*

"Close your eyes."

"Wind Dancer. I can't stay here. He's got to take me away." Terror. *"I'm falling, Melissa."*

"Why are you falling? Are you hurt?"

"I don't know. I'm on the floor. Closing my eyes. I'm going away. . . ."

"Why are you on the floor?" She threw open the door. *"What's happen—"*

And then she saw it.

The emerald eyes looking down.

The pool of blood spreading on the floor until it touched the child's shoe.

Scream after scream tore from Melissa's throat.

She didn't know how she got across the room,

but she was falling to her knees. Stop the blood. She had to stop the blood gushing from Jessica's chest.

"Mellie?" Jessica was looking up at her. "Help . . . Cassie."

"Cassie's fine." She was pressing her hands on the wound. "You'll be fine too."

"She was almost . . . back. I know it. I—did it, didn't I?"

"Of course you did." Oh, God. So much blood. "Now stop talking."

"He's beautiful. . . ." Jessica was looking up at the Wind Dancer. "I can see why Cassie . . ." A thin trail of blood trickled out of one corner of Jessica's mouth. "Beautiful . . ."

She slumped sideways.

"No!"

16

"No use, Deschamps's gone," Galen told Travis outside the museum. "And we'd better get out of here too. Those sirens sound close. It's probably what scared the bastard off."

"Son of a bitch." Travis's hands closed into fists. "He knew this place like the back of his hand. He knew exactly where he was going when he jumped down from that catwalk. How did he get past those guards?"

"That's what I want to know," Galen said grimly. "I'll go find out while you check on Cassie and Jessica. Two minutes and we're out of here."

Travis ran back into the museum and skidded

to a stop when he reached the artifacts room. "Oh, shit."

"She won't wake up." Melissa lifted her head, her mouth smeared with Jessica's blood. "I can't make her breathe." She covered Jessica's mouth with hers again.

"Melissa." He knelt down and put his fingers on Jessica's throat. "It's no use. She's gone."

"Don't you *say* that." She frantically blew into Jessica's mouth. "I won't let her be dead."

He checked Cassie. No wounds. The child hadn't been hit. He hadn't been aware that either of them had been shot when he'd run after Deschamps. He'd glanced at Jessica, but she'd been sitting upright in the chair with the child in her arms.

The sirens were louder. "Melissa, we have to get out of here."

She ignored him.

"Out." Galen was beside them, swiftly picking up Cassie. He glanced at Jessica. "Dead?"

"Yes."

"No," Melissa said at the same time.

Galen nodded. "Dead. I've locked the doors and I'm taking Cassie out through the basement." He carried Cassie toward the steps. "If we don't get moving, we're all going to end up in jail. Both guards are dead, and so is Guilliame.

My man Cardeau was killed too. I found him behind some boxes in the basement. You either get Melissa away from here or leave her."

"She'll come." Travis pulled Melissa away from her sister. "Let's go, Melissa. You can't help her."

"I can help her. I can stop this."

"Melissa, you're lying to yourself. Jessica's dead and you'll be dead too or in prison if you don't come with me. Then we'll never be able to punish the man who did this to her. Do you think it's right to let that happen?"

She stared blindly at him.

"Travis!" Galen called out.

"We're coming."

Melissa whispered, "Dead?"

Travis nodded. He pulled her to her feet. "Come on, Cassie will need you."

"She said 'Help Cassie.' "

"That's right." He pushed her toward the stairs. "But you can't do that unless we get out of here."

"Dead." She suddenly stopped and looked back at Jessica. "Oh, God, it's real." She shuddered. "I wanted it to be another dream." There was a world of pain in her voice.

"Come on, Melissa."

Her gaze slowly moved to the statue. "Bring him."

"What?"

"Bring him."

"No."

"I'm not going without him. Pick him up and bring him."

The sirens were coming from right outside. He knew there was not much time left. "You're not thinking straight. Just come with me, Melissa."

She shook him off and moved toward the Wind Dancer.

"Jesus." He ran across the room, snatched the statue, grabbed her arm, and pulled her after him. "Hurry, dammit. They'll be knocking down the door any minute."

"Is she doing okay?" Galen glanced at Melissa's reflection in the rearview mirror as the car pulled onto A6. "She looks like a sleepwalker."

"She *is* a sleepwalker. With the amount of sedative Jessica fed her, she should be out like a light. She should never have been able to leave the apartment. I don't know what's keeping her going."

"Yes, you do."

"Maybe I do," he said wearily. He took his handkerchief and dabbed at the blood on Melissa's lips. "The body can be made to do amazing things when the will is strong enough."

"Why the hell did you take the Wind Dancer? Did you think we weren't in enough trouble?"

"She wouldn't leave without it." He shrugged. "And what's one more—"

"Straw on the camel's back?" Galen finished. "The French police are going to regard this theft as an insult to their pride. They promised Andreas absolute security for the statue. We could get them off our ass if we find a way of returning it."

"No," Melissa said.

Both men looked at her. It was the first word she'd uttered since they left the museum. "We have to keep it."

"We'll talk about it later," Travis said. "You may not be thinking clearly right now."

"We have to keep it."

"It's dangerous. You saw how the police swooped down on that museum. How did they know we were there? There must have been a leak."

"I called Andreas," Melissa said.

Galen began to swear. "I knew it. I knew she'd do it."

"Be quiet, Galen. It's just as well she did call him. Deschamps was positioned on that catwalk to take us all out. Those sirens scared him off."

"Not in time," Melissa whispered.

"No, not in time for Jessica," Travis said gently. "But it may have saved the rest of us."

"I don't care about the rest of you."

"Not even Cassie?"

She closed her eyes. "Help . . . Cassie."

"She's okay. No different than she was before."

"Help . . . Cassie."

"We'll help her, Melissa." Travis pulled her head onto his shoulder. "Now try to rest. I'll wake you when we get to the cottage."

"Help Cas . . ."

She was asleep.

The shuttered window framed a lavender and scarlet sunset sky.

Beautiful . . .

"Take some water." Travis held a glass to Melissa's lips. "You've been out for a long time. You must be thirsty."

She was thirsty. Her mouth felt as dry as cotton. She drank half the glass. "Out? What do you—"

Jessica.

Pain stabbed through her. White hot. "Dear God."

He caught the glass as it fell from her hand,

and drew her into his arms. "I know. I know. I'm sorry, Melissa." His voice was muffled as he rocked her back and forth. "Christ, I'm so sorry."

"Being sorry doesn't do any good. She's dead." She buried her face in his shoulder. "I couldn't help her. I couldn't stop it."

"No one could help her. Even if we'd gotten her to the emergency room within minutes, the wound would still have been fatal."

"I couldn't stop it. I should have been smarter. I should have realized she'd try to stop me from going along."

"She surprised me too. And if you'd come along, you might have been shot as well."

"No, I'd have found a way to protect her. I knew it was coming. I'd have stopped it."

She felt him stiffen against her. "What?"

"Let me go." She pushed him away and swung her feet to the floor. "I have to get out of here."

"Sure, it will be good for you to be alone." He helped her to her feet. "And this mile or two of beach is deserted. Just don't go far. Okay?"

She didn't answer.

She was running from the bedroom, out of the cottage, her feet sinking into the soft sand. Her shadow cast a spidery imprint on the beach in front of her as she ran toward the far dunes.

Jessica.

She slid down the opposite side of a dune and lay huddled at the bottom.

Jessica.

Sister, mother, friend, savior. Sweet Jesus, why Jessica?

She rocked back and forth as agony tore through her. And, at last, the tears came. Painful sobs racked her body.

Jessica . . .

"Tough." Galen's gaze followed Travis's to where Melissa was sitting on the beach, staring out at the sea. "They were close?"

"You saw them together. What do you think?"

"I think life sucks sometimes."

"Like right now. Everything's going to hell and it's going to get worse." He paused. "You could bail out. I wouldn't blame you. You've done more than I've asked of you."

"So I'm an overachiever. I'll stick around."

"I don't need—"

"Shut up, Travis. This isn't only about you. That son of a bitch killed one of my men last night. Do you think I'm going to bow out before I take him down?"

"He's mine, Galen."

"We'll argue about that when we catch up

with him." He looked back at Melissa. "But she's the one we'd better watch. Once she's over the first shock, she's going to harden into pure steel."

Staring at that fragile, lonely figure silhouetted against the sky, it was difficult for Travis to believe. "You could be wrong."

He shook his head. "She told me once that we were a lot alike. Brother and sister. I think she's right." He turned to go back inside the house. "Since you're keeping an eye on Melissa, I'll go check on Cassie. I'm very good at baby-sitting. Did I ever tell you I once baby-sat a wolf?"

"No, but it wouldn't surprise me." Travis's voice was abstracted as he watched Melissa. So much pain and sorrow. So much loneliness. He wanted to go to her and hold her and try to ease—

Not yet.

You had to face the first grief alone before you could accept comfort. Hell, maybe she wouldn't be able to accept comfort from him no matter how long he waited. After all, he'd been a primary part of that horror at the museum.

Why did he even want to help her? His modus operandi was to be emotionally detached. Yet from the first moment she had shown up on his doorstep, Melissa had managed to . . . involve him. She had aroused interest, anger, desire, amusement, and admiration, and now she was touching something deeper.

Pity?

What difference did it make? Self-examination was bull. He dropped down on the doorstep. So don't think. Just watch and wait and maybe do a little grieving of your own.

"You've been out here a long time," Travis said behind her. "Don't you think you'd better come in? It's almost three in the morning and the wind's coming up, Melissa."

"I don't want to go in. I'm not chilly." It was a lie. She felt ice cold, but it wasn't from the wind. "I have to think about a few things."

"Jessica."

"No, I've thought all I can about Jessica right now. It hurts . . . too much. I loved her. . . ."

"I know."

"You couldn't know. She was everything to me. She brought me out of the dark and taught me how to live again." She rubbed her temple. "She always laughed when I called her Saint Jessica, but there was truth to it. She was so god-damn . . . good." The tears were starting again, and she brushed them aside. "See, I can't think of her without blubbering. I have to stop it so I can think clearly."

"I feel a little like blubbering myself," Travis said. "I didn't know her long, but it was enough to see what a fine person she was."

"You're being kind to me." She didn't look at him. "I wasn't kind to you when your friend was killed. I couldn't let myself soften toward you. You were the one leading Jessica toward the Wind Dancer."

"And I led her right into a trap. I suppose you blame me for her death?"

She shook her head. "No more than I do myself. She was the one who made you promise to bring the statue and Cassie together. It was like being on a runaway train. I knew what was coming, but there wasn't anything I could do about it."

He glanced away from her. "You . . . knew what was coming?"

"I've been dreaming about it for weeks. That was why I came home to Juniper. It was always the same. The Wind Dancer staring down at a pool of blood and Jessica lying dead on the floor."

"You didn't tell her?"

"Jessica never really believed in anything she couldn't see and touch. She wouldn't have paid any attention to me. But she had to pay attention when I joined with Cassie. I thought if I made the Wind Dancer a threat to Cassie, Jessica might keep away from it." Her lips twisted. "And then you offered the statue to her on a silver platter. I wanted to kill you."

"Then you do blame me."

She wearily shook her head. "I guess I never really believed you could stop the train from moving toward its destination, but I had to try. I only hoped I could prevent the wreck at the last minute." Her hands clenched into fists. "If there's a God, it wouldn't make any sense for Him to give me the dreams and take away the power to stop them from happening, would it?"

"Have you had these dreams before? Not about Jessica but about other people?"

"Twice before. The first was right after I started college. A little boy who lived next door to our apartment in Cambridge. Jimmy Watson. Brown hair, a sweet smile . . . I kept dreaming of him crossing the street and being hit by a van. I'd wake up crying. I thought I was going crazy." She paused. "It happened. He jumped out into traffic to get a toy and was run over."

"Killed?"

"No, but he had internal injuries. He was in the hospital for weeks. I went to see his mother and she must have thought I was nuts. She was very soothing and assured me that I had nothing to do with Jimmy's accident."

"You didn't believe her?"

"In my dream it was always a yellow and black florist van. He was run over by a van from Bendix Florist. What are the odds?"

"And the second case?"

"An old man who worked at the college as a janitor. I had a recurring dream that he slipped on the side of the lap pool and hit his head. I could see the blood in the water."

"And what did you do?"

"I went to him and told him about it. He was a nice man, but he didn't believe me. He patted me on the shoulder and told me young people watched too much TV these days. I asked him to at least please take someone with him when he cleaned the locker rooms and the pool area. He said he would."

"But he didn't do it."

She gave a sigh of anguish. "How did you guess?"

"Human nature. If he didn't believe you, he'd go his own way. It happened as you dreamed it would?"

"He drowned. It didn't have to happen. Maybe if I'd kept after him . . ." She shook her head. "Or maybe not. Maybe this is some big cosmic joke. Show me the future and then not let me change it." She turned to Travis and asked unevenly, "Now, wouldn't that be funny?"

"No, and I don't think you've given it a fair shot. The first time you didn't believe in it yourself. The second time it wasn't your fault the old man was too set in his ways to take care of himself."

"And Jessica?"

"She slipped you a mickey. You might have been able to prevent what happened if you'd been yourself." He turned to look at her. "Of course, if you want to think that this is all fate and can't be changed, go for it. It's much simpler. Just turn your back and walk away."

"Simple? You don't know what you're talking about. There's nothing simple about—" Her gaze narrowed on his face. "You're accepting all this much too easily."

"I told you once that I had no problem with talents a little outside the norm."

"Joining with Cassie is a little outside the norm. Dreams of future events are way off the scale."

"I wasn't exactly unprepared for it. It's not totally unheard of in cases involving recovered trauma victims. Dedrick mentioned two cases where authentic foresight was documented. Once in a Greek boy from Athens and once in China. It seems when the barriers are down, anything is possible."

"Dedrick again. I wish I'd gotten my hands on that book when I was going through hell with Jimmy."

"I wish you had too. It might have helped you."

She was silent a moment. "You're trying to help me now. Why? We haven't been the best of buddies."

"Maybe I blame myself even if you don't. I was caught off guard by Deschamps. After the theft and Jan's death, I didn't expect this to happen. I didn't make the connection. Except for my head on a platter, I thought he had what he wanted."

"And he wanted the Wind Dancer?"

"He was up on the catwalk, so he had to know the layout of the museum. Maybe he was planning on stealing the statue himself. He had to have done some pretty thorough advance work."

"Did he follow us from Amsterdam?"

"I believe he knew ahead of time that we might be going after the Wind Dancer. He was waiting for us to set it up for him."

"And how would he know that?"

"Jan's phone was bugged for a time. It had to be Deschamps."

"And he wanted the Wind Dancer enough to run the risk. Why?"

"There could be many reasons. He's a merce-nary. His entire career has been spent in pursuit of money."

"You said he took millions from you already."

"Millions aren't that important anymore. You can make that on one drug deal. Your next-door neighbor can make it e-trading. But the Wind Dancer is priceless. For a man like Deschamps, it could be the ultimate score." He shrugged. "Or it could be something else entirely. Who knows what's important to him?"

"The Wind Dancer is important to him or he wouldn't have been at the museum. But he's not going to get it. Where is it? Where did you put it?"

"In the closet in an old box we found in the shed. It's just going to be an albatross around our necks. We need to return it, Melissa."

"No." She stood up. "Why should we do that? As long as Deschamps wants it, we have the bait to trap him. I won't give it up." She looked him in the eye. "You should want Deschamps as much as I do. You told me you were going after him right after you kept your promise to Jessica."

"I intend to do that. The situation has changed, but as soon as I make sure this place is safe for you and Cassie to—"

"Bullshit. I'm not hiding from the bastard who killed Jessica."

"I guarantee I'll see that he's punished."

"No, I'll see that he's punished." Her lips thinned. "And no one is going to stand in my way, Travis. Now leave. I want to be alone for a little longer."

She's going to harden into pure steel.

Galen was right. She was changing, toughening. Not that she hadn't always been strong, but now you could almost see the steel.

"Go on." She turned to look at him. "Don't worry. I'm not going to walk into the sea and drown or anything. I just have to work my way through this so I can think."

"Come when you're ready and we'll talk." He turned and walked back toward the cottage. Not that talking would do any good.

"You shouldn't be here, sir." Danley opened the limousine door as it pulled up in front of the hangar. "I was going to come and report to you as soon as we got the casket onto the plane."

"You told me you'd kept the removal of her body from the media," Andreas said. "It better be true. Where are you taking it?"

"Arlington." He hesitated. "I wonder if you wouldn't reconsider? We've reports the sister

was very close to the deceased. She might decide to say a last good-bye."

"The more evidence of what happened at the
museum, the more likely the media will find out
about the theft of the Wind Dancer. There may
be a chance Travis wants to negotiate for the
statue. Have you got the in-depth report on the
sister yet?"

"Not yet, sir. Of course, we did preliminary
work after they took Cassie, but she was considered of secondary importance."

"Well, now she's of primary importance."

"We've located the van they rented in
Antwerp. It was abandoned forty miles outside
of Paris. That means they've changed to another
vehicle. We're checking all rental car agencies in
the area. Though with Travis's contacts, he
could have obtained a car from other sources."

"Let's hope you have better luck than you've
had to date." He walked over to the casket.
"Open it."

"Sir?"

"Open it. I want to see her."

Danley motioned to the man guarding the
coffin, and the lid was lifted.

Danley probably thought he was some kind of
ghoul, Andreas thought. He didn't know why
he wanted a last look at Jessica Riley's face.
Maybe just to assure himself that it was really

her. The theft of the Wind Dancer was completely bewildering, and he couldn't put the pieces together with Cassie's kidnapping. And why would Jessica's sister call and tip them off? Some of the fingerprints at the museum had been Melissa's; she had risked being caught in the same trap as Travis and her sister.

There was no doubt this woman was Jessica. In death her face looked as soft and gentle as in life. That gentleness had always been his impression of Cassie's doctor. He had never been sure that her methods were right, but he'd never doubted the fact that she cared about his daughter.

Until she'd taken his daughter away.

Now he had to deal with a wild card. How did he know what kind of psycho Melissa Riley had turned out to be after those years in withdrawal? He'd felt some comfort when Jessica had called and told him Cassie was safe. There was no comfort at all now.

He turned away from the coffin. "Shut it up."

17

Dawn was lighting the sky when Melissa came back to the cottage.

Travis met her at the door with a cup of coffee. She took a swallow before she asked, "Cassie?"

"I just checked her," Galen said from the chair across the room. "I think she's asleep." He grimaced. "Though I'm not sure how you can tell."

"I'll take a look." She opened the bedroom door. Cassie was curled up on the bed across the room. "Cassie."

She sensed a withdrawal, a scuttling away. Melissa didn't know to what extent Cassie had been aware of what was going on at the museum, but it had frightened her enough to make her retreat. How far she'd gone Melissa would have to find out later. "Everything's okay, Cassie. Just rest. We'll talk later." She shut the door and came back into the living room. "She's not asleep, but she's all right for now." She sat down on the window seat and leaned back. "How safe are we here?"

"I've arranged to have some of my guys positioned around the beach, so we'll have warning. On a scale of one to a hundred, I'd give it a sixty," Galen said. "It was a seventy before you made Travis snatch the Wind Dancer. It will go down to a forty if Andreas decides to release the story about the theft."

"He hasn't done that yet?"

"Not yet." Travis sat down on the couch across from Melissa. "He may be waiting for us to contact him and make a deal."

"Why would he do that?"

"It's the smartest way to dispose of an art treasure that's instantly recognized by everyone in the world. The only alternative would be to sell it to some closet collector who would bury it in a vault somewhere."

"Would Deschamps have contacted Andreas?"

"I believe he has another agenda."

"What agenda?"

"It wouldn't be the first time some weirdo fixated on the statue."

"And if Andreas did agree to deal, it would probably be so he could set a trap?"

"That's my reading. Getting Cassie well is what's been driving him all these months. The statue's been in his family for centuries, but he'd give it up in a heartbeat to find Cassie. That's all he really wants."

Melissa nodded slowly. "And to get the terrorist who did this to her. He doesn't know it's Deschamps, right?"

Travis shook his head.

"But he has the power to locate Deschamps for us?"

"Maybe. But it wouldn't be for us. If we told him Deschamps was the man at Vasaro, he'd go after him himself."

"Then maybe we wouldn't tell him. We could just use him for information."

"Use Andreas? He's not that pliable."

"Stop putting roadblocks in my path." Her lips tightened. "You're the one who caused all these damned complications. What's our alternative? I suppose you could spend some of those diamonds and buy the information."

He grimaced. "I'd rather not." He paused. "Actually, I'm going to retrieve the diamond I gave Thomas."

"Why?"

"I need to get Karlstadt off my back. Having

to dodge him will get in my way of finding Deschamps."

"Even if you get the diamond from Thomas, you won't be able to retrieve the ones I gave to Guilliame," Galen reminded him. "They're probably in the possession of either the French police or the CIA by now."

"I can work around that. Karlstadt won't like it, but if the diamonds are in a secure place and not in circulation, I can probably stall and keep him from taking a contract out on me."

"They're still not going to be in his pocket. What difference would their not being in circulation make?"

"All the difference in the world." He took a sip of his coffee. "The diamonds are not exactly what they seem."

Melissa's eyes widened. "They're phony?"

"It depends on how you look at it."

"They're either phony or they're not."

"It's all in the eye of the beholder. Those particular diamonds could meet every test the most qualified jeweler could put them through. For nearly fifty years scientists have known how to transform carbon-rich substances into small industrial diamonds, but they haven't been able to create gem-quality stones. There were all kinds of problems. The amount of pressure needed and the graphite, which is soft but very resistant to change. The bond between the layers is weak, so the graphite flakes apart, but the inner layers are incredibly strong. The carbon atoms—"

"I don't want to hear all this. The bottom line, Travis."

"There's a group of Russian scientists funded by the local Mafia that has managed to create perfect diamonds indistinguishable from those grown in the ground."

"That's not possible. There have to be tests that can tell the difference."

"The diamond industry developed one test that detected the defects caused by nitrogen concentrate in synthetic stones. The residual luminescence was unmistakable."

"But the Russians solved the problem?"

Travis nodded. "That they did, and it's scaring the diamond syndicates shitless. I found out about it from one of my sources and decided to go to Russia and see if there was anything interesting in it for me. I was there for about six weeks when there was a convenient explosion at the lab. The equipment and the scientists were blown to kingdom come."

"You obviously managed to survive and get out," Galen said. "With your pockets full of diamonds?"

"And a disk with the process."

Galen chuckled. "I thought you were only

smuggling. This is much more interesting. And who does Karlstadt represent?"

"He does the strong-arm work for a South African diamond syndicate. Naturally, they don't want the diamonds to appear anywhere. If they did, the bottom could fall out of the market. No one would know whether the jewels they bought were real or made in the lab. Prices would plummet because the element of rarity would be gone. It could spell disaster for the entire diamond industry."

"The Russians could build a new lab."

"I'm sure they're doing that now, but it will take time. Mean-while Karlstadt can negotiate or use muscle to keep the Russians from duplicating their efforts. The diamonds and the process are the only danger to him right now."

"I don't care about the danger to your South Africans," Melissa said. "What's important is that you don't have money to buy information."

"I have some in a Swiss account, but those accounts aren't altogether safe from CIA snooping."

Melissa turned to Galen. "Can you raise the money?"

"Not enough. I can tap some sources, but Deschamps is a dangerous man and wells tend to dry up when you're as hot as we are."

"Then it has to be Andreas." She got up and

put her cup down on the end table. "We have to find a way to deal."

"You have a suggestion?"

"Give him what he wants."

"Cassie?" Travis asked. "What about her nightmares? We can't send her back in the shape she's in now."

"Then we have to give him a Cassie on her way to recovery." Her gaze went to the bedroom door. "Jessica told me to help her. She probably meant for me to save her from Deschamps, but Jessica died trying to bring Cassie back. One of the last things she said to me was how close Cassie had been to coming back." She blinked back tears. "She was so happy that Cassie— Oh, shit." She was silent a moment before she could continue. "Cassie's coming back. I'm going to see to it. And we might as well find a way to screw Deschamps by doing it."

"It's a long shot," Travis said.

"I'm going to do it." Melissa headed for the bedroom. "You just make sure that Karlstadt and all the rest of the baggage around you don't get in my way."

"I'll try to oblige."

"Oh, and I want a set of keys to that new van."

"Is that necessary?"

"You're damn right. Cassie's keeping me tethered, but I'm not going to be any more of a prisoner than I have to be."

"I'll have a set made today. Galen is going to have a small car picked up in town by one of his guys. I'll see that you have keys to that car too."

"Thanks."

"What are the odds she'll be able to help Cassie?" Galen asked Travis when the door closed behind her. "The kid seems almost comatose to me."

"I don't know. She has . . . responses."

"But not when she's awake."

Travis shook his head. "Jessica seemed to sense a response. Like I said, it's a long shot. But maybe it's just as well that Melissa's going to be absorbed with Cassie. It will be safer than having to chase after her while she scours Europe for Deschamps."

"And leaves you free to make a deal with Karlstadt."

"Yes." He paused. "But it will also give you time to track down another missing piece of the puzzle for me."

"And what is that?"

"Henri Claron's widow, Danielle. She disappeared the night of Claron's death. She grew up in the same village as Cassie's nanny, and she may have known more about Deschamps than just his identity. If we have her, we may not need Andreas or anyone else."

"You believe she's still alive?"

Travis shrugged. "It's a chance. Since her body's not been found, she may have gotten lucky."

"And we may get lucky." Galen turned away. "I'm on it."

"Cassie?" Melissa whispered as she gazed down at the child. "I know you're not sleeping. Answer me."

No response.

Melissa hadn't expected it, but she had felt obliged to try Jessica's method. Jessica had been the voice summoning from the ramparts. Melissa had been the guerrilla behind the lines. Cassie had become accustomed to dealing with both of them.

But now there was no Jessica with her gentle voice and persuasive words, and Melissa had to take her place.

Good God, how was she going to do it? It was impossible. She was as different from Jessica as night and day. She wasn't even sure that Jessica's soft approach was the right way to bring Cassie back. The child was strong, perhaps stronger than Melissa had been at that age. She had willed herself away from the world, and persuasion wasn't working. Perhaps if they had the time . . .

They didn't have the time. Melissa had to follow her own instincts, and they were not leading her down an easy path.

Poor Cassie.

"I'll be back. You can play possum while I'm taking my shower and brushing my teeth." She moved toward the bathroom. "Then we're going to talk, Cassie."

It took Melissa two hours to break through the barriers Cassie had erected against her.

"It's about time you stopped hiding from me," Melissa said. *"And why did you go deeper? It was almost too dark for me to find you."*

"I didn't want you to find me."

Not good. *"Why not?"*

"You're . . . different now. You make me feel funny."

"I am different. That doesn't mean that I'm not your friend. People change."

"Not in here." She paused. *"Why did you change?"*

"My best friend was taken away from me."

"That wouldn't have happened here."

"Yes, it would. It happened because you were

here." She added deliberately, "So it's partly your fault, Cassie."

"No, I didn't do anything."

"You hide away and close your eyes."

"I'm afraid."

"We're all afraid. You have to fight what you're afraid of . . . or people get taken away."

Silence.

"Jessica was your best friend, wasn't she? She's . . . gone?"

"Yes."

"I thought so. I've been missing her."

"So have I."

"The monsters took her?"

"Yes."

"I'm not to blame." A pause. "Am I?"

"We didn't fight them hard enough."

"They're too strong."

"They're not too strong. They'll fade away if you face them."

"Won't do it. Blow me apart like they did Jeanne."

"I'll be there to keep that from happening."

"Won't do it." Withdrawal. "Going away . . ."

"I'll follow you. I'll find you and bring you back. I can do it now whether you're awake or asleep."

"Why are you being so mean to me?"

"You have to come back. It's what Jessica wanted most in the world. She wanted you back in the world and not afraid any longer."

"Have to be afraid. The monsters . . ."

What could she say to that? Melissa thought wearily. No one knew better than she did that there were real monsters waiting for Cassie. "You're more afraid now than you will be if you face them. I promise we'll fight them together. I'm your friend, Cassie."

"I thought Jeanne was my friend." Betrayal. Distrust. Hostility.

"She only pretended. I don't pretend. I believe you know that."

"I don't know it." Panic. Terror. "You want to let the monsters into the tunnel."

"They can never come into the tunnel. You're imagining them only so that you have an excuse to stay here. If you faced them, they'd vanish like a puff of smoke."

"No, they come and chase me. . . ."

"They won't do it any longer. Travis and I have stopped them." She paused. "And on the outside the Wind Dancer has stopped them. Didn't you feel it when you were looking at him? You were so happy. For just an instant you were outside and yet you knew you were safe."

"I'll find him again."

"Not in the tunnel. He has no reason to be in the tunnel. He's not afraid and he doesn't want you to be afraid either."

"How do you know? He took me away."

"*Because you needed to be away until you were strong enough to come back and face the monsters.*"

"*I'm not strong enough.*"

"*Yes, you are. Think about it. Jessica told me that you made up all kinds of adventures with the Wind Dancer. Were you ever afraid?*"

"*They were only stories.*"

"*But weren't they about duty and saving the good guys and punishing the bad?*"

"*Maybe.*"

"*Well, that's what life's about too. It's not about curling up in a tunnel. Think about it.*"

"*I won't think about it. I'm afraid and I won't come out. I'll go deeper so the monsters won't hurt me.*"

"*Your friend the Wind Dancer won't let you go deeper. You were searching for him in the wrong place. Did it ever occur to you that he always wanted you to leave the tunnel and come back? He knows it's time for you to come out even if you don't.*"

"*You lie.*"

"*There are no monsters in the tunnel. You'll just stay there until you're ready to come out and fight the bad guys with the rest of us. Your mom and dad and Travis and me. We're all waiting for you. We need you.*"

"*No.*"

"*I'm telling the truth. We do need you. I'm going away now, but I'll be back.*"

"I don't want you."

Poor kid. Melissa couldn't blame her for her anger or panic. She'd yanked away the security blanket Jessica had folded around her and told her she had to be a warrior and not a victim. Pretty tough fare for a seven-year-old.

And what if Melissa was wrong? What if she was inflicting serious damage on Cassie?

"I hate you."

"Right now. But you hate the monsters and the way they make you afraid more."

"You're the one who's making me afraid."

"Because I'm telling you that it's your duty to come out? Didn't you ever want those stories you made up to be true? If you see wrong, you have to fight it. Doing your duty isn't as easy in real life."

"Go away."

"I'm going. But I'll see you soon, Cassie. . . ."

18

"Wake up, Melissa."

She opened her eyes to see Travis's face above her.

"Time to eat. It's almost dark. You've been sleeping for hours."

She had no doubt. She'd been exhausted after that latest bout with Cassie. She glanced at the child. She was sleeping too. Melissa could feed her later. "Ten minutes. I have to wash my face and brush my teeth."

"No hurry. Galen fixed a couple of casseroles before he left. I've just put one in the oven to heat."

She swung her feet to the floor. "Left?"

"He had an errand to do for me." He walked out of the room.

The answer was evasive. She hurried through her washing and was patting her face dry with the towel as she came into the kitchen. "Where did he go?"

"He's searching for word on Danielle Claron."

"Danielle Claron? Who is she?"

"Sit down." He took the casserole out of the oven. "I'll tell you about her over dinner." He spooned two servings onto plates and set them on the table. "Galen would never forgive me if I let it get cold before you could fully appreciate his expertise."

"I want to know—" He was shaking his head, and she sat down at the table and picked up her fork. "I'm eating. Tell me about Danielle Claron."

She was halfway through the meal when Travis finished. She frowned, thinking. "You believe she may know something that will help us find Deschamps?"

"Maybe. It's the only lead we have. Even if she can't locate him for us, she's a witness to her husband's murder, and Deschamps doesn't like witnesses. Chances are he'll want to find her." He got up and poured coffee into their cups. "So we may not need the Wind Dancer to draw him into a trap."

"Danielle Claron is obviously not willing to bear witness if she's been hiding out for the last few weeks."

"If we offer her protection, she might change her mind." He shrugged. "And the worst that can happen is that I'll turn her over to Andreas and let the CIA try to persuade her. If I hand him a witness gift-wrapped, he might be a little more inclined to think twice about throwing me in the clink."

"Why do you have the money to find this woman if you don't have enough to locate Deschamps?"

"If Galen can tap into the right contacts, he may be able to find the woman without spending a dime."

"And I'm sure he has the right contacts," she said dryly. "He seems to be able to manage almost anything . . . criminal. But then, you have the same contacts, don't you? You've been known to sell information too."

"Yes. But we don't have the same sources. Which comes in handy on occasion."

"I thought you had to contact Karlstadt. Why are you still here?"

"I have a telephone. If I need to see him, I can wait until Galen gets back."

"Because you think you have to protect us?"

"Not you," he said lightly. "You could take on

Andreas and Deschamps single-handed. But there's the kid to think about." He glanced at her plate. "Do you want any more? Galen cooked more than enough for a couple of meals."

She shook her head. "I'm not hungry. It was very good though. He's multifaceted, isn't he?"

"More than you know. Or maybe not. He said you'd read him very well. Something about brother and sister?"

She smiled. "It was easy to see that we're a lot alike."

"In what way?"

"Well, we both believe in making the most of every minute."

"And you're both tough and very perceptive. Maybe too perceptive?"

"You think this was in the psychic grab bag I got handed to me? Maybe. Or maybe I'm just a good judge of character." She lifted the coffee to her lips. "Like you are."

"I haven't demonstrated much of that ability lately." His gaze went to the bedroom door. "How's the kid?"

"She's sleeping."

"You're sure?"

"I'm sure." She hesitated. "I can reach her whether she's asleep or awake now. And I can do it when I'm awake."

"What?"

"I tried it on the plane and it worked."

"Why didn't you tell me?" He shook his head. "Never mind. We weren't on the best of terms."

"No, and I couldn't tell you without telling Jessica. She wouldn't have believed me, and if she had, she would have been afraid." She looked down into her cup. "And I didn't know how I was going to use it. I wasn't sure Jessica was handling Cassie right. We were all being so soft and gentle. . . ."

He stared at her thoughtfully, but he didn't speak.

"Cassie's not a gentle child. She's lively and strong and very intelligent, and she was never a shrinking violet until Vasaro. The withdrawal was completely out of character."

"Shock."

"Yes, but I have a hunch that later her nurse's betrayal made her more angry than hurt."

"You sound as if you know her very well."

"Only what Jessica found out from her parents and what I've observed myself."

He smiled faintly. "And maybe you're a good deal like Cassie too. I hope not. It took six years to heal your trauma."

"But I have an advantage Jessica didn't have with me. I know where Cassie's at right now."

"What does that mean?"

"It means that after the first trauma heals, it

takes a really strong push to destroy that world you built for yourself. Jessica never gave me that push. She gave me love and gentleness instead. It might have worked for some kids, but it took a long time for her to get through to a stubborn brat like me." She added, "And it means I understand that Cassie's not really a victim. She was in the beginning, but now she's in that tunnel because she wants to be. She willed herself there, and it's easier to stay."

"Easier? What about the nightmares?"

"She needs them to validate staying in the tunnel." She moistened her lips. "So I'm going to take them away from her."

"How?"

"I've already told her she doesn't have them anymore because the monsters are waiting outside the tunnel for her to come and fight them."

He frowned.

"I know what you're thinking. Yes, it was a risk and yes, it could backfire and keep her in that tunnel for the rest of her life." Her hand was shaking and she steadied it as she brought her cup to her lips. "That's *my* nightmare."

"I don't know if I would have taken the chance."

"She's a fighter. It's her nature. She just has to be forced back into the battle."

"How can you be sure she won't have the nightmares?"

"I'm not sure. She could still will herself to have them. But I'm hoping that the suggestion I planted will take root. I'll reinforce it every time I'm with her. After that, we can only wait and see." She put her cup down. "She'll probably try her damnedest to do anything I tell her not to do. She's not very fond of me right now."

"And you could be wrong."

"Yes, but if I'm right, I'll make her face her demons and bring her back. I'm stronger than she is now, and I'm growing stronger every day. I'll nag her and block her at every turn."

"Tough love?"

"I do love her. You can't imagine how close I am to her. She's like . . . my other self." She closed her eyes. "I know I'm being hard, but I have to make her come out. For her sake and for Jessica. You see, I have one more advantage Jessica didn't have with me. I'll do whatever I have to do." She opened her eyes, now stinging with tears. "Because I'm no saint like her, Travis."

"You don't have to be like her." He covered her hand on the table. "You do fine on your own."

"I hope so." His grasp felt warm and comforting, and she let herself take that comfort for a moment before she moved her hand away. "I hope I'm not rushing Cassie because I want to use her to get Andreas to help with Deschamps."

"I don't think you are."

"But neither of us is sure." She pushed back her chair. "I'm going for a short walk on the beach before I wake Cassie and give her supper."

"I'll do it."

She shook her head. "My job."

"I don't mind helping. Are you closing me out?"

"If I've really managed to get rid of the nightmares, then you're closed out anyway. You should be glad there's a chance your responsibility is over."

"It's not over. It's just shifted." He grimaced. "And I'm not at all comfortable with it. I prefer to be an observer."

"I've noticed that. Then maybe you're living in a tunnel as much as Cassie is."

He smiled. "Maybe I am. It's an interesting thought. Do you see any other similarities between me and the kid?"

"Oh, yes. But you're more complicated. It would be difficult to—" She stopped and looked at him. He was sitting there, still smiling, and yet she could sense . . . what? Pain? Loneliness? She wasn't sure, but he had once again been kind to her. She wanted to do something, but she wasn't even sure what. "I'm . . . sorry your friend died." The words came haltingly. "And I'm sorry I was ugly about it. Since you don't let many people close to you, it must have hurt you very much to lose him."

"Yes, it did."

"Perhaps you'll tell me about him sometime."

"Sometime."

Because the pain was too deep and he wasn't a man to show his feelings.

"Did he know you loved him? Did you tell him?"

"No, I didn't tell him. But I think he knew."

"Good. That was one rule I made for myself after Jessica brought me back. Life's too short not to have every emotion out in the open. If someone deserves love, then they deserve to know they have it."

"That's a very perilous philosophy."

"It's more perilous not to tell someone they're loved. I would have regretted it all my life if Jessica hadn't known I—" She cleared her throat to rid it of huskiness and headed for the door. "I won't be long. I just need to clear my head. Thirty minutes or so . . ."

★   ★   ★

She walked very fast along the beach, her back straight and her head high.

She looked like a soldier going into battle, Travis thought.

She's a fighter.

They were the words she had used to describe Cassie, but they also applied to Melissa. A scarred warrior going forth to fight Cassie's monsters.

What the hell was he doing standing there watching her? She was absorbing entirely too much of his attention, when he needed to focus on getting himself out of this mess and going after Deschamps. He couldn't even give lust as an excuse, although that had been there between them from the beginning. How could you lust after a woman who made you want to heal and protect at the same time? Come on, admit it, he was a man and, hell, yes, he wanted to get her in bed. It didn't matter that she was hurting and he was torn with compassion. Maybe because sex was the safest relationship he could have with her. Anything else would involve him in ways that could change his life, and he had long ago opted out of the path she was traveling. He didn't need to let himself in for the role of knight trailing at the heels of a damsel fending off dragons.

He had his own monsters to subdue, and there was nothing idealistic about that battle. It was going to be dirty and fraught with greed and violence.

And it was time he set about doing it. He reached for his phone and dialed the number Galen had given him for Stuart Thomas.

"I've found a trail," Galen said when Travis answered his phone the next evening. "Danielle Claron's parents, Philip and Marguerite Dumair, still live in the village where she grew up. Jeanne Beaujolis lived on the next block, and she was in and out of Danielle's house all during their childhood. She visited them frequently even after she took the job of nurse to Cassie. From talking to the neighbors, I gather she boasted a lot about her fine position and was a trifle patronizing to the villagers."

"Have you been to see the Dumairs?"

"Not yet. I've been scoping out the neighborhood to find out if anyone's seen anyone of Deschamps's description in the village."

"And?"

"No luck."

"Then talk to the Dumairs and give them your phone number. They don't have to tell us where their daughter is if they don't trust us. They just have to give her the message that we're offering money and protection from

Deschamps if she'll come out of hiding and tell us anything she knows about him."

"How much money?"

"The limit."

"Our pockets are pretty lean right now unless you want to use the diamonds."

"If I have to, I'll tap the Swiss account."

"And chance having the CIA breathing down your neck?"

"I can't use the diamonds and I've already promised Thomas cash in exchange for the diamond. Send him ten thousand from your fund, will you?"

"Thanks. I live to please. Why?"

"It's safer than my going into my accounts. As far as we know, Andreas isn't aware you're involved yet."

"A state that can't go on forever." Galen sighed. "Danley must have heard of my cleverness and brilliant ingenuity. Such perfection doesn't go unnoticed. It's only a matter of time until he decides I'm the only one who could successfully keep you out of his clutches."

"True."

"You're agreeing only because you want me to send Thomas the money."

"Also true."

"Have you talked to Karlstadt yet?"

"After you pick up the diamond from

Thomas. I want to be able to tell Karlstadt it's been retrieved."

"He may decide to cut your throat regardless."

"Not as long as I have the rest of the diamonds."

"Except the ones the CIA are holding."

"I'll have to do some negotiating there. All you have to worry about is negotiating with the Dumairs."

"I'd judge that a little safer." A pause. "I had some other news. I think I'm on track to find out where Deschamps stays when he's in Paris."

"What?"

"You told me to put out feelers. I made contact with Pichot, who was with the Sons of Liberty group about the same time as Deschamps. He may be able to tell me something."

"For money?"

"No, he owes me a favor."

"When will you know?"

"It may take a while. Pichot wants to make sure Deschamps won't find out he was the one who told me." He changed the subject. "How are Melissa and Cassie doing?"

"Better than expected. Cassie hasn't had any more nightmares. Melissa believes there's a chance she won't have them again."

"And she should know. Our Melissa is a little on the fey side."

"Why do you say that?"

"You may not regard her tiny idiosyncrasies as unusual, but my mum taught me to always be wary of things that go bump in the night."

"You never knew your mother."

"You really know how to spoil a story." He paused. "Melissa . . . sees too much, Travis."

"Some people say the same of you."

"But I don't go bump in the night."

"And if you do, they never see you coming."

He chuckled. "Have you noticed that you always defend her? Maybe she's got the old voodoo on you."

"Don't be an asshole."

The chuckle became a laugh. "Just thought I'd call it to your attention. I'm not attacking her. I like her. How could I help it? Except for those little idiosyncrasies, she's just like me. Give her my best. Good-bye, Travis."

"Call me when you've talked to the Dumairs." He hung up.

* * *

Paris

"Ready?" Galen slipped the phone into his pocket after talking to Travis. "Let's do it, Pichot."

"You lied to him."

"My mum never taught me the virtues of sharing." He moved toward the car. "Cardeau was one of mine and Deschamps killed him." He smiled. "Besides, I'm much better at this than Travis. It's one of my specialties."

"I know." Pichot grimaced. "I'm counting on it. I want to get out of this alive."

"You will." Galen started the car. "Now, where is this place?"

"Number fifteen Rue Lestape."

"Was that Galen on the phone?" Travis turned to see Melissa a few feet away, hair tousled, wearing a navy blue Sorbonne nightshirt.

"Yes."

"Has he found Danielle Claron?"

He shook his head. "He's trying to persuade her parents to give her a message if they know where she is. They live in St. Ives, a small village outside Lyon, not too far from Henri Claron's farm."

"There's a chance they do know?"

"Don't we all cling to our parents? It's natural to run to them for safety. Some say it's the strongest bond we have in our lifetime." He looked beyond her to the bedroom. "Cassie?"

"Okay." She rubbed the back of her neck. "Stubborn. It's hell getting in and harder to make her listen. I have to plant myself and keep talking."

"What do you talk about?"

"The outside. Her father and mother. The Wind Dancer." She sat down in a chair and tucked one leg beneath her. "You."

"Me?"

"You're the bridge between the tunnel and the outside." She made a face. "She still trusts you. I'm the enemy right now."

"You can't make her understand?"

"She's seven years old. I'd have dug my heels in too if Jessica had tried the same tactics."

"And you're still sure they're the right tactics?"

"I have to be sure. Otherwise I'm lost. There's got to be a breakthrough soon." She leaned her head back on the chair. "I'm as impatient as you are to get her well."

"I've never said I was impatient."

"You didn't have to say it. I can *feel* it."

He smiled. "I'm glad Galen isn't here. He remarked on the fact that you're a little on the fey side."

"Did he? I thought he'd picked up on a slip I made. He doesn't like anyone knowing him too well."

"Slip?"

She moved her shoulders uncomfortably. "Sometimes I know . . . things."

"Telepathy?"

"For God's sake, no. I'd want to jump in the river if I had that kind of albatross around my neck."

"What about Cassie?"

"That's different. Everything about Cassie has been different. Usually I just . . . sometimes I pick up on things."

"And you picked up on the fact that I'm impatient."

She shifted in the chair. "It's hard to hide that. You have every right to be impatient. You want to be rid of us so that—"

"You're right, I want to be rid of you." He drew a deep breath. "Right now. Go back to bed, Melissa."

"In a few minutes."

"Now."

"I think we should talk this out. There's too much—" She inhaled sharply as she met his gaze. "Travis?"

"It doesn't take much talent to read my mind right now, does it?"

"No."

"Then get yourself back to bed and let me think of something besides those gorgeous long legs and what's between them."

She slowly uncurled herself from the chair. "I can't— It's not the right time, Travis."

"I know that." He tried to keep the edge from his voice. "I'm not a fool. But we both know it's been there from the beginning." He grimaced. "And my mind may tell me one thing, but my body doesn't recognize mourning as a valid reason to go dormant. It's all for propagating the species. So get out of here, will you?"

"I'm going." But she still stood there. "It's not that I—"

"I know. Wrong time." He reached for the book on the table. "And probably the wrong man. We could have a hell of a lot of fun, but I can't see you doing a one-night stand. You have too much Jessica in you."

"I'm nothing like Jessica." She moistened her lips. "But you're right, I do have problems with ships that pass in the night. I need to know where I am with people these days."

"You know. You've seen right through me since the day we met. Most of the time you didn't like what you saw."

"That's not true. It was just that the situation was complicated and you were making it more complicated. I had to do what—" She moved toward the door. "Good night, Travis."

She was gone.

Open mouth, insert foot. Dammit, he should have kept quiet.

Hell, no, they were sharing close quarters and he had never been one to suffer in silence. He was doing enough trying to keep himself sympathetic and in brotherly mode. Let her help. Now that she knew, she'd be on guard.

That's what he wanted, right?

No way.

What he wanted was to have her on his lap, with those long legs wound around him and making sounds that—

Don't think about Melissa. Read this damn book. Or make plans that would get them all out of this situation.

Don't think about her.

Don't think about him.

My God, she had run away. Incredible. She had sworn she would never run away from anything again after Jessica had brought her back. But she had fled like a schoolkid.

Why? It wasn't as if she were a blushing virgin. She had tasted sex with enthusiasm. Sex was joy and pleasure, and she loved it the way she loved the euphoric burn of a good exercise workout.

It's been there from the beginning.

Since that first day she had seen him running at Juniper. She had joked with Jessica about her sexy neighbor, but she had been half serious. If she hadn't been so frightened about her dreams, she might have paid Travis a visit for another reason. She had felt the same spark but had ignored it.

As she should ignore it now.

But she couldn't because she'd sworn to herself that she'd confront any fear. And yet she had run away from Travis.

Because she thought sleeping with him would dishonor her mourning for Jessica? No, life was for living and Jessica would never want her to give up one minute of happiness to convention.

One-night stand.

That must be it. She was afraid she might want more than a one-night stand. She was drawn to Travis on too many levels. Lately she had come too close to him and had seen another side of him. He was right; sometimes she could see through him, and what she saw was not what he thought. She had seen humor, patience, and compassion behind that cool, analytical wall he erected. Something about him . . . touched her.

The thought sent another ripple of panic through her. She was too vulnerable right now and she certainly didn't need another obstacle to overcome. She wasn't about to try to jump over those walls he used to keep everyone at a distance.

So she would keep her own distance from now on.

19

Number 15 Rue Lestape was a small, elegant town house near St.-Germain.

"He's not there now, you know," Pichot said. "I checked it out before I called you."

"He may come back." Galen tested the front door and then strode quickly through the alley to the back of the house. "Or there may be something inside that will tell me where he is." He bent down and examined the lock on the door. Excellent craftsmanship. It took him a couple of minutes to spring it. "Open sesame."

"What if there's an alarm system?" Pichot asked. "Maybe we shouldn't—"

"Deschamps isn't going to want the police to

come pounding on his door." He stepped inside. "Come on, Pichot."

"Maybe I should wait in the car."

"I don't think so." Galen smiled at him over his shoulder as he turned on his flashlight. "Not that I don't trust you, but I like the idea of having company while I'm strolling through Deschamps's lair. You're a little too wary of our absent friend."

"You don't need to worry. I'm more scared of you." Pichot's gaze was wandering around the small hall. "Nice. I wonder what that tapestry cost?"

"You've never been here?"

"Deschamps is not one to get chummy. I always picked him up outside."

It was an exquisitely furnished area. A Persian carpet covered the oak floor and led toward a large room several yards away.

"What are you looking for?" Pichot asked.

"A study, a library . . ." He glanced up at the spiral staircase. "Maybe the bedroom."

"What's that?"

Pichot was staring across the room at a door. But not an ordinary door. Every inch of it was covered with magnificent floral carvings.

Galen started toward it. "Evidently a portal of importance. Let's see what's behind it."

The door was locked.

"Hold the flashlight." He squatted and started to work. With some difficulty, he finally managed to spring the lock. He took the flashlight from Pichot. "Now let's see what we have—" He stiffened. "Holy shit."

"What is it?" Pichot shoved him aside and took a step inside the room.

A red light on the far wall blinked on.

"No!" Galen grabbed Pichot, pushed him through a window, shattering glass, and dove after him.

The house exploded into a fireball.

Deschamps went rigid as the signal button on the warning device that was always with him went off. He took the device out of his pocket, but the red light went out even as he looked at it.

He closed his eyes as waves of pain surged over him. "No," he whispered.

It was gone.

"Damn you." Travis's hand tightened on the phone. "I'm going to break your neck, Galen."

"Why bother, when I nearly managed to do that on my own?" He paused. "I didn't expect it. I thought maybe a desk or a safe would be rigged but not the whole damn house. The switch wasn't triggered until Pichot stepped into the room. It doesn't make sense."

"Did you get a glimpse of what was in that room?"

"It looked like a bloody museum. Like an Aladdin's cave with paintings and sculpture . . . That's what doesn't make sense. One of the paintings had to be a Monet. I'd swear it was the water lily painting that was supposedly burned with the Rondeau estate last year. If that was an example of the quality of art treasures in that room, why would Deschamps blow it up?"

"I'll ask him . . . when we find him." He added grimly, "And if you don't go off on the hunt alone again. I want your promise, Galen."

There was silence on the other end of the line.

"Galen."

"I guess fair is fair. I had my shot. I'll let you have yours."

"Thank you," Travis said sarcastically. "I appreciate the favor."

"You should," Galen said. "I was royally pissed when I picked myself up off that sidewalk outside Deschamps's house."

"Are you coming back here?"

"Soon. I've still got to go see the Dumairs in St. Ives. See you."

Travis hung up and went outside on the porch. Dammit, he should have known Galen would do something crazy if the opportunity offered itself. He was always a law unto himself. Admit it, he was jealous of Galen, who was free to go after Deschamps and not tied up there. Well, at least Galen had gone on the offensive.

They would just have to see what kind of fallout his actions would bring from Deschamps.

Two nights later Cassie had a nightmare.

Melissa jerked upright in her bed at the first piercing scream.

"Cassie . . ." She swung her feet to the floor. "No, baby, don't do—"

"What's wrong?" Travis stood in the doorway. "I thought you said you didn't think she'd have any more nightmares."

"I said I hoped." She turned on the lamp.

Cassie screamed again.

"Don't just stand there. Sit down beside her and start talking to her."

"The usual things?"

She nodded and got under the covers with Cassie. "But when I tell you to stop, do it."

"What are you going to do?"

"I'm going to call her bluff."

"Bluff?"

"I've been telling her she won't have any more nightmares." She closed her eyes. "She's showing me I'm wrong."

"Pretty drastic demonstration."

"She wants me out. If she proves me wrong, she thinks I'll go away." She cuddled closer to Cassie. "Talk to her, Travis."

She closed him out, only vaguely aware of the murmur of his voice. Cassie was keeping her at bay. There was no strong pull cata-pulting her into Cassie's world as there usually was during one of the nightmares. It took her a few minutes to force herself into Cassie's mind.

Terror.

Swirling horror behind her.

Monsters.

"No monsters," Melissa said.

"Liar." Cassie was running, going deeper. "They're here. I have to get away."

"If they're here, it's because you brought them. And you can send them away."

"I told you they'd come."

"Because you want an excuse to stay here."

"Have to go deeper . . ."

"No." Melissa put herself in front of Cassie, blocking her path. "Stop running."

"Get out of my way." Melissa could feel the force of the child's will pummeling her. "Go away."

"There are no monsters behind you. Turn around and see."

"I won't. I won't."

"Turn around."

"They're here. I have to run."

"Turn around." Melissa took her shoulders and forced her to turn around.

"I won't look."

"You will look."

"You can't make me."

"You know that's not true. I'm stronger than you are now, Cassie. Open your eyes."

The child held out for another moment and then slowly her lids lifted.

"What do you see, Cassie?"

"Monsters."

"What do you see?"

"Monsters."

"What do you see?"

"I told you," she said defiantly.

"Then why haven't they hurt you?"

"Michael is keeping them away."

"Go away, Travis."

"No!" Cassie struggled to get away from her. "You come back, Michael!"

But Travis's voice had stopped.

"He's gone, Cassie. And you're still here."

"The monsters are coming. They'll get me."

Jesus, her will was strong. "They're not here. You don't see them."

"Don't tell me what I see."

"Then you tell me. What do you see?"

"Masks and teeth and eyes . . ."

"But they haven't hurt you. Because they're not real. I'm going to hold you right here and let you face them. If they get too close, I'll be here to protect you."

"No, you won't." She was sobbing. "You hate me."

"I love you."

"Then let me go."

"When you tell me what you're seeing."

"Mon—" Her voice broke. "I have to— I can't go back. I have to go deeper."

"What do you see?"

She suddenly whirled on Melissa. "Nothing," she screamed. "Nothing. Nothing!"

"No monsters?"

"No monsters. Are you satisfied now?"

"Oh, yes." Tears were running down her face as she drew Cassie into her arms. "I couldn't be more satisfied, baby."

"Let me go." Her arms tightened around Melissa even as she spoke. "I hate you."

"Soon." Melissa rocked her back and forth. "I'll let you go soon, Cassie. . . ."

★ ★ ★

It was over an hour later when she opened her eyes.

"Hi." Travis was sitting in the chair next to the bed. "How are you?"

"Okay," she whispered. She kissed Cassie's forehead before slipping out of bed. "It took a while to get her to sleep."

"What the hell happened? She screamed like a banshee when I stopped talking to her. It scared me silly."

"I was pretty scared myself."

"But it worked out all right?"

She nodded. "Breakthrough. She admitted to me and to herself that there were no monsters in the tunnel."

"So no more nightmares?"

"God, I hope not. Her imagination is powerful enough to create whatever she wants to. But at least she's aware now that she was lying to herself. The best possible result would be for her to start doubting the reason she thinks she's in the tunnel."

"And what is that?"

"The Wind Dancer wants to keep her there to be safe."

"Can you convince her that's not true?"

"I'll try to nibble away at it." She turned off the lamp on the nightstand. "I only hope it doesn't take long. I'm going to make a cup of decaf and try to get back to sleep. Do you want one?"

"Why not?" Travis followed her to the kitchen and watched her as she made the coffee. "The two of you didn't need me tonight, did you? That's why you sent me away. To prove to Cassie that she could do without me."

"And we did it." She sat down at the table. "That should make you happy. You're free of her."

"That's not entirely fair. I've never begrudged my help with Cassie."

"Even though you used it as a bargaining tool."

"Touché." He lifted his cup to his lips. "It's the nature of the beast. I'm no saint either, Melissa. I've never pretended to be."

No, he'd always been open with them about his character and motivations. The way he thought might be as convoluted as a Chinese puzzle, but they'd always known where they stood with him. "I guess you had your reasons. You said you were worried about your friend Jan. It seems you had cause."

"More than I knew."

"Tell me about him."

"Why?"

Melissa glanced away from him. "I don't

know. I don't believe it's easy for you to draw close to people. I suppose I'm curious what kind of man you would call a friend."

"A good man. He called himself selfish, but he was always there for me when I needed him. Jan was like family. He and my father were in business together. For years."

"What kind of business?"

He smiled. "An occasional art theft, but mostly smuggling. My father was a true adventurer. He thought he was some kind of swashbuckler. He lived for excitement. Jan was always the practical, calming factor in my life. At the time I didn't appreciate him when he tried to keep my father from taking me on the runs. He always said it was too dangerous, and we used to have some gigantic brouhahas."

"Your father actually took you along?"

"Sure, he thought it was educational."

"And was it?"

"You bet. I learned a lot. Of course, very little of it was legal."

"Weren't you in school?"

"Correspondence school. Jan insisted. Then, when my father died, Jan took me to Amsterdam and put me in a formal school there."

"How old were you when your father died?"

"Thirteen."

"With a background like that, you must have been a shock to the other students."

"Not so much. I was fairly subdued at the time. My father's death wasn't pretty, and I got a little roughed up myself."

"What happened to him?"

"He stepped on the toes of the head of a drug cartel in Algiers. They blew up our boat."

Her eyes widened in shock. "And you were on it?"

He nodded. "So was Jan. My father was down below and the blast killed him. Jan and I were on deck and were thrown overboard. I cracked my head on some debris and Jan had to tow me to shore. I was in the hospital for weeks. He never left me. When I was well enough, he took me to Amsterdam."

"And what about your father's murder?"

"Do you mean the police? In the business we were in, unless you wanted to end up in prison, you didn't go to the police. You took care of the problem yourself."

"Not if you're only thirteen years old."

Travis smiled. "I didn't stay thirteen."

She felt a chill as she studied his face. "What did you do?"

"Why, what any kid would do. I studied, I played soccer, I read books." He stood up and took his cup to the sink. "And I waited."

"And then?"

"You don't want to know the details." He rinsed out the cup and set it on the shelf. "I took care of it."

He was right, she didn't want to know the details. It was clear they would be both violent and savage.

"Shocked?" He was studying her expression. "You shouldn't be. You knew I didn't grow up with a silver spoon in my mouth like you. We're as different as we can be."

"Because you wanted revenge?" She shook her head. "We're not different at all."

"Maybe not in feeling, but I guarantee we'd differ in execution. When it concerns someone I care about, I'm not into quick, neat kills." He paused. "So don't think you're going to get in my way."

She stared at him without speaking.

"Dammit, let me do it." His hands clenched into fists. "You think it's easy to kill a man?"

"I don't believe it would be hard to kill Deschamps. Like stepping on a cockroach." She stood up. "Or hitting it on the head with my silver spoon. Good night, Travis."

"Melissa, don't—" He drew a deep breath. "I may be free of Cassie, but she still needs you. You promised Jessica."

"You don't need to remind me. But she's

better now. Have you heard any more from Galen?"

"No."

"But you would tell me?" When he didn't reply, her lips tightened. "I thought as much. You're closing me out. Our partnership was fragile at best. It's good to know where we stand."

"Deschamps will kill you. Listen to me. You're going after this guy as if you were some kind of commando. I know you. I've never seen anyone who loves life as much as you do. How do you think you'll feel taking a life?"

"I'll feel *right*. He killed my sister. And I'll do anything I have to do."

"Leave him to me, Melissa."

Anger suddenly flared in her. "The hell I will." She strode to the bedroom and slammed the door behind her. Shit, she shouldn't have done that. She could have woken Cassie.

No, the little girl was still asleep.

Her anger slowly left her as she sat down on the bed and gazed at Cassie. "You have to get well, baby," she whispered. "You're coming so close. You have to come out. You owe it to Jessica."

Cassie stirred.

Melissa froze. She had never seen her do that when Jessica had talked to her. Jessica had said she could sense a response, but this was actual physical movement.

"Cassie?"

The child turned her head away.

Rejection. But that was a response too.

"Okay." She swallowed. "One step at a time. It seems we came closer tonight than I thought. Now, I'll just sit here and talk to you. And you'll listen, won't you? We're going to talk about the Wind Dancer and you and me and the way to get rid of the monsters forever. . . ."

"Hello, Travis. You're proving to be exceptionally annoying."

He stiffened. "Who is this?"

"Don't you recognize my voice?"

He inhaled sharply. "Deschamps?"

"Do you know what beauty you destroyed?" Deschamps's voice was harsh with pain.

"I don't know what you're talking about."

"It's just coincidence that my house was invaded and destroyed when I know you must be searching for me? I don't think so. It was you, wasn't it?"

"I'm not the one who blew up your place. You set an explosive."

"It wouldn't have gone off if you hadn't tried to enter the room."

"You're the one who destroyed it. Why?"

"It wouldn't have been mine any longer. I'd have had to think of it as belonging to you or whomever you sold it to. It would have spoiled it for me."

"Good God, you're a closet collector?"

"What a pat phrase. You know nothing about it. But you didn't succeed in robbing me of all my treasures. Do you think I'd keep them all in one place? But you're going to pay for that Monet. You're going to give me something in return. Where's the Wind Dancer, Travis?"

"The museum."

"Screw you. You took it with you."

"How do you know?"

"Where's the statue?"

"If I did take it, you know I won't tell you. So why are you calling?"

"I told you."

"Why?"

"Perhaps I thought it was time we got to know each other. I've been looking for you for a long time."

"You found me. But you shot Jan instead."

"I had my reasons. I believe you know what they are."

"The Wind Dancer."

"It was obvious from your conversation with Van Beck that you were going to steal it. All I had to do was wait and watch."

"But you'd already scoped out the museum for yourself."

"I thought it might be necessary after you kept me from getting the little girl. It would have been so easy to ransom her for the Wind Dancer."

"So it was always about the statue?"

"Of course. Always. I've known I had to have the Wind Dancer since I was a boy. All my life I've been waiting for my chance. You've spoiled it for me twice."

Keep him talking. Find out what makes the bastard tick. "What could you do with it? You couldn't sell it, and Andreas would never give up searching for you."

"You and I both know there are still places on this earth where a man can lose himself. I've been looking at the Orient lately. Europe is getting a little too hot for me." He paused. "And a man who would sell the Wind Dancer is a man without a soul."

"Do you believe you actually have a soul, Deschamps?"

"Because I'm not a sentimental fool? What is a soul? My entire being sings when I see a beautiful painting or a magnificent statue. I shed tears when I first saw a picture of the Wind Dancer. Who's to say that my sensitivity doesn't equal yours?"

"I'm not a cold-blooded killer."

"That's a poor argument. You're an intelligent man, but you'd be a much worthier adversary if you didn't let your emotions control you. It was very clear when I killed Van Beck."

He smothered the surge of rage. "You had no reason to kill Jan."

"Of course I did. It hurt you. I always have a reason. I never indulge myself with senseless slaughter."

"Not even when you killed your stepfather?"

"Ah, you've been busy. And what did you find out about my esteemed parent?"

"That you didn't like him and demonstrated that dislike by chopping him into pieces. Just what did he do to you?"

"He put me in prison for the very love he tried to instill in me. I practically lived in his art gallery. Wasn't it natural that I tried to take just a few pieces for my own? I had a lot of time to think when I was in prison. It was like being in a cocoon and turning into a butterfly."

"Hardly. Maybe a cobra. Why are you telling me this?"

"I want you to understand me. I want you to know what's waiting for you." He paused. "You should have died at the museum. I was planning on killing you all and grabbing the statue. I would have done it if it hadn't been for that woman."

"You killed Jessica Riley, the only woman involved in this."

"It wasn't Jessica Riley who called Andreas and had him send the police that night." He paused. "But I find it interesting that you're lying to keep me from knowing about Melissa Riley. I was planning on looking her up in the near future, but I believe I'll have to put her near the top of my list."

"And distract your attention from my humble self?"

"There's time for all of you. Have you killed Cassie Andreas yet?"

"What?"

"You have the Wind Dancer. There's no reason to keep her alive. She must be a burden." He laughed. "My God, you haven't done it. That soft streak is going to be the death of you. It's difficult to be patient. Think about it. Dream about it. I will." He hung up.

Travis swore softly as he punched the end button.

"Problems?" Galen was standing in the doorway.

"It's about time you got back."

"Deschamps?"

Travis nodded. "You struck a nerve when you invaded his territory. Evidently, he's feeling the need to communicate."

"Anything interesting?"

"Just threats." Against him, against Melissa. "Damn, I wish we could have traced the call."

"Who knew he would decide to call you?"

"He may call again."

"If I start trying to get a tech crew together, we'll blow the cover."

Travis knew that. It was just damn frustrating that he couldn't take advantage of the lead. "He has contacts. He had my number and he knew the statue wasn't in the museum. He also knew Melissa was the one who blew the whistle. Can you find out who he's using?"

"I can try." His gaze shifted to Melissa, who was sitting on the beach. "Are you going to tell her?"

Travis hesitated and then shook his head. "Nothing to tell." Nothing but ugliness and blood and a homicidal maniac focusing on her. She had enough on her plate and didn't need another shock. "Maybe if you can get me something concrete."

Galen turned to go back into the cottage. "And maybe not. I can see protectiveness raising its gnarled, interfering head. If she does find out, you can bet she's going to give it a lethal karate chop."

20

"Good news. We've identified the man who was found dead in the basement of the museum, sir," Danley said. "He was Pierre Cardeau. Born in Marseilles, a petty thief, but he's been known to take jobs in a variety of more violent areas. Excellent with guns." He paused. "And he was in Nice at the time of the attempt on your daughter at Vasaro."

"So he could have been in on it," Andreas said. "But on which team? Travis or the bastard who tried to kidnap her?"

"Are you still so sure that they weren't in it together?"

Andreas wasn't sure of anything. "All I know is that I want Travis caught."

"We're doing everything we can. This is a real break. Cardeau had a brother, and we picked him up this morning. They worked together occasionally. If he knows anything, I promise you we'll know it too."

"How long?"

Danley smiled. "Oh, very soon, Mr. President. I guarantee it."

Andreas wasn't going to question either Danley's certainty or his methods. It was the first break they'd had since Cassie had been taken, and he'd take anything he could get, any way he could get it. "Let me know as soon as you hear."

"Good morning." Galen looked up from the stove when Melissa walked into the kitchen the next morning. "Sit down. I'll have breakfast ready in just a minute."

"I didn't hear you come in." She sat down at the table. "Where's Travis? Isn't he up yet?"

"He rushed off the minute I got here. Cannes, I believe." He set a glass of orange juice down before her. "The Karlstadt business. He said he'll be back as soon as he can make it, but it could be a couple of days."

"Did you find Danielle Claron?"

"Not yet. But her father promised to have her call me if she surfaces."

"He doesn't know where she is?"

"He says he doesn't. Of course, he may consider everyone a threat to his daughter." He smiled. "Though who could be less intimidating than me?"

"Attila the Hun."

"Careful, I'll leave the seasoning out of your scrambled eggs. And what's life without the spices?" He set a plate of eggs and bacon in front of her. "How's the little girl?"

"No more nightmares."

"Travis said you'd pulled the plug on them. Congratulations."

"I got lucky. It could have gone either way." She began to eat. "So you're here on guard duty in Travis's place?"

"I just needed a little vacation by the sea. After all, I'm the one who's been doing all the work. How are the eggs?"

"Fine." She sat back, her gaze narrowed on his face. "Will you tell me if Monsieur Dumair or Danielle Claron calls you?"

He stared at her thoughtfully. "What would you do if I said no?"

"Become very frustrated and start thinking of ways to find out for myself."

"I thought so." He nodded. "I'll tell you. Though Travis will not be pleased with me. Now, what do you want for lunch? My abun-

dant talents are at your disposal. Ask me for anything."

She smiled. "You've already given me what I
want."

Cannes
2:50 P.M.

The roof of the hotel.
Possibly the open window above the bakery.
Or the souvenir shop on the corner.
Any of the three or maybe none of them.
Travis stepped farther back in the shadows. He
had already checked out the street earlier in
the day, but he would have to check again before the meeting with Karlstadt that evening. To
be unprepared was often fatal.
Was that movement in the alley beside the
bakery?

6:05 P.M.

Galen and Melissa were sitting down to supper when his phone rang.
Melissa stiffened.

Galen smiled. "It could be anyone. An important person like me has to remain in touch."

"Answer it."

He nodded as he flipped open his phone. "Galen." He listened, his smile fading. "Right. I'll tell Travis. Of course I'm interested. I said, I'll tell Travis. Could I have a number to call you back?" He pressed the end button. "She hung up."

Her heart jumped. "She?"

"Danielle Claron."

"Are you sure? How did she sound?"

"Scared. Very scared. And no, I can't be sure about anything. But she had my number and she knew I'd talked to her parents."

"What did she say?"

"That she needed money, a lot of money. And a safe place to hide. She wouldn't promise anything until we came to terms. She wants to meet with Travis tonight."

"Where?"

"At the old church at the north edge of the village. She said they'd built a new one in the center of town and this one is deserted now. She'll be there after midnight."

"Then we have to go and meet her."

He shook his head. "Travis will go. It's with him she wants to bargain."

"But Travis isn't here, dammit."

"I'll phone him later." He glanced at his watch. "He's supposed to be meeting with Karlstadt in a couple of hours and the situation may be very delicate at the moment."

Even after his "delicate" situation was resolved, Travis would never let her go with him to the church, Melissa thought with frustration. And there was always Cassie to think about. "You stay with Cassie. I'll meet with Danielle Claron. There's a chance she'll feel less threatened with another woman, isn't there?"

He shook his head. "She specified Travis. Besides, she has to be targeted by Deschamps. It will be dangerous to be anywhere near her."

Her hands clenched into fists. "I'm not stupid. I won't barge right up and call for—"

"I know you're not stupid." His lips tightened. "But you don't know this game. I don't agree with Travis that you should be kept in the dark, but I'm not helping you act recklessly."

She could tell by his expression that she wasn't going to be able to move him. She got up from the table and strode toward the door.

Galen jumped to his feet. "Where are you going?"

"For a walk. I'm mad as hell and I need to burn off a little steam." She gave him a grim glance over her shoulder. "Did you think I was going to jump in the car and head for St. Ives?"

"The thought did occur to me."

"Like I said, I'm not stupid, Galen. I know you'd try to stop me and you're probably very good at stopping people." She slammed the door behind her and ran down the steps. She moved quickly, forcefully, her heels digging into the soft sand. She'd had to get out of the house before she exploded.

She wanted to hit someone, dammit.

No, she wanted to hit Travis. He was blocking her at every turn and seeing that Galen would be no real help to her either. This was the first break, a chance to find Deschamps, and she was supposed to sit here and wait for someone else to find Jessica's murderer.

Jessica.

Don't tear up. She had cried too much already, and she couldn't think straight when she let emotion rule her. She stopped at the edge of the surf and looked out at the sea. She felt very small and alone.

Stop thinking like that. Negative thoughts were bull. She was alone, but that didn't mean she couldn't do anything that had to be done.

She just had to work on it.

★ ★ ★

8:35 P.M.

"So I'm here," Karlstadt said grimly as he sat down at the table at the sidewalk café. "It had better be good, Travis."

"Your situation couldn't be worse, could it?"

"Yes, it could. You could still be alive at the end of this meeting. I don't appreciate being double-crossed, you bastard."

"You weren't double-crossed. Not intentionally." He pushed the pouch across the table. "All the diamonds I have at the moment. Unfortunately, the rest are in the hands of the CIA."

Karlstadt didn't touch the pouch. "That's not good enough."

"I'll return the deposit you made to the Swiss account. That means you won't have to pay for the missing diamonds."

"You know that's not the issue. Those diamonds have to be taken out of circulation."

"I have a few ideas how that might be done. In the meantime, you have to admit that having them tucked away by the CIA is the next best thing."

"I don't have to admit anything." Karlstadt's expression was rock hard. "You've put me in a very bad light with my employers. They don't appreciate failure."

"You haven't failed. You've gotten the time to deal with the Russians. They don't know you don't have all the diamonds."

"I don't have the process either. Give me the disk, Travis."

"You'll get it."

"Now."

"I'm not stupid, Karlstadt. It's in a safe place and will go straight to *The New York Times* if I don't call for it in a reasonable length of time. I'll send it to you." His gaze wandered to the rooftop of the hotel across the street. "Otherwise you might decide to signal that gentleman to take me out."

"You expect me to trust you? I trusted you once."

"You didn't trust me. You did what was necessary to please your employers. Just as you'll do what's necessary to please them this time. I'll keep my word to you because it's the intelligent thing to do. I have enough problems without having you after me."

"So I've heard." He was silent a moment. "You could have made a copy of the disk."

"Same answer. I want out, not more trouble."

"When do I get it?"

"I'll call you to let you know where to pick it up." He stood. "Long distance."

Karlstadt's smile was without mirth. "That's

wise. I'd be very tempted to recoup my losses in a very violent fashion if you don't stay out of my way."

"I'll keep that in mind." He glanced at the rooftop again. "I'm leaving now. Please tell our friend not to attempt to follow me. It would be a deal breaker."

"I'll give you two days to get that disk to me. Then I'll come after it." He smiled maliciously. "I can't afford to wait much longer. You're in plenty of hot water. I don't want someone else to kill you before I get my chance."

"That would be unfair. I'll try not to disappoint you." Travis strode down the street and around the corner. His pace quickened as he wound a zigzag path around the town for the next thirty minutes until he was certain he wasn't followed. Then he set out for his car.

So far, so good. It had been close. Very close.

His only advantage had been the fact that Karlstadt was a businessman and knew when to cut his losses. That didn't mean he wouldn't come after Travis if he took too much flak for losing the rest of the diamonds. The sensible thing would be for Travis to get out of Europe and lie low for a while.

Screw the sensible thing.

Not while Deschamps was still alive.

His phone rang as he was starting the Peugeot.

"We have a problem," Galen said. "Have you left Cannes?"

"Not yet. I should be back at the cottage in a few hours."

"Don't come here. Go directly to St. Ives. I got a call from Danielle Claron. She wants to negotiate with you. She'll be at the old church at the north edge of the village after midnight."

"When did she call?"

"After six. I thought I'd give you time to finish with Karlstadt. It's only a few hours' drive from Cannes to St. Ives." He paused. "But you'd better hurry. Melissa may get there before you do."

"What? You told her?"

"Guilty. But I watched her all the time she was on the beach. And she came in from her walk and went straight to bed."

"For God's sake, you weren't suspicious?"

"Of course I was suspicious. I opened the door and looked in on her four times in the past couple of hours. The last time she threw a book at me. Five minutes later I heard the van start. She must have crawled out the window the moment I closed the door. I ran out, but she was already gunning it down the beach."

"I'm going to murder you."

"I may commit suicide. It was most humiliating. Now I'm relegated from being a mighty warrior to being a lowly nursemaid for Cassie."

"You should never have told her. We don't know what the hell is happening with Danielle Claron."

"I wouldn't have appreciated being kept in the dark." He paused again. "And she's not totally without protection. You did give her the gun."

"That's the only weapon she has. She's out of her depth. She doesn't know—"

"That's what I tried to tell her. She wasn't listening. In her place, I don't know if I would have listened either. Call me when you get to St. Ives." He hung up.

Travis glanced at his watch. At least three hours to get to St. Ives from here.

His foot stomped on the accelerator and the car leapt forward.

21

St. Ives

The ancient church on the hill had to have been built centuries ago, and the graveyard stretching behind it looked like the resting place of generations of villagers. The building itself had no windows, and the stone steps leading up to the massive oak doors were splintered.

Melissa was not about to go up those steps. She would be a clear target in the bright moonlight. Her hand closed on the gun in her jacket pocket as she stepped deeper into the shadows beneath the oak tree.

She couldn't just stand there all night. She moistened her lips and called, "Danielle. Danielle Claron."

No answer.

"I'm Melissa Riley. Michael Travis sent me."

No answer.

"He wasn't sure he could make it in time. But I can authorize any money you might need."

No answer.

"For God's sake, would he have sent a woman if he'd wanted to harm you?"

"If he was clever."

Melissa whirled to face the woman coming around the church from the direction of the graveyard. She was petite, dark-haired, and in her middle thirties, wearing a purple sweater and long print skirt. "My husband was never that clever. He never listened. He always underestimated me."

She was pointing a gun at Melissa.

"That's how that bastard managed to kill him. I don't underestimate anyone. I'm not going to die. Put up your hands."

Melissa slowly raised her hands. "I'm not here to hurt you. I'm here to give you what you want."

"Can you give me my husband back?"

"No, but I can give you the money to keep you safe."

"And what do you want in return?"

"Edward Deschamps. Do you know where he is?"

Silence. "Maybe."

Melissa's heart leapt. "Either you do or you don't."

"Maybe," she repeated. "We'll talk again when I see some money. And it better be soon. Do you think I've liked hiding out here all these weeks?"

"Will you put away that gun? You can see I'm no threat."

Danielle stared at her appraisingly before saying finally, "No, you're too soft." She lowered the gun. "I wasn't sure you weren't hired by Deschamps to trick me into coming out in the open." Her lips twisted. "The bastard has a history of using women. Like that bitch Jeanne Beaujolis. That's how I got into this mess."

Melissa put her hands down. "She told you about what was going to happen at Vasaro?"

"No, only that Deschamps was going to help her strike it rich. I put the rest together when I heard what happened there." Her face hardened. "She was crazy about him at first, and then she was crazy only about the money she was going to get."

"Did you meet him before Vasaro?"

"Once or twice."

"Where?"

She shook her head. "The money."

"How much?"

"Travis offered my husband five hundred thousand dollars. I want seven."

"It may take us some time to get that amount."

"I don't have a lot of time. I have to get out of here. I'll give you until tomorrow night to— What's that?" She lifted her head to gaze at the woods behind Melissa. "Did you hear it?"

Melissa whirled around. "Hear what?"

"Rustling. There's someone in the woods." She looked back at Melissa, her eyes blazing. "You lied to me. Deschamps did send you."

"No, it might be Travis. He said he'd—"

"Liar." She jumped toward Melissa. "It's not Travis. It's Deschamps." The butt of her gun was coming down toward Melissa's head.

Melissa ducked, grabbed the woman's arm, and twisted it behind her back.

"Let me go, you bitch."

Melissa released her but pulled the Smith & Wesson out of her jacket pocket at the same time. "When you listen to reason." She pressed the gun to Danielle's back. "One, I didn't hear any rustling, and two, I'm the last person who'd be in league with Deschamps. He killed my sister. I want him as much as you do."

"More," a man's voice said from behind her. "Much more, Ms. Riley."

Pain burst through her head.

She slumped to the ground.

"Is she dead, Edward?"

Danielle Claron's voice, Melissa realized dimly.

"I hope not." He bent down and picked up her gun, which had fallen from her hand. "I have other plans for her. No, I think she's just out."

"You took long enough. I did like you said. I tried to distract her."

"And you did very well, Monique. If I hadn't known Danielle was dead, you would have fooled me. Sorry to make your job harder. I was scouting around for Travis."

"He's not here?"

"Not yet."

"But you're through with me? It's not my fault she came instead of Travis. I can have my money?"

"Of course. I promised you, didn't I? Come along into the church, where I can turn on my flashlight and count it out for you."

"What about her?"

"This will take only a minute."

They were walking away. Something wasn't right. . . .

It didn't matter. Think about it later. Get up. Get away before he comes back.

She struggled to her knees.

Jesus, her head hurt.

Move anyway. Get to your feet.

On the second try she made it.

She staggered to the road. Get to the car.

God, she felt sick.

Find a place to rest for a few minutes.

She had to throw up. She staggered to a tree and leaned against it while she heaved.

A hand fell on her shoulder.

Deschamps!

She whirled and crashed her fist into his face.

"Jesus, what the hell—"

It was Travis.

She collapsed against him. "He's here. We have to go back—"

He stiffened. "Deschamps?"

"He's in the church. There's a woman . . . but it's not Danielle Claron. He called her Monique. I think Danielle Claron's dead. He's paying the woman now." She pushed him away. "We have to go back."

"You don't have to do anything at the moment but sit down before you fall." He frowned. "Are you bleeding?"

"I don't know. He hit me." She looked up the

hill. "We have to go to the church. He and that woman are—" She stopped. "No, there's something wrong. He didn't even check to see if I was unconscious. He would know how hard to hit someone, wouldn't he? He didn't check. . . ." She rubbed her temple and her fingers came away wet. She *was* bleeding. "He wanted me to get away and find you. He wanted you to rush back to the church. It's a trap."

He said slowly, "But if we know it's a trap, then we have the advantage."

Panic soared through her. "No, he'll be waiting for you. He'll kill you."

Travis was ignoring her. "Can you make it back up the hill? I'll go into the church alone, but I don't want to leave you here by yourself."

"Dammit, he's *waiting*."

His expression was grim. "It's my shot at him. I'm going to take it." He repeated, "Can you make it up the hill?"

"I'll make it." She fell into step with him. Damn right she'd make it. She wasn't about to stay here. "But he may have— What's that smell?"

"*Shit.*"

At the top of the hill the old church was blazing. Fire was licking out of every window and the door.

"He torched it?"

Travis nodded, his gaze on the church, which was now an inferno.

That smell . . .

Jesus, she felt sick.

Because she realized what that familiar smell was.

Horrible smell, nightmare smell.

It was the smell of burning flesh.

"Come on." Travis's hand cupped her elbow. "Let's get out of here."

She couldn't stop staring at the flames. "Deschamps."

"He'd be stupid to still be here. There are already villagers running toward the church."

Yes, she saw them now. One old man wearing only pants and shoes and a woman carrying a bucket. What could one bucket of water do to this inferno?

"There's someone inside. I smell—"

"I know. But it's too late to save her. She was probably dead before he started the fire."

He was talking about the woman who had pretended to be Danielle Claron. "He killed her?"

"No big surprise. He doesn't like witnesses." He was turning her, pushing her down the hill. "He torched the Claron house too, to destroy evidence."

"But he could have waited. It doesn't make sense. I *know* he wanted to trap you, Travis."

"Maybe." He stopped at the van. "Can you drive? We have to get both vehicles away. There will be an investigation and we don't want to be connected."

"I can drive." She opened the door.

"Wait." He got in and checked the back. "Okay. You can get in now."

A chill went through her as she realized he had thought Deschamps might be in the van, waiting for her. "He already had his chance at me, and he didn't take it."

He was peering underneath the van. "Circumstances change."

"Where's your car?"

"Around the curve in the road."

She settled in the driver's seat. "Get in. I'll take you there and wait until we're sure he's nowhere around."

"Are you protecting me, Melissa?"

"Shut up and get in the van."

"Right."

No one appeared to be in the Peugeot or anywhere near. Maybe. She'd learned a hard lesson about appearances tonight.

She pulled up next to the car. "Hurry up, get in."

His gaze circled the woods on the side of the hill. "In a minute. I don't think he had time, but there's a possibility . . ." He opened the hood of the car, examined it, and then went around to the back, knelt down, and peered beneath it. "He knows about explosives, and it doesn't take much time to rig a simple bomb." He straightened up and seconds later he was in the driver's seat. "Get going. I'll follow you. If you get dizzy, pull over and we'll leave the van by the road. Galen can arrange a pickup later."

She was dizzy now. Dizzy and sick and confused. Bombs and deception and murder . . .

And that awful smell of burning flesh.

Galen met them as they drove up to the cottage.

"You're lucky I'm a forgiving man. It wasn't a nice thing to— You're bleeding." He lifted her down from the van and called to Travis, who was getting out of the Peugeot. "Deschamps?"

"Yes." He stopped beside Melissa. "Okay?"

"Yes."

"You don't deserve to be." He walked away, leaving her behind.

Galen gave a low whistle. "I'd better take care of that wound," he told Melissa. "In his present humor Travis would probably let you bleed to death."

She hadn't been aware of the anger seething

beneath the surface. She hadn't been aware of anything but disappointment and horror . . . and that smell of burning flesh.

Mama. Daddy.

The forest, safe from horror and the smell of death and burning.

Jessica.

But there was no Jessica to coax her out of the forest now.

"Melissa?"

"I'm all right. But he's right, I don't deserve to be. She fooled me."

"That's no crime, only a mistake. And it didn't hurt anyone but you." They were in the living room by then. "Sit down. I'll put some antibacterial cream on that cut."

"I can do it."

"But I can do it quicker. You don't look so steady." He pushed her down into one of the chairs. "Travis called me from his car and filled me in. Do you want to talk about it?"

Flesh burning . . .

She moistened her lips. "It was a trap. It wasn't Danielle Claron. She was so . . . believable. I don't know how she knew where to call you or the other details."

"It could have been a bug at the Dumairs' home. Deschamps knew we'd be looking for Danielle Claron." He dabbed at the cut. "Travis said he bugged Jan's place and that Jan said he was a bloody expert." He spread a little ointment. "This cut isn't bad at all."

Because Deschamps hadn't really wanted to hurt her. A trap. A trap that had not been sprung. "I was a little dizzy, but I'm fine now. How's Cassie?"

"Fine." Travis came out of Cassie's bedroom. "No credit to you."

"Don't you give me a guilt trip. I knew Galen would take care of her. I didn't think I'd be gone more than a few hours."

"And you almost didn't come back at all," he said fiercely. "I told you that you shouldn't go after him."

"Then you should have let me go with you. The only reason I went alone is that I knew you were closing me out."

"So it's my fault you almost got yourself killed? You were lucky you didn't end up roasting in that church with that woman."

Scorched flesh.

Mama, wake up. Please, wake up.

She was smothering. She had to get out. "I guess I was lucky." She jumped to her feet and headed for the door. "I'm going out on the porch. I'll be back in a few minutes."

★ ★ ★

"You were pretty rough on her, weren't you?" Galen asked. "She's rough enough on herself."

"She could have gotten herself killed." Travis headed for the door. "She's like a torpedo heading straight for a target and not realizing she'll be blown up too."

"Why don't you leave her alone for a while? She may need some space."

"I *can't* leave her alone, dammit."

"No?" Galen studied him a moment and then nodded slowly. "You're that sure he's out there?"

"Like I told you when I called you from the car, Melissa was sure it was a trap, and her instincts are good. She just didn't think far enough. Deschamps wants me, but he also wants the Wind Dancer. He set up the meeting at the church so that he could follow us back here. Did you alert your men guarding the place?"

Galen nodded. "When do you think he'll go for it?"

"When he's sure the Wind Dancer is here. So we have to make him think the Wind Dancer is someplace else and we're planning on picking it up soon. We'll make a couple of dummy calls to one of your guys and lead Deschamps down a false trail. Who's sharpest?"

"Joseph."

"Then fill him in. Deschamps can't use bugs, so he'll probably use long-range amplifiers. I figure he'll have them in place in eight or twelve hours. Have your guys try to locate him. He could set up either onshore or in a boat."

"How do we communicate, then?"

He grimaced. "Very carefully. We'll use the laptop when we don't want him to hear. Does Joseph have one?"

"Get real. This is the twenty-first century."

"Then tell your guys to monitor their E-mail for instructions."

"And what if you're wrong about Deschamps?"

Travis didn't want to speculate about that. "I don't think I'm wrong. He's smart and he's waited this long. You just see that Cassie and Melissa are protected."

Galen's gaze went to Melissa. "And she's not to know?"

"No."

"You're risking her neck."

"I'm risking all our necks. I can't help it." His lips thinned. "I'm going to find a way to trap him, Galen. I'm going to get him."

"How?"

"I'll work on it." He suddenly realized that was Melissa's phrase, the one that defined the bedrock of her character. "You take the first watch, okay?"

Galen nodded. "You'd better make sure she

doesn't decide to start wandering around. Just in case. And you might try being nice to her. She's feeling pretty bad."

"I don't want to be nice to her. I want her to stop—" He drew a deep breath. "Call your guys and get them busy trying to spot Deschamps."

"Come on inside, Melissa."

Travis was standing behind her.

"Pretty soon." She wrapped her arms around herself. Lord, she wished she could stop shaking. Get control. Don't let him see . . .

"Now."

She shook her head.

"I know I was sharp with you, but you can't stay out here."

"You think I'm pouting?"

"That's not a word I'd use in connection with you. I know you're upset." He paused. "Okay, I didn't make it any easier."

"You made it easier."

"How?"

"You stayed alive." She closed her eyes. "I made a terrible mistake. I could have killed you."

"And would you have shed a few tears for me?"

"Oh, yes."

He took a step forward. "Melissa . . ."

"Don't you touch me." Her eyes flicked open and she backed away from him. "I can't let anyone—"

"Christ, you're shaking so hard, your teeth are rattling."

"It will go away."

"Shit." He stepped closer and took her in his arms. "Am I responsible for this?"

"Don't flatter yourself." But her arms closed around him. Warm. Safe. Here. Now. Alive.

"Deschamps?"

"Not Deschamps."

"Then why the hell won't you quit shaking?"

She buried her face in his shoulder. "The smell." Her voice was muffled. "That woman in the church . . . That smell . . ."

He went still. "Christ, I didn't make the connection. Your parents . . ."

"It's the first time since I came out that I felt any pull to go back into my nice little forest. I was so scared. . . . I wanted to go there. I felt so safe there."

"The hell you did." His arms tightened around her. "You were half dead. Now stop it. You're not going anywhere."

"Of course I'm not. It's just . . . I had to work my way through it. I'm glad Jessica didn't see me. It would have scared her silly."

"It scared me."

"Did it?" The shaking was easing. "You can let me go now."

"Can I?" He didn't move.

"No, maybe not. This feels . . . good."

"Yes, it does."

"*You* feel good." Good and right. Completely right. All the tension was leaving her. "Thank you."

"You're welcome . . . I think."

A few minutes passed and then Travis pushed her away. "You'd better go in."

Yes, she'd better leave him. This was too good. "You can't close me out again. We have to talk about Deschamps."

She could feel the tension in his body. "Not now, Melissa."

No, not now, she thought wearily. Too much to think about. Too many emotions to sort out. She backed away. "In the morning."

He glanced at the sky. "That won't be too long."

She looked at the streaks of pearl gray lighting the night sky. "Jessica loved this time of day. She said when she was an intern she'd walk through the park when she finished her duty. Everything was so clear and bright and new, it made her able to face the next night."

"Jessica would want you to be safe."

She shook her head. "Don't try to manipulate me by using Jessica. Good night, Travis. I'm sorry I put you at risk."

"You could have saved my neck. You're not all that gullible, so that woman must have been good. I might have fallen for her story too."

She thought about it and then smiled. "You're absolutely right. You should be damn grateful to me."

She went to her bedroom, where Galen was sitting beside Cassie. She put her finger to her lips and motioned for him to go. He nodded and silently left. She lay down next to Cassie and closed her eyes.

"You left me," Cassie said.

"Not for long."

"I was lonely."

"Then come out and you'll never be lonely again."

Silence. "You were scared. You wanted to run back to your forest."

How had Cassie picked up on that? "But I didn't do it. I'll never go back there again."

"You could come into my tunnel."

"But you won't be there for long."

"You keep saying that."

"Because it's true. Isn't it?"

Silence. "You truly don't want to go back?"

"Why should I? Look at me. What do you see?"

Silence. "I'm going to go to sleep now."

"*Stubborn.*"

"*But you* were *scared. I saw it.*"

"*And what else did you see?*"

"*Michael. I saw Michael. . . .*"

Melissa lay awake a long time after Cassie drifted off to sleep.

Would you have shed a few tears for me?

I saw Michael. . . .

22

Travis's door opened a few hours later.

He tensed.

"It's only me," Melissa said.

"*Only?*" He rose up on one elbow. "What are you doing here?"

"I wanted to be with you."

"Do you want to talk about your parents?"

"Not now."

"Deschamps?"

"I don't need a therapist, Travis." She came toward him. "That's not what this is all about."

He went still. "Then what the hell is it about?"

"What do you think?"

"I think you'd better be very clear."

"You want clear?" She paused to steady her voice. "I'll give you clear." She stopped beside the bed. "I'm going to get undressed. I see you're already naked, and that's very convenient." She pulled her nightshirt over her head and dropped it to the floor. "Now I'm going to get into bed with you. Then I want you to indulge in every carnal act you've ever learned or heard of." She drew back the cover. "Is that clear enough?"

He was silent a moment, and when he spoke his voice was uneven. "I believe that's crystal-clear. But you went through a hell of a lot tonight. Are you sure that you're able to judge—"

"Oh, for God's sake. Of course I'm sure. Stop quibbling. Do you think this is easy for me? Not that I'm some shrinking violet, but it's—"

"Shh." He reached out and probed gently between her legs. "Now I believe you. Christ, you're quick."

"Don't you be." Her voice was trembling as she pressed against him. "I want this to last a long, long time. . . ."

"You're very good." Melissa shifted and then cuddled closer. "For someone who likes to stay on the outside, your inside technique is remarkable."

"If you'd warned me you were going to seduce me, I'd have put some thought into innovation."

"Instinct is better. Besides, I didn't know. I wasn't sure. Not until you actually stopped arguing and touched me." She brushed her lips across his chest. "Then I knew it was the right thing to do."

"It was definitely the right thing." His hand tangled in her hair. "And I'm glad you didn't decide it wasn't the right time and the right man at that late stage."

"I'm no tease. I wouldn't have cheated you." She chuckled. "And I certainly wouldn't have cheated myself. What a wicked man you're turning out to be, Michael Travis."

"I aim to please. You said every carnal act."

"I think we've reached that boundary."

"Nah, we haven't even started." He took her hand and sucked on her index finger. "Have we?"

She felt a surge of heat move through her. Jesus, he was good. Sex with him had been like nothing she had ever experienced. A closeness that was fever hot and more than sensual. "Maybe we haven't." She drew closer. "Show me. . . ."

★ ★ ★

The sun was high in the sky when they walked out on the porch.

"There's Galen, sitting on that dune." Melissa returned his lazy wave and watched him as he stretched, yawned, and then lay back on the sand. "He looks so relaxed, just zoning out, looking at the boats. It's the first time I've seen him lazing around since we got here. He's always bustling, cooking, or on the phone, managing the world."

Travis followed her gaze to Galen and then to the two boats anchored up the coast. "The universe. But maybe he's more tactful than you think. He wouldn't want to disturb us. He understands things."

"What things?" She glanced at him. His hair was tousled, his shirt mussed, and his expression . . . She looked away. She'd thought she'd had enough, but maybe . . . "What do you think Galen understands about us?" She smiled. "Do you believe he thinks I seduced you to get my way?"

"He's no fool." He looked straight ahead. "But would you care to confide in me why I got lucky?"

"I wanted to do it," she said simply.

"It's not that easy."

"Yes, it is. I was the one who was making it

difficult, which isn't like me. Every moment of life should be lived to the max. I wanted you but I wouldn't take you. But I was scared to death last night. I thought I was going to die and then I was afraid you were. It jarred some sense back into me. I feel . . . something for you."

"What?"

"I don't know. Sometimes I feel so close to you, and that . . . intimidated me."

"You could have fooled me."

"What's wrong? Are you insulted? I wanted to be honest with you."

"Oh, you were. I can understand why you fought against feeling anything for me. We're at opposite ends of the universe."

"And you don't want to make any commitment to anyone."

He was silent.

She smiled. "But you're going to have to make a commitment to me. Because I can't turn my back on the people I become close to. So like it or not, I'm in your life."

"You are?"

"Don't panic. There are all kinds of commitment. Friendship is one. You should feel safe with that."

"I believe I'm becoming a little annoyed with your analysis of my character."

"Sorry," she said wearily. "I suppose I'm just

trying to work my way through this. It came as a shock to me that I'd feel this strongly about you. I don't want anything to happen to you. It would make me—"

"Sad?"

Lord, she wished it were only sad. She was so near a great abyss that she had to move very carefully. "I suppose you could use that word." She changed the subject. "What's next? We've lost the only lead we had. Do you think Deschamps—"

He exploded. "Christ, you almost got killed last night chasing after Deschamps. Why can't you leave it alone? And dammit, don't close up." He took her shoulders and shook her. "You listen to me."

"I am listening."

"But you're not hearing. You're running away from me."

"I'm not running away." She met his gaze. "Do you want to go back to the bedroom and make love again?"

"No, I do not. Oh, shit, of course I do. But I'm not going to let you use me to— What the hell am I saying?"

"I didn't use you. I only shared joy. Didn't I?"

He stared at her and then he slowly nodded. "Jesus, what kind of woman are you, Melissa?"

A woman who might love you.

Oh, God, she wished that answer hadn't popped into her head. But there were all kinds of love just as there were all kinds of commitment. She could deal with this. She forced a smile. "You should know by now. I'm pretty transparent."

"The hell you are."

She turned to go back in the house. "Compared to you, I'm clear as glass. I'm hungry. Do you want breakfast?"

"No, I'm going for a walk. I'll see you later."

She watched him walk toward Galen. He was upset. Well, she couldn't do anything about that. She'd been as honest with him as she could. She couldn't forget about Deschamps, and she wasn't going to lie to Travis.

Galen and Travis were talking. Fast. Intensely.

About Deschamps? Probably. If they were making plans, they were leaving her out again. She couldn't allow that to happen. Dammit, Travis was even more protective than before. Last night could have been a mistake.

No, joy was never a mistake. She'd just have to work out the problems.

Galen was coming back to the cottage. He smiled as he walked up the porch steps. "Travis says you're hungry. What do you want for breakfast?"

"I can fix it."

"Nah, it's all in the package." He opened the screen door. "And I imagine you could use an easy time after last night."

She blinked.

He laughed. "Oops. No, I meant the knock on the head."

She looked at Travis, who was still on the beach. "Is he coming?"

"Not right now. He said he needed some time to himself. Pancakes? Ham and eggs?"

She watched Travis start off down the beach. She could tell by the wary, contained way he was moving how tense he was. Maybe she could talk to him when he came back. Or maybe it was better to let him cool down.

She turned back to Galen. "Pancakes. I'll set the table."

Travis glanced back at the porch and watched Melissa go inside. Christ, she was stubborn.

And strong and bold and giving. And so bright and beautiful that she made him feel . . .

Scared to death.

She wouldn't stop. If last night hadn't discouraged her, nothing would. It was only a matter of time until she found out that Deschamps might be in that boat in the cove. If she hadn't been so upset last night, she would have probably already figured out Deschamps would follow them. There was no doubt in his mind that Deschamps would target her again. She had interfered and she was now a witness.

It made him sick to his stomach.

He couldn't let it happen.

"Want to play poker?" Galen asked. "I'm getting tired of solitaire."

Melissa turned away from the window where she'd been watching Travis on the beach. "No, thanks."

"Your loss." He played a queen on a king. "I'm known as the worst player on the Continent. It could be a great ego boost for you."

Maybe she could use an ego boost. Travis had been avoiding her all day. Except for dinner, he'd stayed out on the beach. She supposed it was natural. Besides her refusal to back off on Deschamps, she'd been frank with him about her intention to stay in his life. Travis was probably feeling uneasy.

Well, let him get used to it. He could stay on that beach all night. She wasn't going to wait around for him. "I'm going to bed. Good night, Galen."

He didn't look up. "Good night."

Cassie was asleep and Melissa moved quietly into the bathroom to brush her teeth and wash her face. But the little girl woke when she slipped into bed next to her.

"Melissa?"

"Shh. Go back to sleep."

"I will. So sleepy . . . Why is Michael here?"

"He's not here."

"Yes, he is. I can feel it. Almost always with you now . . ."

She was asleep again.

Almost always with you now.

Melissa stared into the darkness. Was Cassie sensing the new bond that had formed between them? Or was Melissa just thinking more about Travis and the child had picked up on it?

But Cassie was wrong. Michael wasn't with her tonight. He was somewhere outside on that damned beach.

And she was lonely. Funny that she could be lonely after only one night with him. Was he lonely too?

She hoped to hell he was. She didn't want to be this miserable all by herself. But he was probably as happy as a clam. Men weren't as introspective as women, which was entirely unfair.

Go to sleep. Forget him.

But, Jesus, she was lonely. . . .

★   ★   ★

"Monsters!"

Melissa woke with a start. Dammit, she had thought the nightmares were over. But there was no doubting the child's terror.

"They're coming. Why are you lying there? We have to fight them!"

"We've talked about this. You know there are no monsters in the tunnel, Cassie."

"Monsters. Guns. They want to hurt you."

"Not you?" At least that was a breakthrough. Cassie's nightmares had always concerned a threat to herself.

"Don't want to hurt me. Get up. Run away."

"I won't leave you. There's nothing to worry about. The monsters are only in your imag—"

The bedroom door flung open.

Four men. Guns.

"No!" She flung herself on top of Cassie. "Don't hurt her."

"Melissa!" Cassie screamed.

23

"Take the handcuffs off her, Danley," Andreas said. "And I want her in the limo with me."

"I wouldn't advise you to—"

"I think I can protect myself from her." His arms tightened around Cassie. "And I doubt she's any danger to my daughter. You told me yourself that her first move was to try to save Cassie."

"That might have been a clever act on her part to—"

"Put her in the car, Danley."

"Yes, sir." He reluctantly unlocked the cuffs and opened the door.

Melissa got into the limousine.

"Your neck is scratched," Andreas told her. "It's bleeding a little. There's a tissue in the holder." He wrapped Cassie more tightly in the blanket. "Sorry. I told them not to hurt you."

"Why?"

"It was part of the deal." He took out his phone. "If you'll excuse me, I have to call my wife." He dialed the number. "Cassie's safe. Perfectly safe. Yes, I'm sure. She's not been hurt. I love you too. I'll call you later."

"What deal?" Melissa asked when he hung up.

"Michael Travis. He called and told me where you and Cassie were."

Betrayal. She shouldn't be this shocked. She should have known when she'd seen no sign of Travis or Galen while she'd been dragged from the house.

"And the deal?"

"Amnesty for you. You're not to be prosecuted for kidnapping or any other crime. You're to be kept in custody for forty-eight hours and then released."

"And for Travis?"

"He's an intelligent man. He knows I'm ready to cut his throat. The deal was entirely for you. He was very persuasive, and I had little choice when he told me this Deschamps knew where you all were and could come after Cassie at any

minute. He said he would phone me right before he left with the Wind Dancer and we had
to charge in before Deschamps."

Who had followed her and Travis to the cottage, she realized in disgust. My God, why hadn't
she put two and two together? If she'd been leading with her head instead of her emotions, she'd
have figured out what had been evident to Travis.
All that time he and Galen had spent on the beach
. . . "Did you search the area?"

"Of course. I'd have been delighted to find either Travis or Deschamps."

"It's Deschamps you want. He's the one who
staged the Vasaro attack."

"I want them both. But I've had a report on
Deschamps since Travis called me, and that bastard may be marginally worse."

"He's a monster. Ask Cassie."

"Unfortunately, she won't answer." He looked
down at his daughter. "Is it true Cassie's not
having the nightmares any longer?"

She nodded. "It's early days, but I think they
may be gone."

"I'll pray you're right." He looked down at his
daughter. "I wanted to kill your sister that day
Cassie was taken."

She flinched. "Someone else did it for you."

"I know." He paused. "I sent her body back to

Virginia. It was difficult for me to believe that she was an accomplice."

"She wasn't. Leaving Juniper just seemed better for Cassie at the time." Her chin lifted. "And she was right. Cassie is much better now. If she'd stayed at the house, she might have been lost forever, or one of those bouts of hysteria could have killed her."

"I'm supposed to be grateful?"

"Hell, yes."

"She put Cassie in jeopardy."

"And she gave her life for your daughter."

He was silent. "Just as you were prepared to die for her in the cottage today."

"My reaction was pure instinct. If Jessica had known she was going to die, I believe she would have gone to the museum to see the Wind Dancer anyway. She thought she had a chance of bringing Cassie back. She almost pulled it off."

"So Travis told me." He looked down again at Cassie. "How close was she?"

"Very close."

"She asked me to take Cassie back to Vasaro. I refused."

"You should have done it."

"Hindsight. But you'll be glad to know your sister is getting her way."

"What?"

"That's where we're going. We'll stay for two days and you're going to be my guest."

"Why?"

"Didn't you just tell me that it's best for Cassie?"

She studied him. "But why now? I'd think you'd want to rush her back to the States to her mother."

"I have to stay here for another couple of days, and I don't want to let her out of my sight. I'm not about to rely on anyone else to make sure she's safe. You can understand that."

"Yes." But Andreas wasn't telling her everything. "You evidently had this arrangement in place before—"

"No statue, Mr. President." Danley had opened the door. "We tore the place apart."

"I didn't think it would be there. I just had to make sure Travis really had it with him. Tell the driver to go on."

"You were looking for the Wind Dancer," Melissa said as the car started. "I should tell you Travis didn't want to take it from the museum. He said you'd raise all kinds of hell to get it back. I made him do it."

"Why?"

"Deschamps had just killed my sister and he wanted the statue. I wanted to use it as bait."

"Then Travis definitely must have come

around to your way of thinking," he said grimly. "Please stop trying to defend him. Stealing the Wind Dancer is the least of his crimes."

"He didn't hurt Cassie."

"He put her in jeopardy." He added coldly, "And I intend to see him punished."

She wearily leaned back in the seat. Why was she trying to save Travis when she was so angry with him? He had tricked her and was now trying to tie her hands. "Okay, do what you like. But it's best if you don't talk about it in front of Cassie. He's still her hero."

He frowned. "Do you think she's awake now?"

"I know she is. She's listening to everything we say."

"How do you know?"

Evidently, Travis had not told Andreas of the link between Melissa and Cassie, and she wasn't about to do it. Credibility was of the essence. All she needed was for him to think she had a screw loose. "I've been with her almost constantly since we left Juniper. I can tell."

He stroked Cassie's cheek and his voice softened to velvet. "I love you, baby. I'm going to take you home soon. Will you like that? Won't you speak to me? No? That's okay. Maybe later." He cleared his throat as he looked up at Melissa. "But you've succeeded in getting her to talk?"

She frowned. "Where did you get that idea? No, we haven't gotten that far."

"Danley said she screamed your name."

Her eyes widened. "She did? She actually *said* my name?"

"Screamed it."

"Thank God." She could feel the tears stinging her eyes. "Then maybe I shouldn't be so mad at Travis after all. It might have taken weeks to get to that point if Cassie hadn't been frightened." She added deliberately, "And maybe you shouldn't be either."

"I'll think about it . . . later."

Now that she'd warned him, he was not about to upset his Cassie. But that didn't mean he was softening. Andreas was difficult to read, and she was aware of a multitude of undercurrents both in him and the situation. Well, if she had to work her way through them, she'd better begin. There was more going on than Andreas had said. One thing he had thrown out had set off a small flare. Concentrate on that first.

Why were they going to Vasaro?

From Travis's helicopter the limousine and official cars looked like a giant snake as they wound their way to the highway that led to Vasaro.

Galen gave a low whistle. "Andreas brought enough firepower for a battalion."

"He's not about to let Cassie be taken from him again." Travis's gaze shifted to the boat in the harbor that had pulled up anchor and was starting to move. "There goes Deschamps. He's probably gnashing his teeth right now because he didn't go into the cottage and grab the statue when he had a chance." He flipped him the finger. "Screw you, bastard."

"Ready?"

Travis nodded. The Wind Dancer sat on the floor at his feet. He had deliberately not put it in a box. When they'd run down the beach to board the helicopter, the sun had shimmered on the golden statue like the lamp in a lighthouse. There was no question Deschamps had seen it. "Let's get out of here."

Melissa's first glimpse of Vasaro took her breath away. Rolling hills covered with flowers and, dear Lord, the scents . . .

Now she knew why Andreas had rolled down the window. The delicious fragrance of lavender blossoms was enough to make you dizzy.

"Wonderful," she murmured.

Andreas nodded. "Cassie always loved it. I was hoping it might ignite some response."

"She's stubborn." The limousine was going up the road to a big stone house that had nothing grand about it. It looked like what it was, a lovely, spacious farmhouse surrounded by well-kept outbuildings. It was obviously a working farm, but Melissa didn't see any workers. "Did Mr. Danley toss all the employees off the property?"

"Caitlin Vasaro would have been outraged if we had. Her workers are like family. We found them temporary accommodations in the area." The limousine had drawn up at the front door. "The security of this house is going to be tighter than Fort Knox. Nothing is going to happen to Cassie again."

"Deschamps is still out there. Wouldn't it be better to send her to Washington?"

"There's no reason for Deschamps to target my daughter. I no longer have the Wind Dancer." He got out of the limousine and Melissa followed him. "I'm going to take her up to her room. It's the second one at the top of the stairs. Pick any other room you like." He glanced back at her. "You're free to go any-where in the house. The grounds are off limits. Don't go past the veranda or you'll be stopped."

She nodded, her gaze going to the foothills. She could already see dozens of men spreading out, ringing the farmhouse and the outbuildings. "If you need me, call me. Cassie's used to me now."

"She won't need you. I've arranged to have a nurse and doctor in residence. And I'm going to stay with her as much as possible." He made a face. "Who knows? Maybe she'll talk to me."

"I hope she will."

He studied her expression. "You really do."

"I know you won't believe me, but I love her." She paused. "I'm going to make something to eat and bring it up. Neither Cassie nor I have had anything to eat today. So if you want one of your CIA people to watch what I'm putting in your food, you'd better send him to me. Where's the kitchen?"

"Down the hall to the left." He started up the stairs. "And I believe I'll trust you. You haven't hurt her yet."

The huge country kitchen was fully stocked, and Melissa found canned soup and vegetables for a salad. She grabbed a bite for herself, then took a tray up to Cassie and Andreas.

An hour later she was standing at the sink, washing the dishes and looking out the window at the hills. It must be wonderful to live here and be able to look out at all these flowers. Such a beautiful place . . .

A sudden chill went through her.

Such a deadly place.

★ ★ ★

Melissa stood in the doorway of Cassie's room. "May I speak to you in the hall?"

"Not now," Andreas said.

"Now. I don't want to talk in front of her, but I will."

He looked at her face and then glanced at Cassie. "Five minutes." He stood up and followed her from the room. "You're pale as a ghost. What's the problem?"

"You tell me. Something's going to happen here. What is it?"

"I don't know what you're talking about."

"The hell you don't." Her hands clenched into fists at her sides. "Something's going to happen and you're part of it."

"Why do you say that?"

"Because it's true, isn't it?"

"You're imagining things. You and Cassie are perfectly safe."

She knew that was true. "It's Travis."

He turned to go back in the room.

She grabbed his arm. "What's going to happen to Travis?"

"What he deserves." He went into Cassie's room and shut the door.

Damn him. She collapsed back against the wall. God, he was hard and totally unforgiving.

He wasn't going to tell her anything. He'd let it happen. . . .

Well, she wasn't going to let it happen, but she couldn't prevent it by standing there feeling sorry for herself.

She straightened and crossed the hall to the bedroom she'd chosen. She snatched a crocheted throw and wrapped it around her shoulders. Christ, she was cold. She curled up on the window seat and stared out at the hills.

Such a deadly place.

The thought had come out of nowhere and with it a vision of Travis falling, blood pouring from his chest. His eyes had glazed over as life had fled.

He was going to die.

Just as Jessica had died and that nice old man at the university. She had failed to stop both. She wouldn't be able to stop Travis from dying either.

You didn't give it a chance, Travis had said. It's easier to just call it fate.

Travis falling, dying.

"No!" She blocked the image.

Coward. Maybe something there could help her put the pieces together. She forced herself to close her eyes and brought the picture back. Travis falling . . .

Where was he?

Travis falling . . .

He was inside a building or shed, and there was an old lantern with a copper hood on the post beside him. She saw a table behind him with strange containers and on one corner a gleam of gold.

The Wind Dancer.

Terror iced through her.

A pool of blood and emerald eyes staring down . . .

No, that was Jessica. It didn't have to happen like that again. She could stop it.

How could she do it if she couldn't even smother the panic freezing her mind? She wanted to scream with frustration. It's not *fair*. If you're going to let me see anything, let me see enough to stop it.

Travis falling, dying.

Okay, damn you, don't give me any more. I'll figure it out anyway.

4:30 P.M.

"You can't go in there." Danley blocked the way when Melissa tried to enter the study. "The President is busy."

"I'm going to see him. And unless he's order-
ing another attack on Iraq, it's going to be now."

"He said he didn't want to be disturbed."

"Now."

"I can have you removed by—"

"It's all right, Danley." The door had opened
and Andreas stood there. "Evidently, the lady
doesn't know the meaning of the word *no*." He
stepped aside. "Come in, Ms. Riley. I can give
you a few minutes." He added sarcastically, "Iraq
isn't causing me any immediate trouble. But you
might remember that I do have other problems."

"How can I forget?" She whirled to face him.
"Where are you supposed to meet Travis
tonight?"

"I beg your pardon?"

"Don't play games with me. You would have
taken Cassie home right away if you didn't have
a damn good reason to stay. So I asked myself,
what would that reason be?"

His gaze narrowed on her face. "And what
did you answer?"

"The Wind Dancer or Deschamps." She
paused. "Or both."

"It could be something other than personal
business."

"But it's personal business that brought you
here."

"And I got what I came for."

"Not entirely. You'll never feel Cassie is safe until Deschamps is taken out." She drew a deep breath. "And that's what Travis promised you, isn't it? When he called you before he got on the helicopter, he told you to go to Vasaro and he'd meet you there and turn the statue over to you in exchange for amnesty. But that call was all a sham for Deschamps's benefit. Travis had called you before, hadn't he? He asked you to go along with what he said and he'd take Deschamps out for you. Then you'd have everything you wanted."

"Would I? This is all supposition."

"But it's true, isn't it? He chose Vasaro because he and Deschamps would feel more comfortable going after the Wind Dancer here. Deschamps had scoped it out before the kidnapping attempt. What harm can it do you to tell me?"

He was silent a moment and then slowly nodded. "Travis called me after your meeting with Deschamps at St. Ives and told me to come to Cannes to be in position and he'd contact me later by E-mail."

"Where is Travis supposed to meet you?"

He shook his head. "No interference."

"You're not going to meet him, are you?"

"I wasn't supposed to. It was always a trap for Deschamps. Travis promised he'd leave the

Wind Dancer after he got rid of Deschamps for me."

"Leave it where?"

Andreas smiled. "You are persistent."

"Are you going to let Travis escape after he kills Deschamps?"

"We didn't discuss it. I believe he knows he's on his own after I get what's mine. He's a clever man. He might be able to get away."

"But you'll pounce after he leaves Vasaro."

"Naturally, I have to have sufficient security to make sure Deschamps doesn't escape if he kills Travis."

Travis falling, dying . . .

The vision filled her with panic. Keep calm. "But you don't intend to be around if Travis needs any help." She moistened her lips. "For God's sake, you have an army here at the house. You could send someone to see that Deschamps doesn't hurt Travis."

"But that might tip off Deschamps. He might get away."

"You'd still have your statue."

He smiled. "I want it all."

It was what she had been afraid of. "You want Travis to be killed. You regard this as personal business and you don't want to order Danley or one of his men to do it. Because that would compromise your ethics as president. But you're hoping he'll die."

His smile faded. "He took my daughter. He risked her life. For days she was exposed not only to Deschamps but also to any other nut who has a grudge against me. He put my wife through hell. She could have lost the child she's carrying. I believe justice would be served if Deschamps and Travis killed each other. Now, is that all? I have to get back to work."

It was hopeless but she had to try. "Please. Send Danley or someone to save him."

"Let him save himself. He may get lucky."

"He'll die."

"Good day, Ms. Riley."

She drew a deep breath. "Okay, just tell me where he is so I can go help him myself."

"No interference."

"Don't tell me that. I'm not asking much." She rubbed her forehead. "It's got to happen tonight because you told me you were going to hold me for only forty-eight hours. You wouldn't have him anywhere close to Cassie, so he has to be far out on the grounds. He's in some kind of house, isn't he?"

He lifted a brow. "Good guess. Would you care to go for animal, vegetable, or mineral?"

"I'll find him myself."

"You're in my custody. You leave this area and you'll be shot."

"I don't think so. You're an honorable man and you know I helped Cassie. The only way you'll stop me is if you kill me." Her lips twisted. "Though maybe you'll get a bonus and Deschamps will take care of me too."

"Vasaro is a large property. You'll never find Travis."

"I'll find him. You just tell Danley not to use me as target practice. Will you have him give me a gun?"

"You're really pushing the envelope."

"I have to." She tried to keep the desperation from her voice but didn't succeed. "Travis doesn't deserve this. Yes, he did something he shouldn't have done, but he's a good man. You're making a mistake."

He shook his head.

"And you'll regret it."

"In my position I have to make many decisions I regret."

"But this doesn't have to be one of them. He saved Cassie once. Doesn't that have any weight at all?" She wasn't getting through to him, she realized in despair. "Cassie thinks of Travis as her friend. Are you going to be able to tell her later what you did to him?"

He didn't answer directly. "It's clear you have an attachment to Travis, but you'd be wise to have second thoughts. I've no desire for you to be hurt. Stay out of it, Ms. Riley."

"The hell I will." She turned and strode past Danley down the hall. She had to stop shaking. After all, she hadn't had much hope that she could persuade Andreas to help. If it had been her child in jeopardy, she would probably have been just as bitter.

She was lying to herself. She had hoped for a miracle. Well, the miracle hadn't happened and she was on her own. She threw open the door of the library. She couldn't run around Vasaro searching blindly. There must be a map of the property somewhere that showed where all the outbuildings were located.

She only had to find it.

Dear God, help me find it.

It took Melissa three hours to find a map. It wasn't on any of the shelves but tucked in a ledger in one of the bottom drawers of the desk.

She quickly spread it out on the desk. It seemed fairly new, so it should have all the current outbuildings on the property.

Shit.

There were seven other outbuildings besides

the ones surrounding the farmhouse, and they were scattered all over the property. They had to be miles apart. The chances of her being able to find the right place were practically nil.

She glanced at the window. Sweet Jesus, the sun was going down. It would be dark soon, and that's when it would happen. Dammit, she didn't even know how much time she had left.

She sank down in the desk chair and covered her eyes.

24

Travis checked his watch. "Almost time to go." He glanced at the helicopter parked near the hangar of the small airport. "Enough fuel to get us there and to Nice afterward?"

Galen looked at him in surprise. "Of course."

"Just checking."

"Since when do I need to be checked on? Are you a tad nervous?"

"Maybe."

"Natural enough. This isn't your field of expertise. You should really let me go in alone." He paused. "You think he'll be there waiting for us?"

"I'd bet he went straight to Vasaro. It's what I'd do. Get to Vasaro before Andreas arrives with the troops, dig in, and wait. No chance of stumbling on to anyone coming or going from the farm. He's smart enough to figure out that Andreas will seal the perimeter to catch me."

"Then how will he get out? He wouldn't leave a car or helicopter sitting around in the fields."

"He could steal my transportation after he's killed me." He smiled. "Or maybe he thinks he'll fly out of there on the wings of the Wind Dancer after he steals it."

"Where is the statue?"

"I put it in the closet in the back room." He opened the door. "Will you go get it? I'll go start the helicopter."

"Right." Galen went in the back room and opened the closet door. No gleam of gold in the darkness. He turned on the light and glanced up on the top shelf. No statue.

"Son of a bitch."

He ran out of the office, but the helicopter was already lifting off. "What the hell are you doing, you asshole?" he shouted. "You *need* me."

Travis waved a hand.

Galen was still standing on the tarmac, looking up, when Travis turned south toward Vasaro. Jesus, he was pissed.

Well, Travis couldn't help it. Galen had no

stake in this that was worth the risk Vasaro posed. Even if taking out Deschamps turned out to be easier than Travis expected it to be, Andreas would snap him up if he got the chance.

Travis just had to see that he didn't get the chance. Get rid of Deschamps, then take off for Nice and hope Andreas didn't have something lethal to take down the helicopter. If he moved fast, he might get out. Andreas would hesitate if he thought Travis might have the Wind Dancer in the aircraft.

He glanced at the Wind Dancer on the floor in the back of the helicopter. The statue seemed to stare back at him. The light from the setting sun caused the emerald eyes to glitter with a fierce life of their own. At that moment Travis could see why some people believed the statue had supernatural powers.

He smiled at it. "Sharpen your teeth, my friend. We're going hunting."

Cassie!

Melissa slowly raised her head from the desk. She had no idea which building Travis was going to be in, but Cassie might know. Cassie spent her summers here. She'd helped pick the flowers. She'd probably run wild all over the farm. It was possible. . . .

Let it be possible. Please let it be possible.

She closed her eyes.

Cassie.

The child wouldn't let her in. It took several precious minutes to break down her defenses.

"Cassie, I need you."

"I should be mad at you. Where have you been? You haven't been here all day."

"Your father was here."

"He just came back. Before there was only this . . . nurse."

"She's very nice." She had no time for this. *"Cassie, I need you to help me. I need you to find a place."*

"You shouldn't have left me. I've been lonely."

"Cassie."

Silence. "You're scared. You're scared of the monsters."

"Yes." Oh, yes.

Fear. "Coming here?"

"No, I have to go there."

"Because of Michael."

"He's in a house or shed. I don't know where it is. I have to find it. There's a lantern with a copper hood and on a table there are bins."

"What kind of bins?"

"Funny-shaped."

"Show me."

Concentrate on the table. Don't show her Travis dying.

"It's the picking shed in the south field."

Her heart leapt. "You're sure, baby?"

"Of course I'm sure. There's only one like that. Caitlin told me it's been there since the beginning of Vasaro. There was a fire, but it wasn't burned and she—"

"Thank you. Thank you. Thank you, Cassie." She grabbed the map and located an outbuilding in the south field. Damn, at least four miles.

"There's a shortcut. You go through the bunch of trees down the road and over the hill."

"How much time does that take?"

"I don't know. Some."

She couldn't expect the child to be precise. She just hoped her memory was fairly accurate.

Indignation. "There is too a shortcut."

"Sorry." She jumped to her feet. "I have to go. Good-bye, Cassie."

Sudden panic. "Don't want you to go. Stay here. The monsters will get you."

She had to smother her terror. Cassie was seeing too much these days, and she mustn't scare the child. "I'll be fine. We'll all be fine."

"Come back. . . ."

But Melissa was already in the hall. Then she

was running out the front door. The men on
guard didn't stop her, ignoring her as if she
weren't there.

Lord, it was almost dark.

She ran down the road toward the stand of
trees.

Danley knocked on Cassie's door and opened it.
"The woman's gone, Mr. President. A few minutes ago."

Andreas got to his feet and came into the hall.
"What direction?"

"Toward the trees."

"No one interfered with her?"

"You gave us our orders." His lips tightened.
"Though I have to tell you, I disapprove of the
entire situation."

"I know you do. You like everything neat,
and this is much too uncontrolled for you. Don't
worry, Melissa Riley's chance of finding the
shed is extremely slim. Even if she does, it
should all be over by that time."

"It's not efficient. You should have let us go in
and get the bastards."

"Stay out of it. Your job is to make sure my
daughter is safe. Period."

"And the woman?"

"I warned her. She's on her own." Andreas

turned and opened the door. "Let me know when you hear something."

He sat down in the chair beside Cassie's bed again and took her hand. Damn Melissa Riley. She'd be lucky if she didn't get herself killed. Why couldn't she have resigned herself to looking out for her own neck instead of worrying about Michael Travis? She was emotional and unreasonable and thought you could spin the earth on its axis if you cared enough.

And very much like his Chelsea. The thought popped out of nowhere into his head. He could see his wife doing exactly what Melissa was doing under the same circumstances. He'd been having the devil of a time keeping Chelsea from flying out here since he'd told her they had a good chance of getting Cassie back. She would have—

Cassie was squeezing his hand.

He went rigid. His gaze flew to her face. "Cassie?"

Her eyes were closed and her body was stiff, arched as if she were in pain. Her grasp was tightening until it was like a vise.

"Cassie, talk to me," he said unevenly. "Let me help you. Please."

★ ★ ★

Melissa tore through the stand of trees and up the hill.

Go faster.

She slipped and caught herself before she fell.

She heard something. The throb of an engine. A helicopter? Travis?

Jesus, she hoped not.

She was going down the hill on the other side. Lord, she hoped she was headed in the right direction. What if Cassie hadn't remembered correctly? She was only a little girl.

And maybe there was more than one picking shed that had survived the years.

No second thoughts. It was too late now.

The sound of the helicopter had stopped.

Another hill. Was the shed on the other side?

Her lungs hurt and her breath was coming in gasps.

Keep going.

She stumbled. It was fully dark now and hard to see the ground in front of her. She reached the top of the hill.

Nothing. Only another valley and the next hill.

Go on. Don't give up.

But hurry. She had to hurry.

Travis falling, dying . . .

★   ★   ★

Cassie screamed.

Andreas jumped. Another nightmare?

She bolted upright. *"Michael!"*

For the first time, Andreas noticed her eyes were open. "Oh, my God." He snatched her into his arms, tears pouring down his cheeks. "Sweetheart, you've come back to us. I'm so—"

"Michael." Her arms tightened around Andreas. "Daddy, the monsters. Blood. They're killing Michael."

"Shh." Andreas pressed a kiss to her forehead and rocked her. "Everything's going to be okay. Everything's okay now."

"No." She was sobbing. "It's like before. The monsters—and you weren't here."

"I'm here now."

"It's happening again."

"No, you're safe. We're all safe."

"No, it's not true." Her eyes widened in terror. *"Michael!"*

Travis had landed.

Deschamps faded closer to the bushes beside the shed, his gaze on the helicopter several yards away. The anticipation was a twisting hunger within him. It had been too long. Come out. Let me see it. Let me see what's mine.

There was no moon tonight, and in the darkness he could barely discern the shadowy figure of Travis at the controls. Why wouldn't he get out? Then he realized Travis was just being cautious. He'd be vulnerable as he got out of the helicopter; that was why Deschamps was waiting for the pilot's door to open.

Maybe Travis was sensing something wrong.

So he'd have to be very still until Travis felt safe.

Minutes passed.

Why wasn't the bastard moving?

He edged closer and then closer still.

He was almost at the aircraft when he stopped short. The figure wasn't Travis. It was a jacket wrapped around a dummy. The passenger door stood open.

Travis was out!

"Shit." Deschamps dove for the ground. Travis could be anywhere.

A flickering light suddenly beamed from the shed. The door was open. . . .

Melissa saw the light in the shed as she crested the hill. The silhouette of a helicopter was visible nearby.

It was already happening.

She was sobbing as she tore down the hill. Wait for me. Don't let me get this far and not be able to help.

The door was open. Deschamps might be just inside.

Screw him. If she delayed for even a moment, it might be the end for Travis.

She stood in the doorway, her gaze frantically searching the cavernous shadows for Travis.

She saw Deschamps first at the far end of the room. He was moving, stalking, staring at something in the shadows. Travis?

No, Travis was rolling from under the table, gun in hand, rising silently to his feet. His concentration was fixed on Deschamps, who had his back turned to him.

She held her breath. Do it. Shoot him. Don't let him turn around.

No!

Travis was turning his head. She hadn't made a motion, but he must have caught sight of her out of the corner of his eye. His eyes widened as he recognized her.

And Deschamps was turning around!

The next few seconds seemed to pass in slow motion as Melissa tore the short distance across the room. She launched herself at Travis, her arms encircling his waist as she pulled him down.

Too late.

She heard him grunt and felt the jerk of his body as the bullets hit him.

She'd failed, she realized in agony. Deschamps had killed him.

They hit the floor. Wood splintered next to her cheek as Deschamps got off another shot and hit the lantern on the post. The lantern fell and the candle snuffed out.

Darkness.

Travis's gun was beside him. She fumbled for it and rolled under the table. She knocked over a chair and pulled it close as a shield.

"You can't get away," Deschamps called. "I've killed Travis. Who's going to protect you now?"

Her eyes stung with tears as she looked at Travis on the other side of the table.

"You're afraid, aren't you? I might let you go if you give up right now."

"Screw you." Jesus, how could she see to shoot him when it was pitch black?

"You can't stop me. Do you know how long I've waited for that statue?"

Another shot. A hot stinging as the bullet ricocheted off the chair and grazed her left arm.

"Give up. You don't have a weapon, or you would have used it already. I'm getting impatient. I don't have much time before Andreas gets here."

"Andreas isn't coming. He never intended to come. It was all a trick. So that makes you pretty stupid, doesn't it?"

"You're lying. I checked out the area for miles around. Only the main house is guarded."

"I'm not lying. It was a setup. Even if you kill me, Andreas will scoop you up before you get ten miles from Vasaro." A bullet whistled by her ear. He was aiming at the sound of her voice just as she was trying to gauge where he was. "Why are you wasting time? Get out of here and make a run for it."

"I won't have to make a run for it. I'll take the helicopter Travis arrived in . . . after I get the Wind Dancer."

The Wind Dancer. She could see the gleam of gold on the table above her. Would it lure him close enough for her to get a shot at him? Or would one of his bullets strike her first?

Another shot. Very close.

She gasped and then gave a low cry.

Deschamps grunted with satisfaction. "All right. You've gotten in my way for the last time." Silence. "Did it hurt? I hurt your sister, didn't I? I saw the blood spurting out of her before I ran out." He stopped, listening.

He was testing her, hoping she'd break if the bullet hadn't hit her.

"I was hoping to be able to take my time

killing Travis. I admit I'm disappointed. I wanted to see him hurt. I haven't felt this much hatred for anyone since I killed my charming stepfather."

Bastard.

"Did you see him bleed when the bullets hit? There are legends about the Wind Dancer having a fondness for blood. Wars . . . the guillotine . . . Do you think there's anything to those tales?"

She didn't respond. Come on, you son of a bitch. Let me see you.

"You really shouldn't have involved yourself. You're not clever enough. It was pitifully easy fooling you at St. Ives."

He was stirring, moving.

Yes!

She could sense him on the other side of the room. Come closer. See the pretty statue. Come and get it.

He was coming. Very cautiously, but he was coming.

Her hand tightened on the gun.

Another shot.

A hot, deep pain in her upper thigh.

Don't scream. Don't move. He had to think she was no threat.

"I heard that bullet hit home. There's nothing that sounds quite like that soft thud. You're either a Spartan or you're unconscious or dead. I wonder which it is. I'll make sure as soon as I get the Wind Dancer." He was closer, though not close enough. She couldn't move quickly and she'd have only one chance. "My God, what a thing of beauty it is. I can see those eyes glittering at me in the darkness. It's almost enough to make a man believe all the stories about it."

Shock surged through her as sudden light illuminated the room. He'd relit the lantern. Christ, he was only a few feet away! She froze and held her breath. Her hand tightened on the gun half hidden beneath her body.

But he gave her only a glance, his attention focused on the statue with total fascination. "Alexander, Charlemagne, the Borgias," he whispered as he gathered the statue in his arms. "And Edward Deschamps. It has a splendid ring, doesn't— Shit!" He clutched the statue as he fell to the floor. "What the—"

Travis had his arms wrapped around Deschamps's ankles and yanked the legs out from under him. There was blood everywhere. Travis's blood. On Travis, on Deschamps. But, sweet Jesus, Travis was still alive!

Deschamps recovered immediately. His gun swung to point at Travis.

"No!" The thirty-eight exploded in Melissa's hand.

One shot.

Two.

Three.

Deschamps jerked as each bullet entered his body. Blood poured from the wounds in his stomach.

He looked down in disbelief.

She fired again and he dropped the gun. "Bitch." Tears ran down his face. He clutched the Wind Dancer with his bloody hands and crawled toward the door. "Doesn't matter. You still won't win. I've got it. That's all that's important. I've got it. . . ."

And he might still get to the helicopter and get away. She didn't know how he was managing to even move. Yes, she did. He was obsessed and Jessica had told her fanatics sometimes seemed to draw on superhuman stores of endurance and strength.

Jessica.

No way was he going to get to the helicopter. She shot him in the head.

25

"That . . . hurts." Travis opened his eyes as Melissa pressed a strip of shirt to the wound in his lower shoulder.

"Shut up. You're lucky to be alive. Where's Galen?"

"I . . . didn't need him."

"You ran out on him."

"No one knew he was mixed up in this. Andreas . . . he won't be satisfied with . . . statue."

"You gave him Deschamps."

"He's dead?"

"Yes, and you did it. Do you hear me?"

He tried to smile. "Strange, I don't remember that. Are you trying to make me a hero?"

"I'm trying to save your neck." She moistened her lips. "I never thought I'd get the chance. I saw you dying, Travis. I saw the wounds in your chest and your face. . . . You were dying."

"But you'd tackled me and pulled me down. The bullet didn't hit my chest."

"You might not have been shot at all if I hadn't been here."

"Or I could have been shot and killed. Who the hell knows?" He closed his eyes. "Now, if you don't mind, I think I'll go to sleep. I'm very tired."

"Just so you don't die on me." Her voice was shaking. "I went to a lot of trouble to keep you alive."

"Wouldn't . . . think of it."

He was unconscious. Keep the pressure on the wound. She'd put a makeshift bandage on her own leg wound before she'd crawled over to Travis. How to get them both help? Andreas probably wouldn't come near this place. He wanted Travis and Deschamps to both die.

Galen.

She fumbled in Travis's pocket, pulled out his phone, and began to dial.

The door was flung open. "Hands in the air!" A half-dozen men streamed into the room.

Suits. Indisputably CIA. For God's sake, it was

like that break-in yesterday morning at the cottage.

"I'm *not* putting my hands in the air. If I take my hand off this compress, he's going to bleed to death. Where the hell is Danley? Let me talk to Danley."

"I'll have to do. Danley's busy securing the area." Andreas walked into the room. He looked down at Deschamps. "Is this our man?"

"Yes, I'm sure Danley's shown you pictures of him."

"But it's difficult to tell with half his head blown off."

"It's Deschamps. Travis got rid of him for you." She added fiercely, "So you get him some help."

"I have every intention of doing that. How is he?"

"The bullets went through his shoulder. He's lost some blood, but he'll live . . . if you don't screw up."

"I don't dare screw up. You look like you could use some help yourself." He motioned to one of the men. "Paulding, you get a medical team out here." Then he knelt beside her.

"Leave me alone. I'm okay."

"Let Travis go. We're not going to hurt him."

"How do I know that?"

"Cassie won't let me."

"What?"

He smiled. "She woke up."

"Oh, my God."

"That was my reaction. I felt like I could walk on air. . . . It was damn wonderful. Even though she was almost hysterical and screaming at me to save Travis. She must have overheard us talking about him last night."

She had overheard all right. But not the way Andreas meant. "I told you how she felt about him."

"Yes, you did." He stood up. "We'll get you back to the house and get the bullet taken out."

"Not unless you bring Travis with me."

"You don't trust me?" He smiled. "I promised Cassie I'd bring him back to the house. It was the only way I could get her to quiet down. Do you think I'm about to send her spiraling away from me again? I'd move the whole damn world to keep that from happening."

She studied his face and then slowly nodded. "I can see you would."

"And now I'd better get back and tell Cassie that her hero is safe."

"But what about after Cassie is better? Will Travis be safe then?"

"We'll just have to see, won't we? I still want to break his neck." He moved toward the door. "I'll see you at the house." He stopped beside

the body and bent down to pick up the Wind
Dancer Deschamps was still clutching. "There's
blood on it."

"Deschamps said the Wind Dancer liked
blood."

"Ridiculous. How could it like or dislike anything?" He wiped the blood off the Wind
Dancer and then smiled down into its emerald
eyes. "After all, it's only a statue."

"Melissa. The monsters . . . Michael!"

*"Shh. They're gone. Michael is safe. He's hurt, but
he's right here beside me. We're in a van on the way
back to the house."*

"That's what Daddy said."

"Believe him."

"But I saw Michael—"

*"I know what you saw. But it didn't happen. It
doesn't have to happen if we fight it."*

"Scary out here. Maybe I'll go back in the tunnel."

*"Don't you dare! I'll go in and drag you out again.
What if Michael or your daddy or mom needs you?
What if I need you? You didn't like having your daddy
go help Michael, did you? You wanted to do it yourself."*

"Yes."

She had known a child as strong-willed as
Cassie would have that response. *"So would I.*

And how can you do anything while you're in there hiding?"

Silence. "I'll stay awhile. It's kind of . . . nice to be back with Daddy."

That she was already beginning to cling to her father was promising. Tentative acceptance was probably as much as Melissa could hope for. Jessica would have known how to deal with her at this stage; Melissa could only go by instinct. *"I'll come to see you tomorrow morning."*

"Now."

"Tomorrow," she repeated firmly.

"But I want to see you. I've seen you only the way you see yourself."

And she wanted to see Cassie awake. *"Okay, it may be a while. The doctor's going to have to take care of my leg."*

"I'll wait. Will Michael come too?"

Melissa looked down at Travis, who had been given a shot by the doctor who had arrived on the scene after Andreas had left. *"Perhaps we'll both go and visit him tomorrow. He got pretty banged up fighting the monster."*

"But he's alive?"

"Oh, yes, he's alive." Thank you, God. It was a night for thanksgiving. Thanks for Travis. Thanks for Cassie. *"We're pulling into the driveway. I have to go now. I'll see you later."*

★ ★ ★

"You did come," Cassie said. "I told Daddy you would. He said the doctor would put you right to bed."

"He tried." Melissa made her way forward in the wheelchair. "And I can stay only a few minutes."

"Are you hurting?" Cassie frowned. "You *are* hurting. I can feel it."

"It'll go away. The doctor gave me some medicine to make sure it does." She stopped beside the bed and just sat, looking at Cassie. The girl was thin, but the fragility was gone, banished by the sheer vitality in her expression. "You look . . . good."

"And you're prettier than you think you are. Almost as pretty as Mama." Her voice cracked on the last word, and she made a face. "I'm all hoarse. I sound like a frog. Daddy said it's because I'm not used to talking anymore."

"That would cause it." She couldn't get enough of looking at the child. So alive. So wonderfully alive. She'd never seen this Cassie except in photographs and TV news. "It should get better in a few days."

"I don't care. It makes Daddy laugh." She smiled. "And then I laugh."

"That's the way it works."

"I forgot." Her smile vanished. "You're still hurting. You go to bed."

"Yes, ma'am." She turned and wheeled toward the door. "I'll see you in the morning."

"Early. Come early, Melissa."

"Stop it. You don't have to talk to me this way anymore."

"It's easier."

"Don't do it anyway."

"But my throat's sore. You wouldn't want me to hurt my throat."

"Not that sore. And people don't understand when you talk like this. It would worry your mama and daddy."

"Well, then I won't do it with anyone but you."

It was clear Cassie was going to get her way regardless of whatever Melissa said. Accept the compromise. *"That might work."*

"Are you sure Michael is all right?"

She opened the door. *"The doctor said he'll be fine."*

"I've been worried. I've been trying and trying, but I can't reach him. If I stay out, he has to stay out too. It's not fair otherwise."

"What are you talking about?"

"You tell him. It's not fair. . . ."

★ ★ ★

"I want out of here," Travis said as soon as Melissa came into his room the next morning. "And what are you doing in that wheelchair? Deschamps *did* hurt you. I wasn't sure the bastard was lying. I hoped to hell he was."

"Be quiet." She moved close to the bed. "I'm okay. I'm just bound to this blasted chair for a while. Cassie and her father are going to visit you, but I wanted to see you first." A luminous smile lit her face. "She came back last night, Travis."

He stiffened. "My God."

"She was jarred out of the trauma when she thought you were dying."

"How is she?"

"Scared, eager . . . beautiful." She swallowed hard. "So damn beautiful. I went in to see her last night and again this morning, and she smiled at me. I've never seen her smile."

"Neither have I."

She drew a deep breath. "We have to get you out of here. Right now Andreas is all sweetness and light." She grimaced. "As much as he can be. But once he's sure Cassie's okay, I don't know what he'll do. He's finding forgiving you a little difficult."

"That qualifies as the understatement of the year. I didn't expect forgiveness."

"Well, if we get you away, it may be a case of

out of sight, out of mind. He's got Cassie and the Wind Dancer back, and Deschamps is dead. He can't have a pound of your flesh too."

"No?"

"I've called Galen. He's going to come and pick us up within the next half hour."

He frowned. "I don't want Galen involved."

"No one has to know he's anything but a commercial pilot. He's taking us to Nice, and from there we'll go to Juniper."

"You've got it all planned."

"Someone had to do something. Since you got yourself shot up and weren't able to lift your head, much less—"

"Okay. Okay." He started to laugh. "But when Galen sees how banged up we are, I'll never hear the end of it for not taking him. He'll swear it would never have happened if he'd been along."

"Maybe it wouldn't have." She shook her head. "I don't know anything anymore. The only thing I'm certain about is that I have to get you out of here."

"And I'm certain I have to go with you." He paused. "Anywhere. Anytime."

She went still. "What?"

"You heard me. It's amazing the revelations that come to you when you think you're going to die."

"What about staying on the outside looking in?"

"I didn't say it was going to be easy." He smiled. "But I believe it's definitely worth a try." His smile faded. "What do you think?"

She said unevenly, "There's a possibility I might think it's worthwhile. Though you're a very—"

"Michael, I've been waiting to see you." Cassie had burst into the room. "You should have come with— Oh, you *are* banged up. Melissa said you were, but I—"

"I'm just a little torn around the edges." He smiled. "But you look awesome. Welcome back, Cassie. How do you feel?"

She walked slowly across the room. "I can't walk very far or my legs feel funny." She plopped down on the side of the bed. "Daddy says that's because I haven't used them in so long."

"That's probably true."

"Mama's coming here. Daddy told her to stay in Washington, but she was already on a plane when he talked to her. She said she wasn't going to wait any longer to see me." She giggled. "And Daddy said she'll probably have the only baby ever born on *Air Force Two*."

"It sounds like everything's good with you."

"Mostly. It's still scary." Her smile widened.

"But the Wind Dancer's here. He'll keep me safe. Daddy brought him to me last night. Isn't that wonderful?"

Melissa felt a ripple of shock that Andreas had brought the statue from that scene of death straight to Cassie. No, she guessed it wasn't so bizarre. The Andreas family and the statue had seen centuries of death and joy. If the Wind Dancer could bring Cassie happiness and a new confidence in life here at Vasaro, why shouldn't she have it? "Wonderful, Cassie."

Her smile faded. "But Melissa says you're both going away, Michael. I don't want you to go."

"It's best for us to leave," he said. "We'll always be there for you if you need us."

She frowned. "You promise?"

"I promise." Travis squeezed her hand. "You let me know and I'll come running."

"Most people wait for a formal invitation," Andreas said from the door.

Travis stiffened. "Cassie just issued one. But if you take good care of her, she'll never have a reason to send out an SOS, will she?"

"I'll take good care of her." He crossed the room and picked up Cassie. "I take it you intend to leave here?"

"We have a pilot picking us up in ten minutes," Melissa said quickly. "I know you'll be glad to be rid of us with Mrs. Andreas coming."

"There are many ways for me to rid myself of you." He kissed Cassie's cheek. "Where do you intend to go?"

"Juniper."

"What a surprise. Not exactly Travis's cup of tea, is it? He requires a more exciting venue. And it's very close to Washington." His lips thinned. "Maybe a little too close for me."

"We may not stay there," Melissa said. "But I have private business to attend to. Jessica. You'll take care of the release?"

He nodded. "I'll see to it."

"Good." She met his gaze with a boldness she didn't feel. "Then it's decided."

Andreas didn't speak for a moment, staring at Travis. "So it seems. I'll have Danley arrange to bring you downstairs and put you on the helicopter." He started to carry Cassie from the room.

Melissa breathed a profound sigh of relief. She didn't even want to know how close Andreas had been to going the other way.

"Let me down, Daddy." Cassie wriggled out of Andreas's arms, ran back to Melissa and into her arms. "I . . . love you," she whispered. And then she said fiercely, "Don't you forget me."

Melissa hugged her tightly. "I could never forget you." She swallowed hard. "I'll always be close to you, sweetheart."

Cassie stepped back and nodded emphatically. "You bet you will."

It sounded almost like a threat, Melissa thought with amusement. Cassie's insecurities were rapidly vanishing.

Cassie gave her an impish grin and winked before marching over and taking her father's hand. "I'm hungry. Can we have waffles for breakfast?"

"I believe that could be arranged," her father said as he led her from the room.

Melissa chuckled. "Give Cassie another few months and she'll be running the White House."

"She's not the only bulldozer around here," Travis murmured.

"You and Andreas were both arching like tomcats. Someone had to step between you two and distract him." She wheeled her chair toward the door. "I'll be glad to get back to Juniper and away from all this—" She stopped as pain rippled through her. "No, I won't. Every inch of the place will remind me of Jessica."

"After the funeral, maybe we'll go away for a while."

"Maybe." She glanced at him over her shoulder. "But Juniper will probably be safer until Karlstadt forgets about you."

"You're protecting me again." He smiled. "I'm handling Karlstadt. I'll send him the money and the disk as soon as we get to Juniper. I've already given him the diamond I gave to Thomas."

"That should satisfy him, right? The only diamonds missing are the ones the CIA confiscated."

He hesitated. "Well, not exactly."

"What?"

"There are three good-sized ones I had to use to negotiate."

"Negotiate with who?"

"Danley."

She stared at him in disbelief. "Danley? What the hell are you talking about?"

"I made a deal with Danley the night he picked me up in Amsterdam. I thought I might need him."

"Danley took a bribe?"

He smiled. "Most people have their price, and those diamonds would have made him a rich man. Though he was very cagey about the amount of help he'd give me. He agreed to help me escape only if I needed it."

"And he actually knew you were going to take Cassie?"

"No, Galen and I took care of that. But after he learned I'd taken Cassie, he damn well knew he'd better make sure I wasn't caught. I'd already told him that if I went down, I'd take him with me. There's no way he wanted to be drawn in as an accomplice."

"So he put stumbling blocks in Andreas's way?"

"What do you think? Galen is good, but the odds were pretty much against us."

"Are you going to tell Andreas about Danley?"

"Hell no, I might need him. You never compromise a source."

She shook her head in amazement. "You're incredible."

"Well, Karlstadt might demand that I get him those diamonds locked in the CIA evidence room. Danley has access."

"And what if Danley decides to sell those three diamonds you gave to him?"

"I'll just drop him a word, tell him what Karlstadt will do to him if the diamonds surface." He smiled. "So stop worrying. Like I said, I'm handling the problem. We don't have to hide at Juniper. We have to think about you."

"I *am* thinking about me." She opened the door. "I'll see you downstairs."

26

"My God, what a pair of crocks." Galen watched from the pilot's seat as CIA agents lifted Travis's stretcher into the helicopter. "It's hard to believe that you—"

"Take off, Galen," Travis said. "I'm not interested in your insults."

"You should be. I do it so well." He glanced at Melissa. "You should really watch who you hang out with. I'd have kept you from being hurt."

"Hush," Melissa said. "Go."

A moment later the helicopter was rising and turning south.

Melissa looked down to see Andreas and

Cassie coming down the steps. Cassie lifted her hand and waved. Melissa waved back.

"Cassie?" Travis asked.

She nodded. "I'm glad he brought her to say good-bye." She wrinkled her nose. "At least he won't order a rocket launcher to take out the helicopter while she's around."

"He wouldn't do that. I'm the only one he's having a problem with."

"You might be able to solve it sometime. Who knows, you may be able to tap one of your sources and give him a tidbit of valuable information."

"Possibly."

"And Cassie is going to prove a shock to him when he finds out she's brought back the same kind of psychic baggage I did. He may need help with her."

"We're not sure she has. You haven't been able to bond with her since she woke, have you?"

"Once." She paused. "And I found she'd already picked up some very interesting info when she was in the tunnel. Now that she's out, her ability may grow like wildfire."

"What kind of info?"

"When you were unconscious, she said, 'If I stay out, he has to stay out too.'" She looked him in the eye. "Now, what do you think she meant by that?"

He stiffened. "I'm sure you're going to tell me."

"I thought a lot about it last night."

"I'm sorry to have kept you awake."

"Perhaps we should ask Dr. Dedrick."

"That's one solution."

"Except, dammit, there's no Dr. Dedrick, is there? You made him up. What would you have done if I'd called your bluff when you offered to lend me your book?"

"I didn't think it was likely. You were too involved in Jessica's problems." He shrugged. "And I wanted to help you."

"I should have guessed. You were so blasted understanding about what was happening to me. Your information sources weren't the same as Galen's. You knew about the attack on Vasaro but not about Deschamps. And you were able to help Cassie when she was rejecting everyone else. We just assumed it was because you'd saved her at Vasaro, but there was something else too, wasn't there?"

"I don't know. I'm not an expert on how it works. It could have been for either reason."

"No wonder you were so interested in Cassie. You identified with her. You were struck on the head and unconscious in that hospital for months after your father died. Where were you during that time, Travis? A tunnel, a cave, a forest?"

"No, a boat, a very strong, well-built cruiser with the speed of light that could run away from anything or anyone."

"Monsters?"

"I had my share of them. But I had an impetus that sprung me free of the trauma. I'd seen my father murdered, and hatred is a very powerful goad." He looked away from her. "Then the dreams started. And a little later I'd occasionally see . . . things. I never joined with anyone like you did with Cassie. Evidently, it doesn't work the same with everyone. In the first year, I realized what a tiger I had by the tail. I couldn't see something when I wanted to see it. I felt like it owned me."

"Did you tell Jan?"

He shook his head. "I didn't tell Jan or anyone else. I just bottled it up inside. Sometimes I could stop what I saw. Sometimes I couldn't. Sometimes I didn't want to stop it. I thought I deserved a little profit from all the hell I was going through. When I was old enough, I went searching for answers and I found a few, but we belong to a very exclusive club. Which was why

I was so fascinated when I found out about Cassie . . . and you. It's almost enough to make you believe in fate."

"It wasn't fate that made you step in and involve yourself with Cassie."

"No, it started out as curiosity and then I got pulled in."

"Why didn't you just tell me? Why couldn't you share it with me?"

"At first, we weren't exactly friends. No, that's not the reason. It's . . . difficult for me to talk about it. I've become accustomed to handling it by myself." He grimaced. "Okay, you said once that maybe I was in a tunnel just like Cassie. You didn't know how close you came. Maybe you were right. Maybe I haven't learned to deal with it in a sane, healthy way. I just did the best I could."

"Were you ever going to confide in me?"

"Sure. Maybe. I hope so. It wouldn't have been easy for me. I'm not like you. You're open and you reach out to everything and everybody." He met her gaze. "If you needed me to do it, I would have told you. I'll give you anything that you need from me."

"Travis, I could strangle you."

"Does that mean you're going to throw me out of your life?" His tone was light, but his expression wasn't. "I'd find that very difficult to accept. So difficult that going back into a trauma state would be easy by comparison."

She had never seen him this vulnerable. There was so much she didn't know about him. So much still to learn. He was constantly thinking, moving, planning. He'd lived a life of which she had no real conception. This might be only the first of the secrets she'd find out about him. Travis was definitely no angel.

What the hell. He'd never be boring.

"Why should I throw you out? You're probably the only man in the world who understands me. But you do have a few faults that are going to cause us some big headaches." She took his hand and smiled at him. "Oh, well, I guess we'll just have to work on it."